THE DEEP

Books by Peter Benchley

THE DEEP

JAWS

TIME AND A TICKET

PETER BENCHLEY

THE DEEP

DOUBLEDAY & COMPANY, INC., GARDEN CITY, NEW YORK
1976

*All of the characters in this book are fictitious,
and any resemblance to actual persons, living or
dead, is purely coincidental.*

ISBN: 0-385-04742-8
LIBRARY OF CONGRESS CATALOG CARD NUMBER 75-44521
COPYRIGHT © 1976 BY PETER BENCHLEY
ALL RIGHTS RESERVED
PRINTED IN THE UNITED STATES OF AMERICA
FIRST EDITION

for Teddy and Edna Tucker

THE DEEP

1943

It was ten o'clock in the morning when the captain noticed that the wind had begun to die.

In his cabin, leafing through a magazine brought aboard at Norfolk by one of the crew, he sensed a change in the ship's motion, a softening of the hiss of hull moving through water, a distant slapping of luffing sails. He rolled off his bunk, stretched, and started for the door.

Mounted on the bulkhead to the left of the door was a panel of brass weather gauges. The needle on the barometer showed 29.75 inches of mercury. The captain tapped the glass, and the needle dropped quickly to 29.5.

On deck he walked aft, sniffing the sluggish breeze and searching the horizon. The sky was clear, but a dim yellow haze thickened the air. The captain squinted. Way in the distance, high thin strands of cirrus clouds crept across the sky.

The first mate, a young bearded Scot, stood at the helm, guiding the ship through the long swells. He nodded casually as the captain approached.

"Trim the main?" asked the captain.

"Aye, and the mizzen. She's slacked way off."

"Not for long. There's weather."

"How big?"

"Can't tell. Not with this damn radio silence; this war goes on much longer, we'll forget how to use the bloody radio. But big, I'd venture. The glass is takin' quite a plunge."

The mate looked at his watch. "How much farther we got to go?"

"Fifty, sixty mile. That's to the Narrows. We get there, we'll have a look. Maybe try for Hamilton, maybe put into St. George's."

"Nae worry," said the mate, smiling and patting the wheel. "She can ride 'er out."

The captain spat on the deck. "This old wreck? Only fitting thing about her's her name. She's big and clumsy as the other Goliath." He looked at the sky. "Well, at least we're 'cross the bloody Stream."

By one o'clock in the afternoon, thick, gray alto-stratus clouds covered the sky. The wind had risen to thirty knots, and it whipped whitecaps across the surface of the ocean and churned up heavy seas that broke over *Goliath*'s bow, sending shudders the length of the wooden hull. There had been two short blinding rain squalls, and another black mass of clouds was moving in from the southeast.

The captain, dressed now in oilskins, stood next to the mate as he strained to steer a steady course.

The bosun's mate, a small wiry man—shirtless and sopping wet—hurried aft and stood before the captain.

"They secure?" said the captain.

"Aye," said the bosun's mate. "But knowin' what they're worth, why they packed them things in cigar boxes I'll never know. Muckin' about with 'em is like dancin' on eggs."

"Any breakage?"

"Ain't seen any. They're bagged about with sacks of flour."

The first fat drops of rain struck the captain in the face. "Keep her on one-two-oh," he said to the mate. "I'm gonna shorten down some more. If I'm right, this bitch ain't begun to blow."

Suddenly the wind shifted again, backing around to the southeast. It blew harder, howling through the rigging, driving a stinging rain.

"Gimme oh-two-oh!" the captain yelled above the shriek of the gale.

"We could lay off!" the mate called back.

Goliath's bow slammed into a wave. Somewhere forward, a piece of wood snapped free and flew aft, rattling between the stays.

The captain leaned closer to the mate and shouted, "Nobody lays off Bermuda in weather like this! There are places them reefs come out twelve miles!"

Goliath struggled northeast for another hour, yawing before the following wind. With each thudding sea, the hull groaned and creaked. At three o'clock the wind let up a little, and the rain, which had been slashing almost horizontally, fell more vertically. The dead-gray sky began to brighten.

The captain changed course again, heading southeast for half an hour to try to clear the southern coast to the Narrows—the only safe channel into the shelter of the Bermuda archipelago.

"We may beat this bugger yet," he shouted to the mate, who smiled and licked salt spray off his lips.

An hour later, the storm exploded out of the northeast.

The wind roared down on the ship, ripping the tops off the waves and creating black mountains that towered over the masts. Only two sails were still flying. The forestaysail went first, tearing off its stays and leaving shreds that whistled in the blow.

A huge wave caught the bow and flung the ship skyward. At the crest of the wave, the captain spied a lighthouse—not lighted, for the wartime black-out was in effect, but conspicuous as a thin white stripe against the blackening sky.

He turned to yell something to the mate, as the ship slid off the crest into the trough between waves. A wall of water struck, surged across the deck, and battered the captain to his knees. He thrashed frantically, groping for a handhold. His arms found the wheelbox, and he clung to it.

Hearing a scream, he looked up. The wheel was spinning free, and as he watched, the mate was hurled into the frothy blackness. The captain lurched to his feet and grabbed the wheel.

The ship rose high on another crest, and again he saw the lighthouse. The spanker was still flying; he could make way. If he could reach the lighthouse, he could get into the safety of St. George's harbor.

The spanker held. Careening into the seas, the ship began to move due north. At the crest of each wave, the captain shielded his eyes against needles of rain and spray. He fixed his bow a few points to starboard of the lighthouse.

Something moved in the darkness amidships.

At first, the captain thought it was flotsam washing aft. Then he saw it was a man, the bosun's mate, crawling toward him, moving from handhold to handhold, winch to cleat to stay, to keep from being washed overboard.

When he was a few feet from the captain, the bosun's mate yelled. All the captain heard was the word "David's." He nodded and pointed ahead. The bosun's mate grimaced and came closer. "That ain't Saint David's light!" he screamed.

"It is that!" the captain called back.

"I tell you, that ain't Saint David's! That's bloody Gibb's Hill!"

"No!"

"It's Gibb's Hill! Look dead ahead!"

The captain peered into the darkness. Beyond the bow, not fifty yards away, he saw what the bosun's mate was pointing at: a jagged line of surf, marking the reef. Confused, blinded by rain, the captain had let his ship be blown twelve miles off course to the southwest.

He spun the wheel hard to port, and the ship began to bear off the wind. For a moment, the captain thought he had cleared the reef. And then he felt the first sickening crunch of timber cracking on coral. The ship jolted to a stop, then jerked forward. It stopped again, and again moved forward. The bow rose, then seemed suddenly to drop away. The deckhouse amidships heaved up; the stern rolled off to port. The captain stumbled, reached for the wheel, and missed. His arm slipped through the spinning spokes, his wrist jammed against the wheelbox. For a second, his elbow fought the wheel. Then the elbow broke, the arm was cast free, and the captain was pitched into the sea.

By morning, the storm had passed.

A British naval officer was walking his dog on the beach below the high cliffs from which the Orange Grove Club overlooked the ocean. Always after a storm the beach was littered with debris, but this morning's accumulation was extraordinary. The dog sniffed curiously at pieces of wreck. It started to lift a leg on a piece of wood, then scented something unusual. The dog whined and grew excited, darting forward and back. It stopped at a large hatch cover and dug at the sand beneath it. The navy man followed the dog and, to humor it, lifted the hatch cover.

Underneath, half buried in the sand, was a man, clad only in torn remnants of a pair of shorts. Water ran from his mouth, and from his ears when his head rolled to the side. The navy man bent down and touched him, and the man emitted a rasping, gurgling sound. He moaned, and his eyelids fluttered. The man's name was Adam Coffin.

1

In sea water more than a few feet deep, blood is green. Water filters the light from above, seeming to consume the colors of the spectrum shade by shade. Red is the first to succumb, to disappear. Green lasts longer. But then, below 100 feet, green, too, fades away, leaving blue. In the twilight depths—180, 200 feet, and beyond—blood looks black.

David Sanders sat on the sandy bottom and watched green fluid ooze from the back of a wounded fish. It was a big porgy, with long fanglike teeth; it was at least two feet long, and mottled blue and gray. A crescent of flesh had been gouged from its back—by another fish, perhaps—and blood pulsed from the wound in stringy billows that quickly dissipated in the water. The fish swam erratically, apparently confused by pain or by the scent of its own blood.

Sanders pushed off the bottom and swam toward the porgy, expecting it to retreat. But the fish continued to dart back and forth.

He swam to within three feet of the struggling fish; when the fish did not retreat, Sanders decided to try to catch it. With his bare hand, he grabbed for it, just forward of the tail.

His touch triggered panic in the fish. It began to thrash in a flurry of convulsive writhing. Sanders held on.

The fish was a shuddering gray blur. Sanders closed his eyes and tightened his grip. And then suddenly he felt a stab of pain. Shocked, he opened his eyes and tried to release his grip, but now the fish had him: its front teeth sank into the palm of Sanders' hand.

He yelled into his face mask and yanked his hand downward. The teeth came free, and the fish darted away. Green fluid billowed from two blue puncture marks in his palm.

He looked up, fighting the urge to shoot for the surface. On the surface, twenty-five or thirty feet away, the Boston Whaler bobbed at anchor. He took a deep breath, cursing himself. Trying to remain calm, he thought: Don't panic; don't rush for the surface; don't hold your breath; let it out nice and easy. He kicked upward, trailing blood, forcing himself to rise no faster than the bubbles vented from his air tank.

Gail Sanders, sitting in the Whaler, heard her husband before she saw him: his bubbles popped and burbled on the surface. When his head broke water, she grabbed the neck of his scuba tank and, after he had unfastened the belt and one shoulder strap, hauled the tank aboard the boat. "See anything?" she asked.

Sanders pushed his face mask up onto his forehead. "Nothing. Sand and coral. There's no wreck down there." He was holding the Whaler with his right hand, and Gail saw blood trickling down the gunwale. "What happened?"

Sanders was embarrassed, and he said, "It's nothing." Kicking with his flippers, he heaved himself into the boat and looked toward shore, two or three hundred yards away. Atop the cliff beyond the beach, the pastel orange buildings of the Orange Grove Club shone brightly in the afternoon sun. He raised his arm and pointed straight ahead, then aimed with the other arm at a lighthouse in the distance. "The lifeguard said ten o'clock, right? Put the club at twelve o'clock and Gibb's Hill light at ten o'clock, and we should be right on top of it."

"Maybe it's gone. After all, thirty years under-water . . ."

"Yeah, but he was pretty positive you can still see the keelson and some of her frames."

Gail hesitated, then said, "The bell captain did say we could hire a guide."

"The hell with that. I can find it if it's here."

"But . . ." Gail gestured at Sanders' bleeding hand. "It might be smarter to have a guide."

"I don't need a guide," Sanders said, ignoring the gesture. "Water's water. As long as you don't panic, you're all right."

Gail looked off the stern. Forty yards away, a line of breakers indicated another reef. Behind that reef was another, and behind that one, still another. "If a ship was going to go on the rocks, wouldn't it hit the first rocks it came to and sink right there?"

"Maybe not. If there was a hell of a wind behind it, it could be driven over one or two reefs, bounce from one to another."

"So it could be on any of those reefs."

"It could. But the lifeguard said it was behind the first line. Maybe we're not far enough behind it." Sanders uncleated the anchor line and let the boat drift backward toward the second line of reef. When the boat was within ten yards of it, he secured the line again and adjusted the straps on his scuba harness.

Gail said, "Are you sure you should dive again?"

"Why not? I told you, that hand's nothing. I'll wrap it so it doesn't bleed in the water and attract any enemies."

Gail began to assemble her equipment. She screwed her regulator to the valve on the top of her air tank, then turned the knob that opened the tank. With a sharp *pfft* air rushed into the regulator. She pressed the purge button, to flush any residual water from the mouthpiece, and air hissed loudly from the rubber tube. She adjusted her weight belt, a nylon strap with three two-pound lead weights threaded on it; then dipped her flippers in the water and slipped them on her feet, rinsed her mask, spat on the inside of the faceplate, and rubbed the saliva around the glass to prevent fogging. She stood her tank upright and checked the lengths of the harness straps. "Ready to give me a hand?" she asked. She looked at Sanders and saw that he had not started to put on his tank. He had been watching her. "What's the matter?"

He smiled and shook his head. "Nothing. I think I'm losing my mind, that's all."

"What do you mean?"

"I've been sitting here, getting turned on just watching you spit in your mask."

Gail laughed. "You want to dive naked? We could conduct an experiment."

"My research indicates," Sanders said gravely, "that an ejaculation occurring more than thirty-three feet below sea level could cause a backup in the system, resulting in the blowing out of the brains."

He stood, picked up her tank, and held it until she had put her arms through the straps.

She said, "There are no reserves on these tanks."

"You won't need a reserve. There's only twenty or twenty-five feet of water here, and you should be able to get an hour out of a tank. More, maybe, if you're careful."

Gail sat on the gunwale, her back to the water, and took a breath from her mouthpiece. "Good air."

"It better be. If they're giving us bad air, this'll be one short honeymoon."

"How long will you be?"

"A minute. Go ahead over, but don't go down till you've had a good look around. You don't want to be surprised by anything waiting down there."

Gail rolled backward off the gunwale and disappeared in a cloud of bubbles.

Sanders found a piece of rag and wrapped it around his hand. Then he gathered together his gear, put it on, and went over the side.

It took several seconds for his bubbles to dissipate and his vision to clear.

Shafts of sunlight streaked through the blue, dappling the sand and coral. The water was pellucid; Sanders guessed he could see for more than a hundred feet. Treading water a few feet below the surface, he turned slowly around, searching the crepuscular limits of his vision for any potential danger. A pair of jacks darted in and out of the rocks. He looked down and saw Gail on the bottom, digging in the sand with her fingers. A small grouper hovered beside her, waiting for any morsels—worms or tiny crustaceans—that might float toward him in the cloud of sand stirred up by her digging. Sanders kicked slowly downward, swallowing to clear his ears as the pressure increased.

When he reached bottom, he saw that they had landed in a kind of amphitheater, a bowl on three sides of which coral and rock rose steeply toward the surface. The fourth, the seaward side, was open. There the boat lay placidly on the surface, the anchor line angling down from way forward of Sanders to a spot in the rocks behind him. The only sounds he heard were the soft whistle of his inhalation and the bubbly rattle as he exhaled.

He looked around, trying to discern shapes in the distance where transparent blue dwindled into dim mist. As always when he had not dived for several months, he felt a tingle of excitement, a mild but thrilling blend of agoraphobia and claustrophobia: he was alone and exposed on a wide plain of sand, certain that he could be seen by creatures he could not see; yet he was encased, too, by thousands of tons of water whose gentle but insistent pressure he could feel on every inch of his body.

He rose off the bottom and swam to his right, to the end of the line of rocks. Creeping along the rocks, he looked for anything that might signal the presence of a wreck: metal or glass or wood. He swam around the whole bowl and found nothing. Moving to the center of the bowl, toward Gail, he tapped her on the shoulder. When she looked up, he spread his hands and raised his eyebrows, as if to say: Where do you think it is? She shrugged and held up a piece of glass, the bottom of a bottle. He waved a hand contemptuously: Forget it, worthless. He motioned for her to follow.

Together they swam to the left. At the edge of the bowl, the rocks and coral continued in a fairly straight line. A school of bright blue-and-yellow surgeonfish fluttered by. A streak of sunlight danced over a piece of mustard-colored coral, its surface smooth, inviting touch. Sanders pointed to it and shook his index finger, warning her away. Then he pantomimed the sensation of being burned. Gail nodded: fire coral, whose mucous skin caused terrible pain.

They kicked their way along the reef, followed by the grouper, which evidently still harbored a primitive hope that something edible would result from their visit. Sanders felt a tug at his ankle. He looked back at Gail. Her eyes were wide, and she was breathing much faster than normal. She pointed to the left.

Sanders followed her hand and saw, hanging motionless, staring at them with a white-rimmed black eye, an enormous barracuda. Its body was as sleek and shiny as a blade, its prognathous lower jaw ajar, showing a row of ragged, needle teeth.

Sanders took Gail's left hand, turned her diamond ring so the stone faced her palm, and balled her hand into a fist. For emphasis, he held up his own clenched fist. Gail nodded, tapped herself on the chest, and pointed upward. Sanders shook his head: No. Gail insisted, frowning at him. *I'm* going up, she was saying; you stay here if you want. She kicked hard for the surface. Sanders blew an annoyed breath and followed.

"You want to quit?" he said as they boarded the boat.

"No. I want to rest for a minute. Barracudas give me the creeps."

"He was just passing by. But you should have left your ring in the boat. Flashing that stone around is asking for trouble."

"Why?"

"They'll mistake it for prey. The first time I ever dove on a reef, I had a brass buckle on my bathing suit. The instructor told me to cut it off. I said the hell with it; I wasn't about to ruin a fifteen-dollar bathing suit. So the guy took a knife and tied it to the end of a stick and set it in the sand, blade up. We were five or six feet away from the knife, and the instructor kept wiggling the stick, which made the blade flash in the sunlight. He only had to wiggle

16

it four or five times before a big barracuda came by and stared at the knife. The instructor wiggled it again, and bango! Faster'n you could see, that fish hit the knife. He hit it again and again, cut his mouth to ribbons, but every damn time the blade moved he'd hit it again. And every time he hit it I imagined he was hitting my belt buckle, or right nearby. I never wore that suit again, except in a pool."

Gail removed her rings and tucked them in a cubbyhole in the steering console.

"One more thing," Sanders said. "When there are just the two of us diving, one of us has to be the leader of the pack."

"Why do we need a leader?" Gail thought he was kidding. "Are you on a power trip?"

"No, dammit," Sanders said, more sharply than he had intended. "It's just that underwater we have to do things together. We have to know where each other is, all the time. Like then: If that had been a shark instead of a barracuda, and you wouldn't listen to me and shot for the surface, we'd be in a hell of a mess."

"A shark! Around here?"

"Sure. Chances are they won't bother you, but they're around. And if one does come along, you don't want to do something stupid."

"Like?"

"Like panicking and rushing for the surface. As long as you have air, the best thing to do is stay on the bottom and find shelter in the reef. As soon as you start for the surface

—especially if you're scared and swimming in a hurry—you become prey. And *on* the surface, you're lunch."

"Suppose I run out of air."

"You share my air and we wait for a chance to come up together. Unless he's a real monster, we'd have a pretty good chance of making it to the boat." Sanders saw that the talk of sharks was making Gail nervous. "Don't worry," he said. "Just don't do anything without checking with me."

Gail looked at him and drew a deep breath. "Okay." She put her face over the side and looked through her mask into the water. "You think that barracuda's gone?"

"Probably."

She continued to look underwater for a moment more, scanning the bottom. She was about to take the mask out of the water when she saw something big and brown behind the boat. "Hey, what's that?" she said, passing the mask to Sanders.

"Where?" He leaned over the side.

"Behind us. About as far as you can see."

"It's a timber. I'll be damned. There it is."

Sanders uncleated the anchor line and let the boat drift backward a few more yards. "Let's have a look."

"What did the bell captain say it was called? *Goliath?*"

"Yes. *Goliath.*"

They went overboard together, and as soon as their bubbles had risen away, they could see debris on the bottom. A long thick timber lay at right angles to the reef. Rotten wooden planks littered the white sand. Sanders touched Gail's shoulder and she looked at him. He grinned and put

thumb and index finger together in the "okay" sign. She responded with the same sign.

They swam along the bottom at the base of the reef. Gail found a rusted can, its seams burst and jagged. From a crevice in the rocks Sanders pulled a Coke bottle, intact. Gail lay on the bottom and dug beneath the near end of the big timber. She found a fork and part of a plate. Sanders saw something sticking out of the sand at the far end of the timber. He dug around it until he discovered what it was: the fluke of a huge anchor. Gail motioned that she was going up. He followed her.

Treading water on the surface, Gail spat out her mouthpiece and said, "Let's go over the reef."

"Why?"

"It looks like this is just the last bit of the bow. There's got to be more of her on the other side."

"Okay. But be careful of the surge as you're going over, and once you start to run out of air, don't screw around. Head for the boat."

Seaward of the reef, the bottom looked like a trash heap. Pieces of wood, rusted iron, and coral-covered metal were scattered everywhere. From the sand Gail plucked a pewter cup. One side was caved in, and the handle was rippled with dents, but otherwise the cup was undamaged. At the foot of the reef, Sanders saw an impossibly round ring of coral. He picked it up, held it to his face, and smiled at Gail. It was the remains of a brass porthole. Gail dug in the area where she had found the cup, and soon she had amassed a small pile of flatware—forks and spoons and knives, all gnarled and scarred.

She swam over to Sanders, who was poking in the crannies of the reef. Near the bottom of the reef there was a coral overhang: the coral stopped two or three feet from the sand, and there seemed to be a small cave underneath. She tapped Sanders and pointed to the overhang. He shook his head—no—and held one hand with the other, telling her that something might be living in the cave, something that would grab a probing hand.

They separated. Gail swam back to the area where she had found the forks and spoons; Sanders continued to poke in the reef. He came to another cave, slightly larger than the one he had warned Gail away from. He bent down and peered beneath the coral overhang. It was forbiddingly dark inside, and he was about to turn away and look elsewhere when a glint, a tiny flicker of reflection, made him look again.

Holding a rock to steady himself, he stared at the shimmering object, trying to guess what it could be. He looked at his rag-wrapped hand, and an image came to mind: a photograph he had seen of a man's hand soon after it had been bitten by a moray eel. The flesh had been tattered, and the bone showed sickly white. He hesitated, hearing the pulse thumping in his temples, and he knew he was breathing too fast. He felt fear; he detested the feeling. He stared at his hand and willed it toward the mouth of the cave.

Taking a deep breath, he shot his hand forward to the glitter. His fingers closed on something small, fragile; he snapped his hand back out of the darkness.

In his palm was a glass container about three inches long, tapered at both ends. It was full of a clear, yellowish liquid.

As he backed away from the cave, Sanders noticed that drawing breath was becoming difficult. He swam over to Gail—stopping briefly to collect a few relics he had left at the base of the reef—and touched her. When she looked up, he drew a finger across his throat. She nodded and repeated the gesture.

Sanders rose toward the surface. Gail lingered long enough to gather a handful of forks and spoons—already, after only a few minutes, the gentle current had covered one spoon with a patina of sand—then followed him. Together they crossed over the reef and swam to the boat.

"Beautiful!" Gail said, as she removed her weight belt and flippers. "That is *fantastic*."

In the bottom of the boat, next to Gail's forks, spoons, and pewter cup, were the items Sanders had collected: a chipped, but whole, butter plate; a rusted, dented flare pistol; a straight razor; and what looked like a pebbly lump of coal.

"What's that?" she said, pointing to the lump.

"There could be metal in it. When they stay in sea water for a long time, some metals develop this black stuff around them. Later on, we'll bang it open with a hammer and see if there's anything inside." Sanders opened his right hand and withdrew the ampule from beneath the rag wrapped around it. "Look," he said, and passed it to Gail.

"What is it?"

"Medicine, I guess. It looks like the ends were meant to be broken off so a syringe could be stuck in to draw off the liquid."

"I wonder if it's still good."

"Should be. It's airtight, God knows."

Sanders looked over the stern. "Tomorrow let's bring a bag. I think there's a lot more stuff down there."

When they reached the beach, the lifeguard—blond, deeply tanned, wearing a white T-shirt with a red cross on the back—was waiting for them in hip-deep water. He grabbed the bow, eased the boat up onto the sand, and helped them unload their gear. "See you got some goodies," he said to Gail as he watched her pile their finds on a towel and twist the ends of the towel together, fashioning a sack.

"Some," Sanders answered. The lifeguard had annoyed him at their first meeting that morning, when Sanders had rented the Whaler from him. He was cocky and young, and Sanders was sure he was closer to Gail's twenty-six years than to his own thirty-seven. And when the lifeguard spoke—even in answer to a question asked by Sanders—he looked at Gail. Sanders was convinced that the lifeguard was more interested in the sway of Gail's breasts as she bent over than in any relics they had brought from the wreck.

Sensing Sanders' pique, the lifeguard said to him, "You find any shells?"

"Shells?"

"Artillery shells. Depth charges. You know. Explosives."

"Live explosives?"

"I've always heard *Goliath* had a bunch of munitions on board. Maybe it's all talk."

Sanders said, "We'll look tomorrow. We'd like to use the boat again."

"Sure, as long as the wind doesn't go around to the south and start blowing. You don't want to be on that reef in a strong south wind."

"No. Neither did *Goliath*."

Carrying their gear, Gail and David trudged up the beach. The sand was pink—tinted by millions of tiny hard-shelled sea animals, called Foraminifera—and so fine that walking in it was like shuffling through talc.

By the time they reached the base of the cliff, Sanders was sweating. His palms were wet, and he had difficulty holding the necks of the scuba tanks. He looked up at the cliff, one hundred feet of sheer coral and limestone. To the right was a narrow, twisting staircase that led to the top. To the left was an elevator—a four-foot-square cage that rode up and down on a steel pole embedded in a concrete base—installed decades earlier in a crevasse cut in the cliff.

On a control panel in the cage there were two buttons, marked "up" and "down." If the elevator malfunctioned, there was no alarm bell, no emergency button: the passengers (three, at most) had no choice but to wait until someone spotted them and called for help. At breakfast the Sanderses had been told a story about an elderly couple who were trapped in the elevator as they rode up from the beach at twilight. They were the last to leave the beach, so there was no one below to see them. During the night, the wind swung around to the southwest and freshened into a moderate gale. The pole quivered in the wind, shaking the cage and the couple within, like a pocketful of loose change. When in the morning they were finally found, the woman (so went the story) was dead from fright and exposure, and the man had gone mad. He babbled to his rescuers about devils who had called to him in the darkness, about birds that had tried to peck out his eyes.

On their way down to the beach, Gail had refused to ride in the elevator. "I get claustrophobia in office-building elevators," she had said. "I'd be a basket case before I reached the bottom in that thing."

Sanders had not argued, but he insisted on sending their air tanks down in the elevator, for, as he pointed out, "If we let one of them bong into the rocks and rupture, we'll go up like a Roman candle."

Now he had no intention of walking up the staircase. He turned left, toward the elevator. Gail turned right.

"You're not going to walk up those stairs," he said.

"I sure am. What about you? I thought you were afraid of heights."

"I'm not *afraid* of heights, any more than I'm *afraid* of airplanes. I don't like either one, but I'm not about to let them ruin my life."

"Well, I'm still not getting in that bird cage. Come on. It's good for your legs."

Sanders shook his head. "I'll see you up there." He loaded the gear into the elevator, closed the gate, and pushed the "up" button. There was a click, then the motor whirred, whined, and lifted the cage off the ground. Sanders stood facing the cliff, staring at the gray rock as it moved slowly by. When he had seen enough of the cliff, he turned around and faced the sea, forcing himself to look down. He saw the lifeguard wheeling the Whaler up the beach on a light dolly, and a couple lying on colored beach towels arranged next to each other in perfect symmetry—looking, as they receded, like a postage stamp stuck to the pink sand.

His mind barely registered the change in the pitch of the electric motor, rising from a whine to a complaint.

When the cage bucked once, then stopped, he was not afraid; he assumed that someone, somewhere, had pushed a "stop" button, and soon that same someone would push a "go" button. He waited.

The motor was still racing, like an automobile engine in neutral with the accelerator pushed to the floor. Sanders pressed the "down" button. There was a click, but no change in the sound. He pushed the "up" button. Another click. The elevator did not move. He looked up. There was no roof to the cage, and he could see the top of the cliff, perhaps fifteen feet away.

When Gail got to the top of the stairs, she was breathing hard, and her thighs ached. She walked along the path for a few yards and was surprised to see that the elevator wasn't there. Her first thought made her smile: David chickened out and was following her up the stairs. She returned to the staircase and looked down; it was empty. Her next thought made beads of sweat break out on her forehead. She ran to where the elevator should have been and, supporting herself on a guardrail, leaned over the edge of the cliff. She was relieved: the cage was still there—at least it hadn't pulled away from the pole and crashed to the bottom. Sanders had reached his hands through the bars in the cage and was gripping the pole.

"Are you all right?" she called.

"It just stopped."

Gail looked at the machinery by the top of the elevator shaft. Two steel arms extended from concrete bases and encircled the pole. There was a large metal box, containing, she presumed, the motor. But there were no obvious controls, no buttons. "Don't move!" she said. "I'll get help."

She ran into the lobby of the Orange Grove Club, ignoring sternly worded signs prohibiting "bathing costumes and bare feet" in the public rooms of the club.

"The elevator's stuck!" she shouted as she approached the front desk. "My husband's caught inside."

The elderly clerk at the front desk was dressed in a morning coat, and he seemed more concerned about Gail's lack of clothing than about her alarm. All he said was "Yes."

"The elevator's stuck! My husband's—"

"Yes," the clerk said again. He picked up a telephone and dialed one digit.

"Well, *do* something!" Gail said.

"I am, madam." He spoke into the phone. "Clarence? It's happened again," he said, with a teasing I-told-you-so tone. He hung up and said to Gail, "Help will be along presently."

"What do you mean, 'presently'?"

"Madam," the clerk said stiffly, "if you'd care to wait on the veranda . . ." He cast a disapproving eye on Gail's bare midriff.

As soon as Gail was outside, she started to run, and then she saw Sanders, waiting for her at the top of the cliff, a grin on his face. Gail ran to him, put her arms around him, and kissed him.

"I was so worried . . . ," she said. "How did you make it work?"

"Make what work? I shinnied up the pole."

"You did *what?*"

"Shinnied. You know . . . shinnied."

Unbelieving, Gail looked over the edge of the cliff. The elevator was where it had been, their diving gear still inside. "*Why?*"

"I'd never done it before."

She looked at him and felt a sudden rush of anger. "Are you trying to kill yourself?"

"Don't be silly. It was a calculated risk. I thought I could do it, and I did."

"What if you'd been wrong."

"Yeah, well, those are the chances you take." He noticed the fury in her face. "C'mon, everything's . . ." He saw her hand coming at him, and he ducked. Her fist grazed the top of his head. "For Christ sake!" he said, raising his arm to ward off the second blow. He grabbed her, pinned her arms to her sides, and brought her to him. "Hey . . . nobody got hurt."

She struggled briefly, then stood still and let him hold her. "Who are you trying to impress?" she said.

As he started to answer, Sanders heard footsteps behind him. He turned to see an old black man carrying a ring of keys. The man was muttering.

"What went wrong?" Sanders asked.

"Temp'amental like a baby." The man searched for the key to open the metal box.

"Does this happen often?"

The man didn't answer. He opened the box, reached inside, and flicked a switch. Immediately, the pitch of the motor dropped back to normal. The man pushed something else, and, after a couple of clicks, wheels began to turn. Within seconds, the elevator was at the top of the cliff. The man shut the door, turned the key in the lock, and started away.

"Hey," Sanders said. "What happened?"

"Never know. Maybe too hot, maybe too cold."

"It's not going to fall off the pole, is it?"

"Never happen. If something ain't just right, there's clamps that suck right down on that pole like a old octopus. No, all that ever happen is she get stuck. If people just be patient, they be okay."

When the man had left, Sanders unloaded the diving gear. "Give me a hand with this?" he said to Gail.

She didn't move. She looked at him and said flatly, "Don't you ever do something like that again."

II

Sanders stepped out of the shower, dried himself, and stood before the bathroom mirror. He tightened his pectoral and stomach muscles and was pleased to see the muscle fibers showing through the skin. He patted his stomach and smiled.

The bathroom door opened behind him, and he felt a cool breeze that carried the aroma of Gail.

Gently, Gail pinched the insignificant flesh that sat above his hipbones. "Don't exercise too much," she said. "I'd hate it if you lost your love handles."

"Never." Sanders turned and kissed her.

They dressed for dinner, and as they left the cottage, Sanders slammed the door, turned the key in the lock, and jiggled the doorknob to make sure the lock was fast.

"Who's going to steal anything?" Gail asked.

"Anybody. Cameras, diving gear—it's expensive stuff. No point in making it easy to get at."

"Well, locking the door won't do any good. The maid has a key."

Holding hands, they walked along the path to the main building of the Orange Grove Club. It was like walking through a tropical nursery. Oleander, hibiscus, bougainvillaea, poinciana, and poinsettia, in a fusion of colors, crowded the sides of the path. Oranges and lemons dropped from trees in small well-tended groves. They passed a cluster of cottages similar to their own. The limestone buildings were painted orange—all but the roofs, which shone soft white in the evening sunlight.

Gail said, "Have you ever seen cleaner roofs?"

"They'd better be clean. That's what you drink off of."

"What do you mean?"

"There's no well water on Bermuda, no underground streams, no rivers, no nothing. All the water comes from rain. It runs off the roofs into cisterns."

"I thought you said it never rains here."

"What I said was, there's never been a year with less than three hundred and forty days of *some* sunshine. It rains a fair amount, even in summer. But the storms are sudden and squally, and they don't last long."

"For someone who's never been here, you're full of groovy facts."

"*National Geographic* training," Sanders said. "Life is nothing but the pursuit and capture of the elusive fact."

"Why did you quit the *Geographic?* Writing for them sounds like it'd be fun."

"*Writing* might have been." Sanders smiled. "*Doing* anything might have been. I didn't do, and I didn't write. I only made up captions. Legends, they call them. I went there because I wanted to live with wild apes, fight with crocodiles, and dive for wrecks no man had ever seen. Instead, I spent my days thinking up lines like, 'Calcutta: In-Spot for India's Teeming Millions.' I never *did* anything. I was paid to abbreviate what other people did."

As they neared the club's main building, another couple, younger, appeared on the path, walking toward them. Their gaits were awkward, for they had their arms around each other's waists, and since the man was much taller than his bride, he had to shorten his steps into a mincing trot so she could keep up with him. As soon as he saw the young couple, Sanders dropped Gail's hand.

When the couple had passed, Gail said, "Why did you do that?"

"Do what?"

"Drop my hand."

Sanders blushed. "Honeymooners make me nervous."

She took his arm and touched his shoulder with her head. "You're one, too, you know."

"Yeah. But I've already had one honeymoon."

"It's my first, though," Gail said. "Let me enjoy it."

They passed through the lobby—large, sedate, paneled in gleaming, close-grained cedar—and walked by the billiard room, game room, card room, reading room, and bar on their way to the outdoor patio overlooking the ocean. They were shown to a table at the edge of the patio. The sun, setting behind them, lit the clouds on the horizon and made them glow bright pink.

A waiter came to take their drink order. He was young, black, and there was a name on the tag on his breast pocket. He spoke in monosyllables and addressed them both—not disrespectfully—as "man."

As the waiter turned and left, Gail glanced after him and said quietly, "That must be a lousy job."

"Why?"

"What's he have to look forward to? Maybe, if he's really good, he'll become a headwaiter."

"What's wrong with that?" said Sanders. "It's better than being out of work."

"Did you notice his name? Slake. That doesn't sound Bermudian."

"I don't think there's any such thing as a Bermudian-sounding anything. There are black people with names like Bascomb who speak Saville Row British, and there are white folks who sound like they came out of a ghetto in Jamaica. I remember checking a *Geographic* caption with a guy, a fisherman, who was quoted as saying, 'Holiday tomorrow. There's going to be a tempest.' I thought, nobody says 'tempest' any more. But by God, the man really talked that way. Ethnically, this place is a mess."

When their drinks came, they sat in silence, listening to the waves below them, looking out at the few patches of reef visible on the windless evening.

Sanders reached into his pocket and took out the ampule he had found.

"In the morning, let's see if anyone around here can analyze this for us. I'll bet you a dime it's penicillin—from the sick bay. All ships carry that kind of stuff."

"I don't think penicillin was that common till after the war. It looks more like a vaccine. Anyway, you're on for a dime."

He started to hand the ampule to Gail to put in her purse when a voice behind them said, "Where did you get that?"

They turned and saw the waiter. Slake had menus in his hand. "I beg your pardon?" Gail said.

He seemed embarrassed by the abruptness of his question. "I'm sorry. I saw the little glass, and I wondered where you found it." Slake spoke in a musical accent that sounded Jamaican.

Sanders said, "On the wreck right off there."

"*Goliath?*"

"Yes." Gail held up the ampule so Slake could see it more clearly. "Do you know what it is?"

Slake took the ampule and held it between his finger tips. A gas lamp burned behind him, and he twirled the ampule before the light. He gave it back to Gail and said, "I have no idea."

Sanders said, "Then why are you so interested?"

"I am interested in glass. It looked old. It is pretty. Excuse me." Slake put the menus on the table and walked toward the kitchen.

After dinner, the Sanderses walked, hand in hand, along

33

the path back to their cottage. A quarter moon had risen, casting golden light on the leaves and flowers. The bushes were alive with the croaking of frogs.

Sanders unlocked the door to the cottage and said, "Let's have a brandy on the porch."

"We'll be eaten alive."

"I don't think so." He pointed to a yellow light above the door. "These things are supposed to keep the bugs away."

He poured brandy into the two bathroom glasses and carried them out to the porch. Gail was sitting in one of the two rattan chairs that flanked a small table.

"It's nice," she said, sniffing the air. "There are a thousand different smells."

For several minutes, they sat and gazed at the sky and listened to the rustle of the breeze in the trees.

"Are you ready for another thrilling fact from the files of the *Geographic?*" Sanders said.

"Sure."

"Back in the seventeenth century, this place was known as the Isle of Devils."

"Why?"

"How would I know? My contract only calls for me to give you the 'whats.' Someone else is paid to find out the 'whys.'"

Gail said, "I'm going to yawn now."

"Feel free."

"It will be the most sensual and suggestive yawn you have ever heard. It will promise wild, unimagined pleas-

34

ures that will make me forget that you are a suicidal maniac. In short, it will be a real turn-on."

"Do it," said Sanders. He closed his eyes and listened. He heard her embark on a low, moaning, feline yawn. It stopped—as suddenly as if someone had jammed a cork in her throat. "What's the matter?" he said. "Swallow your tongue?" He opened his eyes and saw her staring out into the darkness. "What?"

"Someone's out there."

"It's the wind."

"No, it isn't."

Sanders walked to the edge of the patio. The path was empty. He turned back to Gail and said, "Nobody."

"Look." Gail was pointing to something behind him.

When Sanders looked again, he saw a man stepping out of the bushes onto the path. He walked toward them, stopped a few yards from the porch, and said, "Excuse me." He was a black man, dressed in a black suit. All Sanders could see were his eyes and a patch of white shirt.

"How long have you been there?" Sanders said.

"Sir? I arrived this very moment."

"From the bushes?"

The man smiled. "That is the shortest way. The path is very roundabout." His accent was crisp, establishment British.

"What can we do for you?"

"I would like a word with you, if I may."

"Okay. But come up into the light."

The man, who looked about fifty, stepped onto the porch. His blue-black skin was wrinkled, and there were flecks of gray in his black hair. "My name is Tupper. Basil Tupper. I am the manager of a jewelry store in Hamilton. Drake's. Perhaps you've heard of it. No matter. My hobby is antique glass."

Sanders looked at Gail. "Lot of glass freaks in Bermuda."

Tupper said, "I understand you recently acquired a small item of glass from the wreck of the *Goliath*. I would like very much to see it."

"Why?"

"What's all the curiosity about?" Gail said, reaching for the purse beside her chair. "It's just a medicine bottle."

"No curiosity, really," said Tupper, "except to those of us interested in fine glass. A chap named Reinhardt worked with glass in Norfolk in the mid-1940s. His work is relatively scarce. It's not worth much in the open market, but in our small circle it's quite a coup to have a piece of Reinhardt glass."

Gail found the ampule and handed it to Tupper. He held it to the light. "A nice piece," he said. "Not outstanding, but a nice piece."

"It's an ampule," said Sanders. "You see them all over the place."

"True, but there is a tiny bubble at one end of the glass. That was Reinhardt's signature."

"What's in it?" Gail asked.

"I have no idea. It could be anything. That's not my concern."

Gail smiled. "For someone who doesn't care what's inside, you're studying it awfully carefully."

"I am studying the container, not the contents. The liquid looks yellow, but it might be quite clear. Reinhardt glass often imparts its own hue to liquids." Tupper returned the ampule to Gail. "Very nice. I'm prepared to offer you twenty dollars for it."

"Twenty dollars!" said Sanders. "But it's—"

"I know, that sounds like a lot. But as I said, in our little coterie there is a certain rivalry. I'd like very much to be the first to have a piece of Reinhardt's work. Frankly, the piece isn't worth more than ten dollars, but by offering you twenty I know I'm offering more than most of the others could pay. Someone like your acquaintance, Slake, couldn't possibly go higher than ten dollars. I am making what could be called a pre-emptive bid."

"Would you mind if we draw off some of the liquid?" Gail said. "We're interested in knowing what's inside, even if you're not."

"No," Tupper said. "That's quite impossible. To draw off the liquid, you would have to break an end of the piece. That would ruin its value."

"Then I'm afraid there's no sale," Sanders said.

"Thirty dollars," Tupper said, abandoning his deferential charm.

"No," said Sanders. "Not even for fifty."

"You're making a mistake, you know. No one else will offer you anywhere near that much."

"Then I guess we'll just have to keep the piece ourselves," Sanders said. "After all, you said yourself that it's quite a coup to have a piece of Reinhardt glass."

Tupper glared at him, then nodded to Gail, said good

night and backed off the porch. A few yards down the path he parted some bushes, stepped into the underbrush, and was gone.

"What the hell do you make of that?" Sanders said.

Gail stood up. "Let's go inside. If he could hang around in the bushes without our hearing him, God knows what else is creeping around out there."

They went into the cottage, and Sanders locked the door. "You believe him?"

"No. Do you?"

"Who knows from Reinhardt glass?"

"If there's such competition between glass nuts," Gail said, "why would Slake have told him about the ampule? He'd have offered to buy it himself. No. I bet he isn't interested in the glass. He's after what's inside."

"I wonder why he didn't say so."

"I don't know. I guess it's pretty hard to pass yourself off as a liquid-collector."

"Have you got the rest of the stuff we found?"

"Sure," Gail said. "Why?"

"Tomorrow, let's see if we can find someone who knows something about the wreck. Maybe there's an old manifest; at least that'd tell us what *Goliath* was carrying."

III

"There were no survivors?" Gail said.

"One," replied the bell captain, a corpulent, middle-aged Briton, "but he's about gone by these days."

"Gone by?"

The bell captain touched his head. "Dotty. He'd tell you volumes, but two thirds of it would be fancy. There is one man who might be able to help you, Romer Treece. He's been on every wreck off Bermuda; found half of them himself. If anyone knows these waters, he does."

"Is he in the phone book?" Sanders asked.

"He has no telephone. The only way to contact him is to go out to his home, on St. David's Island."

"Okay. I saw some motorbikes out front. Are they for rent?"

"The little ones—the mobilettes—yes." The bell captain paused. "Mr. Sanders . . . do you know about St. David's?"

"What's to know? I've seen it on the map."

"They're not exactly . . . hospitable . . . out there. They don't consider themselves Bermudians; they're St. David's Islanders. There's a bridge, the Severn Bridge, connecting the island to the rest of Bermuda. They'd as soon it fell down and was never rebuilt."

Sanders laughed. "What are they, hermits?"

"No, but they're a proud people, and a bit bitter, too. They make their own rules, and the Bermuda Government looks the other way. There's a mutual agreement, I guess you could say a recompense for slavery."

"Slavery?"

"The ancestors of St. David's Islanders were slaves. Half of them were Mahican Indians, troublemakers sent down by the American colonists. The other half were unruly Irish, shipped over by the British. Over the years they intermarried, and they created as hard a bloodline as you'd care to see."

"They sound fascinating," Gail said.

"In daylight, ma'am. Don't linger in St. David's after dark."

Sanders said, "Thanks for the advice. I left our air tanks down in the equipment shed. Can we get them filled again?"

The bell captain didn't answer. He looked uneasy. "I

. . . I meant to ask you, Mr. Sanders." He held up two wallet cards. "The cards you gave me. Forgive my ignorance, but I'm not familiar with NIDA."

"Oh sure," Sanders said smoothly. "National Independent Divers Association. There are so many divers these days, NAUI and the Y can't handle them all. NIDA's a new group."

"Of course." The bell captain made a note on a pad. "It's regulations. I hope you understand."

"No problem."

Gail and David went outside and ordered motorbikes from the Orange Grove cycle shop. While the clerk was filling out forms, Gail whispered, "What was that business with the cards?"

Sanders said, "I thought that might happen. They're getting tighter every year. You can't get air without a certification card."

"But we've never been certified."

"I know. I had the cards made in New York."

"What's NIDA? Is there such a thing?"

"Not that I know of. Don't worry. They never check. They just have to have something to put on file."

"We probably should have taken the Y course," Gail said. "Yesterday was the first time I've dived in a year."

"Who's got fourteen Tuesday nights to waste in a swimming pool?" Sanders put his arm around her waist. "You'll be fine."

"It's not just me I'm worried about."

They listened to instructions about how to operate the

motorbikes. The clerk pointed to a row of helmets and said, "What are your hat sizes?"

"Forget it," Sanders said. "I hate those things."

"It's the law. You have no choice. The police can confiscate the bikes."

"It seems to me," Sanders said irritably, "that I should be able to decide for myself . . ." He stopped, feeling Gail's hand on his arm. "Oh, all right."

Gail put the towel full of artifacts from *Goliath* in the basket on the rear fender of her bike and patted her shirt pocket to make sure the ampule was there.

They set off, heading northeast on South Road. The wind had gone around to the southeast, and as they putted along the road overlooking the south shore, Sanders pointed to the reefs: what yesterday had been a calm anchorage for the Whaler was now a churning boil of foam. Waves crashed on the rocks. Even shoreward of the reefs, the wind-whipped water gathered enough force to make surf on the beach.

The road was crowded with small slow taxicabs, whose drivers—though they had known each other all their lives and saw each other every day—impulsively waved and honked their high-pitched, bleating horns at each other.

There seemed to be no social order, no evident neighborhoods, among the houses they passed. Generally, the houses on the right side of the road, with spectacular ocean views, were large, well kept, and obviously expensive. Those on the left, nestled close together on hillsides, were smaller. Every puff of breeze was rich with thick aromas, sweet and sour, spicy and fruity.

They passed through Devonshire and Smith's Parishes, turned left on Harrington Sound Road, and followed the long causeway across Castle Harbour to St. George's Island. A sign indicated the town of St. George to the left; they went right, across the Severn Bridge, and rode along the narrow road paralleling the airport toward St. David's.

They had expected to ride into a tidy, contained community. What they found, instead, was a random assembly of limestone cottages connected by dirt paths. It was as if someone had taken a bagful of cottages ten thousand feet up into the air, and then emptied the bag carelessly, letting the contents scatter on the hillsides. Only one building seemed properly placed: a lighthouse at the top of a cliff.

They stopped on the side of the road, and Sanders unfolded the map he had gotten at the hotel. "This is it," he said. "It has to be. That's St. David's light up there."

"Let's ask somebody."

"Sure. Ask any one of those thousands of people." He waved his arm at the hillside. There were no bicycles, no cars, no pedestrians. The town seemed deserted.

Fifty yards away, beyond a turn, they saw a hand-lettered sign that said, "Kevin's Lunch."

"It looks empty," said Gail.

There was no door on the frame of the shack, but the remains of a bead curtain hung in tatters from a reed pole across the top of the doorway. Sanders rapped with his knuckles on the wall. There was no response. "Anybody there?"

They walked through the doorway.

"What you want?" said a voice at the far end of a long

counter. The man wore no shirt, his skin was dark brown, his belly fat and hairless. His eyes were black holes above globular cheeks.

Sanders said, "We're looking for Romer Treece."

"Not here."

"Where can we find him?"

"He not a bloody goddamn tourist attraction."

"We're not tourists," Sanders said. "That isn't why we want to see him. We want to ask him about a ship."

"He know ships," the man said, less belligerently. "For sure. How bad you want to talk to him?"

"What?" It took Sanders a moment to realize what Kevin meant.

"Oh. Yes." He took a five-dollar bill from his wallet and put it on the counter.

"You not want to see him very bad."

Sanders started to say something, but he looked at Gail, and her expression said, Let's get out of here. He put another five on the counter. "Is that bad enough?"

"Top of the hill, by the light."

Gail said, "He lives in the lighthouse?"

"Right there by. It's his light."

The lighthouse sat on a flat promontory, so high above the sea that the light itself needed to be only fifty or sixty feet above the ground. There was a well-marked path directing tourists to the front of the lighthouse. A small white house, surrounded by a picket fence, was nestled in the lee of the light. The word PRIVATE was painted on the gate. The Sanderses leaned their motorbikes against the fence, opened the gate, and walked down the short path toward the house. On each side of the front door, where there might have been flower beds, was a bathtub-size vat filled with a clear liquid. In the vats the Sanderses saw dozens of pieces of rusty metal—spikes, buckles, boxes, pistol barrels, and countless unfamiliar objects.

Gail held up the towel-wrapped bundle. "You suppose that's stuff like this?"

"Looks like it. That's probably a chemical bath, to clean stuff off."

The front door to the house was open, but there was a screen door, closed and latched from inside. Sanders knocked on the frame and called, "Hello? Mr. Treece?"

"There's pamphlets in the bloody lighthouse! Tell you all you want to know." The voice was deep, the accent similar to, but not identical with, English or Scots.

"Mr. Treece, we'd like to ask you about some things we found." Sanders looked at Gail. When he turned back to the screen door, he found himself staring up into the face of the biggest man he had ever seen.

He was nearly seven feet tall, and his chest was so immense that the sleeves of his T-shirt had begun to separate at the seams. His hair was black, cropped in a crew cut that rose from a sharp V in the middle of his forehead. His nose was long and thin, and it had a noticeable bend in the middle—as if it had been broken and never set. His face seemed triangular, an upside-down pyramid: wide, high cheekbones above hollow cheeks, a thin-lipped mouth above a sharp, jutting chin. His skin was brown and dry, like overdone bacon. The only facial feature that betrayed the presence of blood other than Indian was the eyes: light powder-blue.

"We're not tourists," Sanders said. "The man at Orange Grove said you might be willing to look at some things we got off a ship."

"What man?"

"The bell captain."

"Briscoe," said Treece. "I'm not his bloody hand-maiden."

"He only said that no one else could help us, and that you might."

"What ship?"

"*Goliath*."

"Nothing worth a damn on that scow. Least if there is, no one's ever found it." Treece looked beyond them to the gate. "You rode all the way out here on those things?"

"Yes."

"Well, what'd you find?" Treece unlatched the screen door and stepped out onto the path, closing the door behind him. "Is that the stuff there?" he said, pointing to the bundle in Gail's hand.

"Yes." Gail handed him the bundle.

Treece squatted down, set the towel on the path, opened it, and looked at the forks and spoons, the pewter cup, the razor, and the butter plate. "That's *Goliath* trash, no question." He stood up. "You got your answer. Was it worth the ride?"

Sanders said, "There was one other thing." He motioned to Gail, and she took the ampule from her shirt pocket and passed it to Treece.

46

Treece let the ampule rest in the palm of his hand. He stared at it, saying nothing. Sanders saw the muscles in his jaw move, as if he were gritting his teeth.

Finally, Treece closed his hand around the ampule. He raised his head and looked at the sea. "God bloody damn!" he said. "Thirty-two years, and finally the sonofabitch comes true."

"What—"

Treece spun on Sanders, cutting him off. "Who else has seen this?"

"Well . . ." Sanders stammered.

"I said *who else!*"

"Last night," he said, "a man tried to buy it from us. A black man. He said he was interested in the glass. And a waiter at the hotel saw it, too."

Treece laughed—a laugh of anger and contempt. "Glass." He held his fist under Sanders' face and opened it, forcing him to look at the ampule. "You know what's in there? Morphine, pure and sweet, enough to give a man a week's holiday in the stars. It's no surprise someone tried to buy it from you. It's proof of the legend."

"What legend?"

Treece looked at Sanders, at Gail, then back at Sanders. "I'd as soon not tell you, but now they know you found it, they'll be letting you know soon enough. Come along."

They followed Treece around to the back of the house. He led them into the kitchen, a large and airy room with a view of the sea. Bottles and vials of chemicals, Bunson burners and tools—dentist drills, forceps, knives, hammers, chisels—were strewn about everywhere, on the counters

47

and on the one round table. He motioned them to chairs at the table.

Gail's throat was dry, and she said, "Could I have a glass of water?"

"If I can find a glass," Treece said, rummaging around in the clutter on a counter.

Gail saw a half-full glass on the table. "This'll be fine," she said, and she reached for the glass. "It doesn't have to be cold."

Treece watched her, waiting until the glass was within an inch or two of her mouth. Then he laughed and said, "Jesus, girl, don't drink that stuff. One sip and you'll be in the history books."

Gail was startled. "What is it?"

"Hydrochloric acid. Clean your pipes out, that's for certain." He found a glass, filled it with tap water, and handed it to her. "Here. All this'll do is rust you."

Sanders heard a growl behind him. He turned, not knowing what to expect, and saw a dog sitting on the window sill. It was a terrier of some kind, medium-size, its muzzle grizzled, and it snarled at Sanders.

Treece said, "It's all right, Charlotte, you dumb bitch."

The dog's eyes did not move from Sanders. She growled again.

"I said it's all right!" Treece grabbed the glass from Gail and flung the water in the dog's face. The dog wagged her tail and licked the water from her whiskers. "You be nice. They're not tourists. At least, not now."

The dog jumped down from the window sill and sniffed around Sanders' pants.

"She's feeling pissy because you got in here without her seeing you," Treece said. "She likes to get her licks in first."

"Does she really bite?" Gail asked, as the dog's cold nose explored Sanders' ankle.

"I guess so! She's purebred tourist hound." Treece leaned against the wall and said, "What do you know about *Goliath?*"

"Nothing, really," Gail said.

"Maybe one thing," said Sanders. "The lifeguard on the beach said he had heard she was carrying ammunition."

"Aye," said Treece. "That, too. *Goliath* was a cargo vessel, a wooden sailing ship carrying supplies to Europe during World War II. There was a sound purpose to using wooden ships, slow as they were. The hull wouldn't attract magnetic mines, and, under sail, she made no screw noise for U-boats to home on. *Goliath* was loaded. Her manifest listed a boodle of munitions and medical supplies. She went down in the fall of 1943, broke her back on the rocks, and dumped her guts all over the place. For weeks, folks gathered every Christ kind of crap you ever saw off the beach. I went down on her two-three times in the fifties and hauled a ton of brass off her—depth charges and artillery shells. There were radios all over the bottom. You never saw anything like it. But nobody ever found those medical supplies."

"What were they supposed to be?" asked Gail.

"Nobody knows for sure. The manifest said medical supplies, period. It could have been anything—sulfa, bandages, iodine, chloroform—anything. A couple of years after the war, though, forty-seven I think it was, a bloody great hurricane beat it all to rubble. Most people forgot about *Goliath* after that, but some didn't."

Sanders said, "The bell captain told us there was a survivor."

"Aye, one. He was damn near in worse shape than the wreck, but he lived. For a time after he got out of hospital he sold scraps from *Goliath*, and for drinks he'd tell tales of the wreck. One night, he was in his cups and he spun a web about a fortune in drugs aboard *Goliath*. Thousands and thousands of ampules of morphine and opium, he said, carried in cigar boxes. He claimed to have been personally responsible for them, said he knew where they were but he'd tell no man. A day later he was waylaid and thrashed by people wanting to know more about the drugs. He swore he'd forgotten what he'd said, claimed he didn't know anything about any drugs. He never told that story again. But once was enough. Rumor spread, and before long the rumor was that there were ten million dollars in drugs down there. People looked—Jesus, they did a bloody autopsy on the wreck with everything save tweezers—but they never found a single ampule. Not till now."

"Why would one turn up now?" Sanders asked.

"The bottom of the sea is a living creature. She's whimsical, the sea, a tease. She loves to fool you. She changes all the time. A storm can alter her face; a change in current can cause her to heave her insides out. You can dive on a wreck one day and find nothing. The wind blows that night, and the next day, in the same spot, you find a carpet of gold coins. That's happened. And we've had four juicy blowups in the past six weeks."

Gail said, "David thought this ampule could have come from the sick bay."

"*Goliath* didn't have a sick bay. They likely carried some medicine for the crew, and if this were any other ship, I'd write the ampule off as from the medicine chest. But not this one. The best hope is that you found the one and only ampule left."

"Why?" asked Sanders.

"Because there are people who'd slit your throat for a fraction of what the rumors say is down there. How much did you tell that fellow last night?"

"Nothing. We didn't *know* anything, except that we found the ampule in the general area of *Goliath*."

Treece looked out the window. Finally he said, "Would you be willing to take another plunge, have another look? Not today. The sea'd turn a diver to hash. But tomorrow?"

Sanders looked at Gail. "Sure."

"It's important to know if there's anything more down there. If there isn't, fine. But if there is, I'll want to get it up before every hophead between here and the Bahamas finds out about it and starts diving for a cheap charge. I'd go myself, but that would be like running a flag up a pole." Treece began to search through some cabinets. "Any time I get my feet wet, the papers start trumpeting about treasure. And now that someone knows there may be something on *Goliath*, for me to go down would be a dead giveaway." He reached deep into the back of a cabinet and brought out two fist-size rocks, which he put on the table. "If you come across another ampule, set one of these on the spot. The shiny chips are infrared reflectors. I'll go down of a night with an infrared torch and poke around."

"Okay," said Sanders. "We'll go tomorrow."

"If the wind behaves."

Gail stood up, and as she lifted her bundle from the table, she noticed the black lump David had found. She pointed at it and said to Treece, "Is that coal?"

"No." Treece picked up the lump. "It's a sulfide of some kind. I can look inside for you, but there's a risk of ruining it."

"That's okay."

Treece took a hammer and chisel from the counter, sat down at the table, and set the black lump in front of him. The hammer looked like a toy in his huge, scarred hand; his thumbnail was as big as the face of the hammer head. But he used the tools as gently and deftly as a gem-cutter. He probed the lump, chipping here and there, found a hairline crack near the center, and lined the chisel blade on the crack. He banged the chisel once, and the lump fell apart in two pieces. Examining the two halves, he smiled. "It's a nice one. Can't quite read the date, but otherwise, it's a dandy."

"What is it?" said Sanders.

"The bones of a piece of eight, ancestor of the bloody dollar."

"I don't understand."

"Look." Treece held the two halves of the lump to the light. In the black mass, Sanders saw the faint imprint of a cross, a castle, and a rampant lion. "That was once a silver coin. When it hit the briny, it began to oxidize. Then it became silver sulfide. That's all that's left, a shadow. Silver does that, unless there's a heap of it, or it lies up against iron. Then it's preserved pretty well."

"You mean a *Spanish* piece of eight?" said Gail. "It can't be."

"It is that, girl. Eight silver reals, as common as a shilling in those days."

Gail said, "It was worth a dollar?"

"No. What I meant was that it's from the piece of eight that the dollar sign came. Look here." Treece spread the dust from the black lump and drew in it with his finger. "Spanish accountants used to register pieces of eight like this: a P next to an 8. That got to be a burden, so they shortened it like this." He drew an 8 and a P together, rubbed out a few lines, and was left with: $.

"How old is it?" asked Gail.

"I don't know. I couldn't read the date. A couple of hundred years, anyway."

"It can't be!"

Treece laughed. "Do tell," he said tolerantly. "Where did you find it?"

Gail said, "We found it on *Goliath*."

"Not possible." Treece paused, then said quietly, "*Goliath* went bubbles in 1943. She was carrying no Spanish coins."

"Well, that's where we found it. David did. In the rocks."

"Ah well," Treece said. "You do find them now and again. Sometimes they even kick up in the surf."

"Could there be more?" Gail asked.

"Aye." Treece smiled. "And beneath that could be Atlantis. You found one coin—not even a coin, a skeleton of one. Imagine: Suppose there was an earthquake right now that broke off this bloody cliff and plunged us into the sea. And suppose three hundred years from now some divers come across the wreckage, and the first thing they find is a penny that spilled out of my pocket. Now, they'd be fools to conclude that they'd come upon the treasure hoard of some Bermuda panjandrum."

Sanders said, "But there *could* be more."

"Possible, aye, I won't deny it. There's more mysteries hidden by the sea than you or I can fathom, and once in a while she unravels one, in her own time. But usually she just teases you, gives you trinkets to keep you interested. Then she spits in your eye."

"I read somewhere about a kid who was walking in the sand and scuffed up a fifty-thousand-dollar gold chain."

Treece nodded. "It happens. But if you wait around for it to happen to you, you'll go mad."

"Should we look for more coins tomorrow?" Gail asked.

"No. You wouldn't recognize them if they fell on your foot. Don't go picking up every Christ lump of black rock you see."

Treece led the Sanderses out the back door and around to the front of the house. The dog followed, sniffing and wagging her tail.

"How will we get in touch with you?" Sanders said.

"As you did today. A long ride it may be, but it keeps visitors infrequent and sincere. In an emergency, you could ring my cousin Kevin."

"Not Kevin's Lunch. We stopped for directions."

A hint of displeasure must have shown on Sanders' face, for Treece laughed and said, "How much did they cost you?"

"Ten dollars."

"He is some kind of mercenary bastard, Kevin is. He's all right, but if there's a way to suck money from dirt, he'll find it."

Gail said, "He seemed very . . . protective of you."

"He is. Most folks here are. It's a tradition."

"To protect you?"

"To shield whichever one of us Treeces is keeping the light. When the bloody bastards dumped us here as slaves in the eighteenth century, they put a sheriff and a band of thugs in charge of keeping us in line. But we didn't take well to slavery, and after a bit we scalped the sheriff and threw him and his lot to the fish. Then they jolly well let us be. We set our own order. A Treece was elected chief, for two reasons: We were always bigger than anybody else, and there were more Treeces around than anybody else, so we always had ample blood kin to help put down any dust-ups. It's been this way for over a century."

"You're the chief now?" Gail said.

"In a way. The job doesn't amount to much. I arbitrate disputes, and I deal with the Bermudians whenever we have something to deal with them about, which is blessedly seldom. And I keep the light, which is the only part of the job that pays. But it's not a bad job, especially in the years before you take it. It's like being the bloody Prince of Wales. When my father was alive, the Islanders paid for my education in England. There's a feeling that the chief should be educated. I don't know why: a degree isn't much help in thumping a rascal or returning a fellow's stolen goat."

"There is crime here, then," said Gail. "We were warned not to stay after dark."

"Not to speak of, at least not among St. David's people. But the warning has merit: Off-islanders are fair game."

"And when you retire," Gail said, "your son takes over?"

"He would," Treece said evenly, "if I had a son."

The flatness of Treece's tone embarrassed Gail. Sanders noticed her discomfort, and he said, "We'll leave the ampule with you?"

"I would," Treece said. "Nobody'd be fool enough to come in here after it, and it's for sure no dizzy bugger's going to knock me down and try to rifle my pockets." He moved to the gate. "Be sure you want to do this. You're on holiday. There's no reason for you to muck about with this if you'd rather not."

"What could happen?" Gail asked.

"I imagine nothing. But you're never sure what people will do when they smell money. Especially some of the black bastards around here."

Treece noticed that Gail started at the words "black bastards" and he said, "Racist. Prejudiced bugger. Fascist. No. I have no prejudice. But I do have my biases. And my reasons. The blacks on Bermuda have ample to complain about, and they do ample complaining. But they've got a way to go before they earn my respect."

56

"But you can't—"

"Come on," Sanders said, cutting her off. "Let's not turn this into a symposium on ethnic attitudes." He said to Treece, "See you tomorrow."

"Good." Treece opened the gate for them and shut it after them. As soon as the gate was closed, the dog reared up on her hind legs, put her front paws on the fence, and began snarling and barking. Treece laughed. "You're tourists again."

They walked their motorbikes down the hill toward the road in front of the lighthouse.

"We *should* be sure we want to do this," Gail said.

"*I'm* sure. What an opportunity to *do* something. I'm sick of reading about what other people have done or writing about other people's good times. You can't live your whole life vicariously. It's like masturbating from cradle to grave. Anyway, all we've agreed to do is dive tomorrow, which we want to do anyway, and see what's there. If we find anything—then we can worry about what to do next. But I'm not walking away from this before we know more."

When David Sanders was seventeen, a junior in high school, his English class had been assigned *Walden*. Most of Sanders' classmates found the book dull and lifeless, a collection of maxims to be underlined, memorized, regurgitated on an exam paper, and forgotten.

But Sanders had found Thoreau's attitudes toward life so inspiring that he had two plaques made. One said, "The mass of men lead lives of quiet desperation"; the other:

57

". . . I wished to live deliberately, to front only the essential facts of life, and see if I could not learn what it had to teach, and not, when I came to die, discover that I had not lived." Though they had chipped and faded with time, the plaques still hung over his desk.

When he was a junior in college, Sanders went to a lecture by Jacques-Yves Cousteau, and by the end of the evening he knew that Cousteau's was the life he wanted to live. He wrote letters to Cousteau (none was ever answered) and drove two hundred miles or more to hear Cousteau lecture and see one of his films. Once, after a lecture, he had spoken to Cousteau, who told him—graciously but firmly—that there were hundreds of applicants for positions aboard the *Calypso* and that unless Sanders had credentials as a marine scientist or underwater photographer, he had no chance of being considered.

Immediately after graduating, Sanders entered the Army's six-month program. When his active duty was over, he married the girl he had been dating since his sophomore year. He didn't particularly want to get married, but, now that it was obvious that he would have to seek routine employment, Sanders thought of marriage as an adventure: at least it was something he had never done before.

David and Gloria moved to Washington. The romance of Camelot was in full flower, and David fancied himself in the Kennedy style. He swam, sailed, played touch football. He even brought with him a letter of recommendation from one of his history professors who had been a classmate of JFK's at Harvard. He thought he might become a speech writer—junior, of course—sitting at Ted Sorenson's right hand, writing quips for the Leader of the Free World. He was advised that the best way to get into the government was to take the Foreign Service examination. He passed the written exam but failed the orals. He never knew why he had failed, but he guessed that one of the examiners had disapproved when he responded to a question about his outside interests by saying, "Scuba diving and killer whales."

A letter from a friend of his father's got him a job at the *National Geographic*. After a year of writing captions—chafing at the sight of full-time writers returning, tanned and leathery, from exotic assignments—he asked his boss how long it would take him to become a staff writer. He was told there was no guarantee he would *ever* become a staff writer. The best way to demonstrate his talent to the editors, said his boss, was for him to write a free-lance piece for the magazine.

He quit his job and began to deluge the editors with one-paragraph story ideas about far-off places, but he soon discovered that before the editors would consider assigning a piece, they wanted an outline so extensive and so detailed that only someone intimately familiar with the place in question could prepare the outline. Sanders had never been west of the Mississippi, and the only place he had visited outside the continental United States was St. Croix. He started to work on a novel. He had written nearly twenty pages when Gloria announced that—despite the diligent use of every birth-control device known to science except abstinence—she was pregnant.

Sanders first considered Wall Street during a glum, drunken evening with a college classmate. The bull market of the mid-sixties was just beginning, and Sanders' classmate was making thirty thousand a year for doing, by his own admission, practically nothing. Certainly, Sanders reasoned, he was no less qualified than his classmate, and he found a roguish appeal in the stories about the young "gun slingers" on the Street. He moved to New York, rented an apartment in the East Seventies, read a few books, made a few contacts, and found a job—all in less than a month.

To his surprise, Sanders liked the work. It was easy and exciting and remunerative. He was gregarious, liked to take chances with money, and his early successes (accomplished simply by following the advice of more experienced brokers) brought him as many clients as he chose to service. He was bright enough to realize that though the Dow might hit the fabulous 1,000 mark, something would eventually happen to bring the market down, so he learned about hedge funds and selling short. The slide that began in 1968 made him, on paper, reasonably well off.

He took himself off salary and became a "customer's man," surviving solely on commissions received from buying and selling stocks for his clients. He was very good at his job (he believed he had a special gift for sensing impending changes in the market, and he relished taking risks based on hunches), and three rival firms tried to hire him at handsome salaries. He refused, preferring the unpredictable life of the customer's man. The fact that he never knew, from one month to the next, how much money he would make, excited him. He viewed it as freedom. If he failed to make a living, he had no one to blame but himself. If (as was the case) he succeeded, there was no one with whom he had to share credit.

His wife, Gloria, however, regarded this freedom, this so-called courage, as madness. She was an orderly person who did not take chances, who liked to know exactly how much money would be in each of the envelopes she kept in a file drawer labeled "budget." There was envelopes for food, clothing, toys, entertainment, and schoolbooks.

By 1971, Sanders had two children, a co-operative apartment on West Sixty-seventh Street, and a house in Westhampton. He knew he should have been a happy man, but he was bored. Gloria bored him. She was interested in, and knowledgeable about, only two things: clothes and food. Their sex life had become routine and predictable. Gloria professed a fondness for sex, but she refused to discuss—let alone attempt—ways of making it more interesting. Sanders found himself, during love-making, fantasizing about movie stars, secretaries, and Billie Jean King.

Soon his work began to bore him. He had proved to himself that he could make money in every kind of market, and he enjoyed both the making and the spending of money. But the challenge was gone. He grew restless and began to do careless things.

He still dreamed, from time to time, of working with Cousteau. He kept himself in excellent physical condition, as if in anticipation of a phone call from Cousteau. But he was not satisfied with fine-tuning his body: he liked to test it. Once, he intentionally gained ten pounds, to see if,

61

as he believed, a special diet he had concocted would strip off the poundage in three days. Another time, on a bet, he set out to run ten miles. He collapsed after six miles, but took consolation in a doctor-friend's statement that—considering that Sanders hadn't trained for the marathon—he should have collapsed after two or three miles. He saw a television show about hang-gliding—soaring through the air suspended from a giant kite—and determined to build himself a hang glider. He built it and intended to test it by jumping off an Adirondack cliff, until a hang-gliding expert convinced him that his kite was aerodynamically unsound: the wing struts were too weak and probably would have broken, causing the kite to fold up and Sanders to fall like a stone down the side of the mountain.

There was only one week a year when he wasn't bored, the week in winter when his children visited their grandparents, his wife went to an Arizona health spa, and he went diving at one of the Club Méditerranée resorts in the Caribbean.

He met Gail at the Club Med on Guadalupe—or, rather, under the Club Med. They were on a guided diving tour of some coral gardens. The water was clear, and the sunlight brought out all the natural colors on the shallow reef. After a few minutes of following the meticulous guide, who stopped at every specimen of sea life and made sure each diver took a long look, Sanders left the group and let himself glide down the face of the reef toward the bottom. He was vaguely aware that he was not alone, but he paid no attention to the figure who followed him. He let himself float with the motion of the sea, turning in lazy circles.

He swam along the base of the reef, peering in crannies. A small octopus darted across his path, squirting black fluid, and disappeared into the reef. Sanders swam to the hole the octopus had entered and was trying to coax it out of its den, when he felt a tap on his shoulder. He turned and saw a woman's face, white with fear, her eyes wide and bulging. She made the divers' signal for "out of air," a finger drawn across the throat in a slitting motion. He took a breath and handed her his mouthpiece. She breathed deeply twice and passed the mouthpiece back to him. Together they "buddy-breathed" to the surface.

They reached the support boat and climbed aboard. "Thanks," Gail said. "That's an awful sensation—like sucking on an empty Coke bottle."

Sanders smiled and watched her as she dried herself with a towel.

She was the most attractive woman he had ever seen—not classically beautiful, but vibrantly, viscerally appealing. Her hair was short and light brown, streak-bleached by the sun. She was almost as tall as Sanders, nearly six feet. Her skin was smooth and flawless, except for an appendectomy scar that showed above the bottom of her bikini. Her tan seemed impossibly even: the only patches of skin that were not honey-brown were between her toes, the palms of her hands, and the tips of her breasts, which Sanders saw as she leaned over to stuff the towel under the seat. Her legs and arms were long and lithe. When she stood, the sinews in her calves and thighs moved as if her skin were paper. Her eyes were deep, brilliant blue.

Gail saw him staring at her, and she smiled. "You deserve a reward," she said. The tone of her voice was not extraordinary, but the way she spoke—with a breezy confidence—gave her words authority. "After all, you saved my life."

Sanders laughed. "You weren't in any real trouble. If I hadn't been there, you probably could've made it to the surface okay. There was only about fifty feet of water."

"Not me," she said. "I would've panicked. Held my breath or something. I don't dive enough to know how to handle trouble. Anyway, I'll buy you lunch. A deal?"

Sanders suddenly felt nervous. Never, not in high school or college or the years since, had a woman asked him for a date. He didn't know what to say, so he said, "Sure."

Her full name was Gail Sears. She was twenty-five, and she worked as an assistant editor at a small, prestigious New York publishing house that specialized in nonfiction books about social, economic, and political affairs. She was a member of Common Cause and Zero Population Growth. For the first year after her graduation from college she had shared an apartment with a friend, but now she lived alone. She described herself as a private person—"I suppose you could say selfish."

After lunch, they played tennis, and if Sanders hadn't been at the top of his serve-and-volley game, she would have beaten him. She stood at the base line and slugged long, low ground strokes that landed deep in the corners. After tennis, they swam, had dinner, went for a walk on the beach, and then—as naturally as if the act were the next event in the day's athletic schedule—made noisy, sweaty love in Gail's bungalow.

When they had finished, that first time, Sanders raised himself on one elbow and looked at her. She smiled at him. Beads of perspiration glued strands of hair to her forehead. "I'm glad you saved my life," she said.

"So am I." Then he added, without really knowing why, "Are you married?"

She frowned. "What kind of dumb question is that?"

"I'm sorry. I just wanted to know."

She said nothing for a long moment. "I almost was. But I came to my senses, thank God."

"Why 'thank God'?"

"I would have been a disaster as a wife. He wanted kids; I don't, at least not yet. I'd resent them for strangling my life."

Two days after he returned to New York, Sanders moved out of his apartment and filed for separation from his wife. He knew he would miss his children, and he did, but, gradually, his guilt faded and he was able to enjoy his afternoons with them without suffering such painful regret that they no longer lived with him.

He had neither sought nor been offered a commitment of any kind from Gail. Though he knew he was in love with her, he also knew that to pursue her like a heartsick adolescent was to invite rejection. He took her to dinner twice before telling her he had left his wife, and when finally he did tell her, she didn't ask why. All she wanted to know was how Gloria had taken the news. He said she had taken it well: after a short, teary scene, she had acknowledged knowing that Sanders was unhappy and that the marriage was a shell. In fact, once her lawyer had convinced her that Sanders' offer of a one-time settlement was as generous as he had claimed—so generous that it left him without a single stock or bond—she hadn't seemed upset at all.

For the next several months, Sanders saw Gail as often as she would permit. He knew she was seeing other men, and he tortured himself with wild fantasies about what she was doing with them. But he was careful never to ask her about them, and she never volunteered any information. Though he and Gail talked about the future, about things they wanted to do together, places they wanted to go, they never discussed marriage. Practically, there was little point: Sanders was still legally married. Emotionally, he was afraid to talk about marriage, afraid that to suggest limiting Gail's freedom might make her regard him as a threat to that freedom.

Sanders had always thought of himself as a normally sensual person, but in those first months with Gail he discovered a reserve of raw lust so enormous that he occasionally wondered if he might be certified as a sex maniac.

To Gail, sex was a vehicle for expressing everything— delight, anger, hunger, love, frustration, annoyance, even outrage. As an alcoholic can find any excuse for a drink, so Gail could make anything, from the first fallen leaf of autumn to the anniversary of Richard Nixon's resignation, a reason for making love.

The day Sanders' divorce became final, he decided to ask Gail to marry him. He had examined his motives, and they seemed logical, if old-fashioned: he adored her; he wanted to live with her; and he needed the assurance—however symbolic—that she loved him enough to commit herself to him. But behind the curtain of logic there also lurked a shadow of challenge. She was young, widely courted, and, by her own admission, averse to marriage. If he proposed and she accepted, he would have achieved a certain conquest.

He was terrified of, but prepared for, rejection, and he wanted to phrase his proposal in such a way that she couldn't take it as an all-or-nothing request. He wanted her to know that if she declined marriage, he would rather continue their current arrangement than stop seeing her. He intended to remind her of their several areas of compatibility. He compiled a list of twelve points, ending with the undeniable fact that it made financial sense for them to live in one apartment instead of two.

He never got a chance to present his brief. They were having dinner at an Italian restaurant on Third Avenue, and after they had ordered, Sanders took the divorce papers from his pocket and held them up to Gail.

"These came today," he said. He picked an anchovy from the antipasto plate.

"Wonderful!" she said. "Let's get married."

Stunned, Sanders dropped the anchovy into his glass of wine. "What?"

"Let's get married. You're free. I'm free. I've gotten everyone else out of my system. We love each other. It makes sense, doesn't it?"

"Sure, yeah," Sanders stammered. "It's just that . . ."

"I know. You're too old for me. You think I'm a sex fiend and that you'll never be able to keep up with me.

You don't have any money any more. But I have a job. We'll make out." She paused. "Well, what do you say?"

They decided on Bermuda for their honeymoon because neither had been there and because it had good tennis courts, good swimming, and good scuba diving.

IV

The lifeguard stood at the water's edge, holding the Boston Whaler on its dolly. "Going after more forks and knives?" he said as the Sanderses approached.

"Sure," said David, "and we'll look for some of those artillery shells you mentioned."

"You get a pretty good price for the brass. But be careful. From what I hear, they're still live."

They slipped the boat into the water, loaded their gear, and shoved off. As they cruised toward the reef, Sanders asked Gail to take the wheel. He took a small flashlight from his pocket and sat on the forward seat.

"What's that for?" Gail asked.

"To see in the cave where that ampule was."

"It's not waterproof. It'll short out in a second."

"Watch." Sanders took a plastic sandwich bag from another pocket, put the light into the bag, made a knot in the open end, and pulled it tight, then touched a switch on the light. It blinked on. "That should last."

"Genius," Gail said. "Crude, but genius."

They found a niche in the reef, guided the boat through, and backed around until the bow faced the shore. Gail stood on the forward seat, ready to throw the anchor overboard, and sighted along her arms, reassuring herself that they had returned to the correct spot.

As soon as the anchor had caught in the rocks, they put on their equipment and went overboard.

They swam to a patch of clear sand several yards seaward of the reef, sat on the bottom and peered at the rocks and coral, looking for the cave where the ampule had been found. The sun was almost directly overhead, and its light cut vertical rainbow shafts through the water. Shadows shifted, appearing and disappearing as spots of darkness in the reef. Sanders moved to the right. At the end of his vision, where the blue water darkened and the shapes of rocks grew fuzzy, he saw a shadow that seemed to remain constant. He tapped Gail and pointed to the shadow. She took the flashlight from her weight belt and pressed the switch. A beam of yellow light flashed on the sand.

The cave was much farther to the right than they had thought, but now, clinging to the coral overhang and looking around, they recognized several pieces of wreckage.

They crowded together at the mouth of the dark hole. Gail swept the flashlight's beam from left to right. The cave was only a few feet deep, and it was empty, carpeted with smooth sand. Sanders looked at Gail and shook his head, saying: Nothing here. Gail handed him the flashlight and pointed to a spot in the sand. There was nothing visible, but as Sanders held the light for her, she waved her hand over the sand, fanning it into a cloud that cut visibility to six inches. She kept fanning in the pool of light, and soon she had made a depression two or three inches deep. She fanned again, and there—at the bottom of the dent in the sand—was a glimmer.

Sanders put his face into the depression and with the tips of his fingers brushed sand away from the glint. It was an ampule, filled with a colorless liquid. It might have been empty, except that when he moved it, a bubble shifted within. Gently, he pried it from the sand, passed it to Gail, and backed away from the hole he had made. He pushed sand into the hole until it was level once again, and then placed a rock marker on the spot.

They left the cave and swam along the base of the reef. Now and then, Gail would stop by a rock or timber and flash the light beneath it or fan away the sand beside it. They found nothing.

Gail moved farther along, then stopped to look for Sanders. He was behind her, digging at something in the reef. She swam to him and saw that he was using a rock to break off pieces of coral. Every few seconds he would stop hammering with the rock and would try to fit his hand into a hole. Finally, he managed to squeeze three fingers into the hole and, using them as tongs, picked out a piece of yellow metal. It was bent and dented, roughly the size of a fifty-cent piece. But as Sanders held it up for Gail to examine with the flashlight, he saw that it was not a coin: there was a concave lip around one edge, as if something had once been held inside. At four points on the lip there were empty pockets, each perhaps a quarter of an inch in diameter. The metal shone brightly, evidently undamaged by corrosion or marine growth. Sanders turned it over, and in the beam of light he saw the etched letters "E.F." Holding the ampule in one hand and the piece of metal in the other, he started for the surface.

When they were back in the boat, Sanders said, "I thought for a minute we might have found a gold doubloon."

"What do you think it is?"

"I don't know." Sanders thought. "Jewelry, I suppose . . . but Jesus, it's awful clean to be old. You'd think it would be worn away, or at least covered with something."

Sanders put the piece of metal aside and looked at the ampule. He held it to the sunlight, and the glass sparkled. "Different color from the other one."

His eyes focused on the ampule and did not see the figure standing on the Orange Grove cliffs.

It was after six when the Sanderses reached Treece's house.

Treece came out and gestured for the Sanderses to follow him around to the back. "Did you find any more ampules?"

"One," said Sanders. "It looks like there's different stuff in it."

Gail handed Treece the ampule. "It was in the same place as last time."

Treece nodded at Sanders. "You're right; different chemical."

"What is it?"

"I'm not sure. It could be a number of things. A heroin mixture or some other opium-based liquid. Might even be another morphine solution. Did you mark it?"

"Yes," Gail said. She gave Treece the remaining rock marker.

"There were no others sprinkled around?"

"No, and that one wasn't on top of the sand. We had to dig for it."

Treece said, "I best have a look tomorrow night."

"Do you want us along?" Gail asked, half-hoping Treece would say no.

Treece sensed her reluctance. "It's up to you. You're welcome to come if you want. Or, you can cut now."

"You bet we're coming," Sanders said. He pointed to Gail's purse. "Show him the other thing."

Treece studied the piece of metal carefully, running his finger around the lip on the inner edge. He squeezed it between thumb and forefinger, and the metal bent easily. "You found this where?"

"In some rocks," Sanders said. "It was lodged pretty tight. I had to break some coral to get at it."

"You might have used the other rock to mark the spot."

"Why?"

Treece grinned at Sanders. "It's gold."

"Gold? Christ, it looks like somebody threw it away."

"No man threw that away. If you'd dug deeper, you'd like have found his bones."

"How come it isn't all crapped up?"

"That's one of the marvels of gold," said Treece. "It's chemically impervious. You could put a fresh-minted gold coin in sea water and leave it there till the end of time, and when you went to fetch it on Judgment Day, it'd be as good as new. Nothing grows on it; nothing eats away at it."

Gail asked, "What was it?"

"A cameo of some kind." Treece pointed to the inner circle. "The picture or etching was in here. These"—he touched, one by one, the four pockets on the rim—"held pearls, the symbol of purity. The lad might have worn it around his neck."

"What does it mean?"

"Finding it? Not anything, necessarily. Chances are, a ship went up on the rocks out there, somewhere—God knows where—and the tide washed this and the coin you found in over the reefs. Or a survivor might have tried to swim to shore and didn't make it. This is personal stuff, not ship's treasure." Treece seemed to ponder his own words. "But, dammit, those answers don't sit right."

"Why?"

"I've been all over those reefs for twenty years and more. I'm not saying I know every inch of every Bermuda reef, but because of *Goliath*, that area I know. If there's a ship out there, I'd have seen a trace of it by now. Guns, the anchor, ballast rock—something."

"How old is it?" Sanders said.

"The cameo? A couple of hundred years." Treece turned it over in his hand. "It's Spanish. And damn fine workmanship. Very carefully made."

"If it's a couple hundred years old, Bermuda would have been inhabited when the ship went down—if there is a ship. There could be records."

"It depends: if anyone saw it go down, if anyone survived, or if anyone's salvaged it since. That's the likeliest—salvage."

"Why?"

"The incident would be over and done with. No need to prolong it with searches or detailed survivors' accounts, so no pile of records. If I had to guess at the story, I'd say the ship heaved up on the rocks during a storm, but didn't sink. Maybe a few people—this E.F. included—were washed overboard. When the wind died, they might have caulked her and refloated her. Or, if they couldn't, they'd've stripped her clean—guns, cargo, personal effects, everything—and left her on the rocks. Next big wind'd hash her up and scatter the pieces all over the place. There'd be damn little left of her to spot."

Sanders was disappointed. "So you think we've found all there is?"

"That's just a guess." Treece handed the cameo to Gail. "What do you plan to do with it?"

"I hadn't thought. Can I keep it?"

"Aye, but legally you can't take it off Bermuda, not un-

75

less you offer to sell it to the Bermuda Government and they decline."

"I don't want to sell it; I want to keep it."

"Then, girl," Treece said with a smile, "you have two options: You can smuggle it out or you can become a Bermuda resident."

Sanders said, "When do you want to go tomorrow night?"

"Come up around sunset. My boat's in a cove below. We can be on *Goliath* by full dark."

They rode down the hill, through St. David's, and across the Severn Bridge. On the causeway separating St. George's Island from Hamilton Parish they were overtaken by two taxis coming from the airport, but otherwise the road was empty. As they passed signs directing tourists to the dolphin show at the Blue Grotto, a green Morris Minor pulled out of a dirt alley and closed to within twenty yards of them.

The car had been behind them for several minutes when Sanders first noticed it in his rear-view mirror. He pulled as far to the left as he could without striking the coral wall by the side of the road. Ahead, the road bent to the right. As he rounded the turn, Sanders saw two motorbikes and a small truck coming toward them. He put out his right hand and signaled the green car to stay back.

The vehicles passed, and now David and Gail were on a straight stretch of Harrington Sound Road. There was no oncoming traffic, so Sanders waved the green car ahead. But the car stayed back. Sanders heard the honk of a horn, and he looked in his mirror. A black taxi was behind the green car. The taxi driver honked again, and Sanders waved it forward. The taxi pulled out and passed the green car and the two motorbikes.

Sanders throttled down and dropped back parallel with Gail. "That jerk won't pass!" he called to her.

"I know. There's a driveway up ahead. Let's pull over and let him go by."

Fifty yards ahead, Sanders saw a break in the thick bushes and a narrow road that led up a hill to a house; there was a sign, "Innisfree." He put out his arm to indicate a left turn and cut the motor until his bike was barely moving. He expected the green car to pull out and pass, but it slowed with him.

Sanders and Gail stopped at the entrance to the driveway. The Morris moved ahead and turned sharply left, nosing into the bushes and cutting off any avenue of escape. A tall black man in a mechanic's outfit opened the left-hand door and stepped out. The driver, another black man, stayed in his seat.

"What do you want?" Sanders said.

"Man want to see you," the tall man replied.

"What man?"

"Make no mind. Get in the car."

Sanders heard an engine noise, and he glanced down the road to his left. A station wagon was rounding a bend, coming toward them. It was heavily loaded and moving slowly.

"Move!" said the man.

The station wagon was about twenty yards away; in a

couple of seconds, it would be abreast of the Morris. As if obeying, Sanders took a step toward the Morris, then suddenly darted sideways, sprang onto the hood of the Morris, and, before the man could stop him, leaped into the air at the oncoming station wagon.

He had a quick glimpse, through the windshield of the station wagon, of the driver's shocked face. He heard the squeal of skidding tires.

The station wagon was barely moving when Sanders landed on its hood, so he was not hurt by the concussion. But his momentum prevented him from stopping; he rolled off the hood and struck his face on the pavement. He tasted blood.

Sanders scrambled to his feet and yelled, "Help!"

The station wagon was full of cricketers, all dressed in white. The driver, a young black, stuck his head out the window and screamed, "You crazy, man!"

Sanders pointed to the Morris. "They're kidnaping us!"

"What?"

The tall man, now standing next to Gail, called, "Don't pay him no mind, man. He's smokin' bad shit."

"No!" Sanders said. "Help us! They're—"

"Crazy bastard!" the driver yelled. "You gon' get killed one day." Then he said to the tall man, "You tourin' some crazy bastards, Ronald." He ducked his head inside the window and pressed the accelerator to the floor.

Sanders reached for the station wagon as it lumbered by him, but his hand slipped off the steel. The road was empty in both directions. He debated running, but he did not want to leave Gail.

The tall man, Ronald, snapped a switchblade knife open and held it at his waist, pointing at Sanders. "Move!" he said. "Or I cut your ass." He took Sanders' arm and roughly pushed him toward the Morris.

Sanders said, "At least let her go."

"Her, too." Ronald opened the front door of the car and shoved Sanders inside.

"What do I do with this?" Gail said, holding the handle bars of her motorbike.

"Drop it."

She released the handle bars, and the motorbike clattered to the pavement. She climbed into the back seat of the car.

Ronald pushed both motorbikes into the underbrush, got in the back seat next to Gail, shut the door, and, cradling the knife in his lap, said, "Okay."

The driver pulled out onto the road.

V

They traveled in silence. The windows were shut, and the air in the car quickly grew acrid with breath and sweat. As they passed a sign for the botanical gardens in Paget, Sanders rolled his window down. He felt the point of the knife press at the base of his neck and heard Ronald say, "Up." He closed the window.

They approached a traffic circle, where signs pointed to the right for Hamilton, straight ahead for Warwick and Southampton. A policeman stood in the center of the circle, directing the early-evening traffic. Sanders wondered if, as the driver slowed for the circle, he would have time to open the door, roll out, and yell for help. Then he saw the driver wave at the policeman, and the policeman smiled and waved back.

It was growing dark, and as they drove along South Road, never exceeding the 20 mph speed limit, Sanders could barely decipher signs for Elbow Beach, the Orange Grove Club, Coral Beach, and the Princess Beach Club. High on a hill he saw the huge Southampton Princess Hotel and then the Gibb's Hill lighthouse. They had traveled almost the whole length of the island.

The stuffy silence increased Sanders' nervousness. "How much farther?" he asked.

"Shut up," said Ronald.

They crossed Somerset Bridge, and another fact from his *Geographic* past occurred to Sanders. He half-turned toward Gail and said, "That's the smallest drawbridge in the world. It only opens wide enough to let a sailboat's mast pass through."

Gail did not answer. Sanders' escape attempt had shaken her, and she did not want to encourage another confrontation.

Ronald motioned with his knife for Sanders to face front.

"For whatever that's worth," Sanders said, turning back.

The car went left off the main road, onto a dirt track, following a sign that said "Public Wharf." They entered a clearing—a crowded square, filled with fish-and-vegetable stalls and ramshackle shops. At the far end of the square was a rickety dock to which half a dozen weathered, patched boats were moored. There were no other cars in the square, and children scampered so carelessly in front of the Morris that the driver had to creep along in first gear. He parked in front of what seemed to be a grocery store. Canned goods and fruit were piled high in the window. A penciled placard advertised bait and pork rind. Faded letters on the gray limestone said, "Teddy's Market."

Two young black men were lounging by the doorway. One was casually flipping a hunting knife into the dirt. The other leaned against the doorjamb, arms folded, watching the green car; his shirt was open to the waist, displaying a fresh red scar that ran from his right clavicle to below his left pectoral muscle—macho graffiti. There was something familiar about the man; Sanders tried to place him, but couldn't.

"You come quiet," said Ronald. "No smart stuff, or they fillet you." He jerked his head toward the men at the door, then got out of the car and held the back door open for Gail.

Sanders opened the front door and stepped out onto the dirt. A breeze was blowing across Ely's Harbour, and it felt cool as it dried the sweat on his face.

"Inside," Ronald said. He followed them through the door, saying to the man with the scar, "What's doin'?"

"Waitin' on you, man."

It was the inflection on the word "man" that made Sanders realize who the bearer of the scar was: Slake, the waiter from Orange Grove. Reflexively, Sanders turned to look at him, but he was pushed forward into the store.

Stepping into the darkness of the store, David could see nothing. There seemed to be rows of merchandise on both sides of an aisle. Gradually, as his pupils adjusted, he saw a faint light shining under a door at the rear of the store. "Where?"

Ronald brushed past him. "You follow me." When he reached the door, he rapped once, then twice.

A voice inside said, "Come."

Ronald opened the door and motioned Gail and David through. He followed them, shut the door, and leaned against it.

On the far side of the room was a desk, and behind it sat a young man—in his late twenties or very early thirties, Sanders guessed. The sweat on his forehead caught the light and made his black skin shine. He wore gold-rimmed spectacles and a starched white shirt. There was no jewelry on his hands, but around his neck was a thin gold chain that held an inch-long gold feather. Two burly men —older than the ones outside the store—flanked him in formal symmetry, arms folded, beside the desk. The room was cluttered with cartons and boxes and file cabinets, and smelled of fish and dirt and sweat and overripe fruit. Two bare light bulbs hung from the ceiling.

The man behind the desk stood up. "Mr. and Mrs. Sanders," he said, smiling. "I am glad you agreed to come."

Sanders recognized the man's accent; he had heard it in Guadalupe; the accent of one whose native language is Caribbean French and who has learned English in a church school.

"We weren't exactly invited," Sanders said.

"No. But I'm glad you chose not to resist. I am Henri Cloche." He paused, expecting the Sanderses to recognize the name. When they did not react, he went on. "The name means nothing? So much the better." He looked at Gail. "Forgive me, madam. You would like a chair?"

"No." Gail looked directly at Cloche, hoping he would not see she was afraid. "Why are we here?"

"Of course," said Cloche. He held out his hand. "The ampule."

Sanders said, "We don't have it."

Cloche looked back and forth, from David to Gail, smiling, holding out his hand. He snapped his fingers.

Sanders felt strong hands grip his arms and pin his elbows back. One of the men beside the desk stepped over to him, grabbed the collar of his shirt, and tore it open, stripping the buttons away. The hands behind him pulled the shirt off his back.

The other man made a move toward Gail, but Cloche stopped him with a wave of his hand. "Take your clothes off," he said. "Both of you. Now."

Gail forced herself to keep looking at Cloche. Slowly, she unbuttoned her blouse and dropped it to the floor. One of Cloche's men picked it up and examined it, feeling along the seams, bending the built-in collar stays. She unhooked her short, wrap-around skirt. The man held out his hand for it, but she dropped it on the floor at his feet. Still looking at Cloche, her eyes locked on his, she undid her bra and dropped it. The man caught it before it hit the floor, and he picked through the cups, checking the thin padding.

Sanders undressed less meticulously, shedding his clothes and letting the hands behind him take them from him. It was not until he was naked that he noticed Gail staring at

84

Cloche. Her thumbs were hitched in her bikini underpants. He tried not to look at her, but the palpable excitement of the gawking men was contagious, and he sensed heat rushing into his groin. He closed his eyes, fighting the absurd tumescence.

Cloche had not taken his eyes off Gail's face.

"Nothing," said the man behind Sanders.

The word broke the trance, and Cloche's eyes dropped down Gail's body. He looked away. "Put your clothes on," he said.

Gail bent over to gather her clothes.

"I could conduct a proper examination of you both," Cloche said testily, "but never mind. I assume Romer Treece has the ampule. One alone is of no importance."

"Then why all this cloak-and-dagger stuff?" Sanders said as he pulled on his trousers.

"Do you know Bermuda, Mr. Sanders?"

"Some."

"Then you will recall, perhaps, the ex-governor—the late governor, I should say—the one who was so fond of great Danes."

Sanders remembered. On a warm night in 1973, Sir Richard Sharples, the British governor of Bermuda, had gone for a late-night stroll with his pet Dane. Man and dog were found slaughtered in the gardens of Government House. "What does that have to do with us?" he said.

"He was a meddler. He refused to do business. I don't like it when someone I approach refuses to do business."

"Business?"

"I wanted to see the ampule solely to confirm my suspicions about it. The fact that you don't have it, that you have entrusted it to Romer Treece for safekeeping—I assume that is what you have done—confirms those suspicions quite adequately. How many more ampules are there?"

"I don't know."

"How many did you find?"

Sanders looked at Gail, but her impassive expression did not change. "Two."

"Do you know what they contain?"

"Not for sure, no."

"But you know the legend. Or, rather, the story, since the legend seems to be coming true."

"Yes."

"Mr. Sanders, I am determined to acquire every ampule down there. Every last one of them."

"Why?"

"They are valuable. We need them."

"For what?"

"Never mind. It's no concern of yours."

Gail said, "Who are you going to sell them to? Kids?"

Cloche smiled. "How nice to see your interest finally piqued. But that, too, is no concern of yours. In fact, the less you know, the better for you."

"Then why bother us? You don't need us," Sanders said.

"You dive. And you know exactly where they are."

"No. We know where two of them *were*. There's no saying that there are any more. Besides, there are divers who know this area a hell of a lot better than we do."

"Perhaps. But it is testimony to British foresight that very few of those divers are black. Just as they have successfully kept the blacks from the professions, so they have kept most of them from becoming first-rate divers. I could import someone, but any qualified diver who came through customs—any black diver, that is—would come under immediate suspicion. You are here, you are tourists, you are white. You are above suspicion."

Gail said, "We're not pushers."

"Pushers?" Cloche was unfamiliar with the word. "Ah, *vendeurs de mort*. Nor am I. I am first a politician, and politics is the business of using means to achieve ends. I am also a businessman, and I am aware that in dealing with people unacquainted or unsympathetic with one's political ends, one must appeal to different desires. Therefore, I am prepared to deal with you." He paused and looked at Sanders. "You will discover how many ampules there are. If there are only a few—if the legend is, indeed, a legend— you will tell me and no one else. Your reward will be continued good health and a carefree Bermuda holiday. If, on the other hand, there is a multitude of ampules, you will recover them. We will, of course, provide you with whatever assistance you need." Cloche turned toward Gail. "Once the ampules are in our hands, you will leave Bermuda. You will go to New York and you will call a telephone number I will have given you. You will leave instructions as to where in the world, six months from that date, you would like to collect one million dollars in the currency of your choice."

Gail drew a quick, startled breath.

Cloche smiled, then looked at Sanders, who gazed back at him without expression.

"No," said Sanders.

"Don't be hasty, Mr. Sanders. I see by your lip that you have a tendency to be hasty."

Sanders ran his tongue over his lower lip. A tender lump had risen, and the saliva made it sting.

"Think about it," Cloche said. "Think about freedom, about the freedom you can buy . . . with a million dollars." He gestured to Ronald. "Where are their mobilettes?"

Ronald made a throwing motion. "The brush."

Cloche said to Sanders, "They will be returned in the morning. A final word: Make no mistake about it—should you still be inclined to be . . . hasty . . . and go to the authorities, you will find that, officially, I do not exist. And should you try to get out of this by leaving Bermuda, you will also discover that, in reality, I exist everywhere." His back stiffened. "There will be no haven." He turned to Ronald. "Take them home."

There was no conversation in the car during the thirty-minute ride to the Orange Grove Club. Ronald and the driver sat in front, David and Gail in back. As they pulled onto the main road, Sanders rolled down his window. When Ronald did not object, Gail rolled hers down, too.

The only sounds on the deserted road, other than the wind and the engine noise, were the calling of tree frogs and the chirruping of cicadas. The driver stopped the car at the entrance to Orange Grove. He did not offer to drive them to their cottage; they did not ask. They walked silently up the driveway, stopping where the footpath to their cottage turned off to the right.

"You hungry?" said Sanders.

"Hardly."

"We can order a sandwich from the room. I could sure use a drink."

Inside the cottage, Sanders tossed the key on the dresser and walked toward the bathroom, where there was a refrigerator. "Scotch?" he said.

"Fine."

He went into the bathroom, opened the refrigerator, pried some cubes loose from an old-fashioned ice tray, and dropped them into the two bathroom glasses. He heard Gail pick up the telephone, and he called, "I'll have a turkey on white with lettuce and mayonnaise."

Gail did not answer.

As he poured whiskey into the glasses, he heard Gail say into the phone, "Get me the police, please." There was a pause. "Yes, that's right. No, there's nothing wrong." She sounded annoyed. "Just get the police."

Sanders set the scotch bottle on the sink and hurried into the bedroom. "What are you doing?" he said.

"What's it sound like?" She spoke into the phone. "What's my room number have to do with anything? I assume this is a local call."

"Hang up," Sanders said. "Let's talk about it."

"What's to talk about? We were kidnaped, for God's sake! Threatened."

"Hang up!" Sanders ordered. "Or I'll hang up for you." He held his index finger above the phone cradle.

Gail looked at him.

"I'm not kidding. Hang up!"

Gail hesitated for a moment, then said into the phone,

"That's all right, operator. I'll try again later." She hung up. "Okay. So talk."

"Calm down," Sanders said. He put his hand on her shoulder.

She brushed the hand aside. "I won't calm down! Don't you realize what we were asked to do?"

"Sure!" Sanders said as he went back into the bathroom to get the glasses. He handed one to her. "But calling the cops is no answer. What are they going to do?"

"Arrest him."

"For what? How are we going to prove anything? You heard what he said: He doesn't exist. At least not officially. Didn't you see that cop wave at the driver? He's probably got the whole damn police force in his pocket."

"Then let's call the government. He sure as hell doesn't have the British Government in his pocket."

"And tell them what?"

"We were kidnaped. That's—"

"For an hour. By a phantom. We'd have a hell of a time making a case out of that."

"Assault, then. You can't go around sticking knives at people and tearing off their clothes. And what about what he wants us to do? Sell him *narcotics*."

"Not exactly. More like *find* them for him."

Gail looked at him for a long moment without speaking. Then she shuddered. "You think he'd really follow us?"

"I don't know. We'll have to find out if he could. Maybe Treece'll have an idea."

"And maybe you'll end up dead."

"C'mon, let's not . . ."

Gail sneezed. As she folded her handkerchief, she noticed a smear of blood. "I've still got a bloody nose," she said.

"What do you mean, 'still'?"

"There was blood in my mask when I came up today."

They left Orange Grove after breakfast the next morning. Sometime during the night, as promised, their motorbikes had been returned and parked in front of their cottage. When she saw the motorbikes, Gail shivered involuntarily.

"What's the matter?" Sanders said.

"They were here."

"Who was?"

"Those men. While we slept."

"Sure they were. How else would they get the bikes back to us?"

"I know. But it's creepy."

When they arrived at Treece's house, they waited outside the gate and called to Treece. When he told them to come in, the dog bounded down the path and escorted them to the kitchen door.

The kitchen table was covered with photostats of old documents. Treece saw Sanders looking at the papers, and he said, "Research."

"What are they?"

"Logs, manifests, bills of lading, diaries, letters. A dividend of my study in Europe. I spent my holidays in the archives of Madrid, Cádiz, and Seville. Friends send me new papers as they surface."

"What do they tell you?" Gail asked.

"What ships went to what ports, what they were carrying, who was on board, where they sank if they sank, how many people survived. They're indispensable tools. Without them, you can dilly around on a wreck for months and not know what you're looking at."

Sanders picked up one of the pieces of paper. The writing was in Spanish, and he could decipher only a few words—like *artillería* and *canones*—and the date: 1714. "What are you looking for?"

"I'm indulging myself in a bit of nonsense."

"What do you mean?"

"I'm trying to figure out if it's possible that another ship did sink out there. That it went down with everything on it, and that it was never salvaged."

Gail said, "Is that possible?"

"It's happened before. Two storms, a hundred or two hundred years apart, spring up from the same quarter, catch two ships in the same circumstance, making for the same shelter, and drive them up on the same reefs." Treece shook his head. "What a mess."

"I think it sounds fantastic," said Gail.

"You do, do you? Take a nice clean wreck—nothing else around, fairly well contained, maybe even find a coin or two that'll date her for you. You can spend a year mucking about in the sand and still not find a bloody thing. Now add to that another whole ship, all busted to pieces, and with a cargo of live ammunition. That's some way to get your jollies."

"Have you found anything?" said Sanders.

"No. Not sure I will." Treece patted the pile of papers. "All I'm doing with this stuff is rooting around to see if I can find someone with the initials E.F. Probably a waste of time, but you have to start somewhere, and E.F.'s all we've got. Now . . . tell me what brings you all the way out here this early. We're not going anywhere till tonight."

They told him about their meeting with Cloche. At the first mention of Cloche's name, Treece started, as if a long-awaited piece of bad news had finally arrived. "Oh, Jesus," he said. Otherwise, he sat, tense and quiet, and did not interrupt.

When they were finished, he said, "You were right not to ring the police."

"Why?" said Gail.

"They couldn't have done anything. He's a shadow, that man. He has friends in many strange places. I know what he can get away with." He shook his head. "Damn. It is a robust piece of bad luck that we're faced with him so soon. You've never heard of him?"

"No," Sanders said. "Should we have?"

"I suppose not. He's got a dozen different names. He comes from Haiti, originally. That's the myth, at least. It's hard to separate fact from fancy about Cloche; he's built himself into a kind of folk hero among island blacks. A lot of them think he's the reincarnation of Che Guevara. And not just here. All over. In the Windwards and Leewards, his mother is still powerful bush."

"Bush?" Gail said.

"Magic, voodoo. You'll see little statues of her in the huts on the hillsides of Guadalupe and Martinique. They adore her, like . . . well, I imagine Eva Perón is a parallel. She was a chambermaid in a hotel in Haiti. At the age of forty-three, she came down with glaucoma, and when it got so bad she couldn't see to work, the hotel fired her without a sou. Cloche himself was nothing but a busboy then, but he was clever. He took mamma into the woods and set her up as a symbol of white oppression. He spread stories about her, made her into an all-knowing black princess, said she cured the incurable and raised the dead—all the standard stuff. People wanted to believe in her—Christ, 'wanted' isn't the word: *longed* to. Once mamma was established, Cloche began to pass himself off as her messenger. He's been all over the islands, thrown out of most of them two or three times, spreading the message. Nobody knows if mamma's still drawing breath, but Cloche is still spreading the word."

"What's the word?" asked Sanders.

"It's time for the blacks to get the biscuit. I suppose it was only a matter of time until he came back here."

"It doesn't look to me like Bermuda's ripe for revolt," Sanders said.

"It's hard to tell."

Gail said, "The blacks aren't exactly what you'd call equal here."

"No, but there's been no serious trouble since the sixty-eight riots—aside from the Sharples assassination, and there's still no proof about that one."

"Cloche as much as admitted that his people killed Sharples," said Sanders.

"Of course. Why shouldn't he? No one else has been

arrested, and it makes him seem like a bigger threat. It's like those Arab fringe groups. Every time a plane crashes, some bunch of birds jumps up to take credit, claiming the crash was a revolutionary act. Crap. Of course Cloche *may* have killed Sharples; I wouldn't put it past him. But the fact that he says he did doesn't make it true." Treece looked at Gail. "In any event, Bermuda has been fairly peaceful for some time. It's a dicey peace, though. Blacks are the majority here, and they get less of the pie than the whites. For my money, they get more as they merit more, and they're getting more all the time. But a chap like Cloche can rile them, convince them that they're oppressed, that numbers alone are enough to merit more. Manipulate them for his own purposes. He's a persuasive speaker, and they're scared of him. Besides, there's no trick to convincing people that they deserve more than they've got."

"Is he a communist?" Gail asked.

"Hell, no. He spouts a good Marxist line—'from each according to his abilities, to each according to his needs,' and all that. I think what he really wants is to set up some sort of island kingdom. He won't call it that, of course. It'll be the People's Republic of some goddamn thing."

"And the drugs?"

"Money. Power. I imagine he'll try to sell the drugs in the States." Treece paused. "I don't want him to get them." He looked at Sanders. "A million dollars? He *is* anxious. Were you tempted?"

Sanders looked at Gail. "No," he said. "Though God knows we could use the money."

"It's a decent amount of cash, no doubting it," Treece said, slapping the photostats in front of him. "But if I can find some parts to this puzzle and we really get lucky, there might be a like amount of *real* goodies down there."

"Do you think there may really be a treasure?" Gail said.

"No. But I'm not convinced there isn't. You never know till you've had a good look."

"What do we do about Cloche?" Sanders said. "Is there a way to get around him? I don't like the thought that he might follow us to New York."

"For the moment, there's nothing to do. You're stuck either way, until we know what's really down there. We'll have a look around tonight. If we don't find any more ampules—and it's possible these two are a fluke—you can deliver the two you found to Cloche and wish him well. If there's nothing else there, I don't think he'll bother with you any more. With luck, that's what'll happen. But before we go down again, I want to talk to Adam Coffin."

"Who's he?"

"The *Goliath* survivor. I imagine he's still chary about talking about the drugs, but perhaps the sight of a couple of ampules will jar his memory." Treece put the two ampules in his pocket. "Leave your bikes here. You'll be coming back later to dive. We can all fit in Kevin's car."

"About the diving," Gail said. "My nose has been bleeding since yesterday."

"Bad?"

"No."

"Not to worry. When you haven't been wet in a while, a day or two of ups and downs will irritate the tissues in your sinuses. Stay out of the water for a bit, and it'll clear up."

"What about tonight?"

"I wouldn't. There's no sense pushing it. The two of us can manage." Treece opened the kitchen door for them. "You go ahead on your bikes, then. I'll come by the hotel, and you can follow me down to Coffin's."

The house was tiny—a limestone cottage perched on a neatly tended patch of weeds overlooking Hamilton Harbour. There was no driveway, only a dirt shoulder wide enough to permit one car to pull off the road and stop without risking a rear-end collision with the passing traffic. Treece nosed the Hillman into the brush beside the shoulder, leaving room behind for the two motorbikes. His immense frame looked ridiculous in the car: he was hunched forward so his head wouldn't jam into the roof, and his legs were so long and so cramped that he could not put them out of the car first. The only way he could get out was to open the door and fall to the right, supporting himself with his hands on the ground, dragging his legs after him.

"Damn fool things," he said as he wiped his hands on his pants. "Built for bloody midgets."

"If you ever had an accident in that car," Sanders said, "they'd have to cut you out with a torch. Why don't you ride a motorcycle?"

"Suicide machines. Only good thing about them is they

97

keep the black population down." Treece looked at Gail and smiled. "Forgive me. I'm a relentless bastard."

They walked up the dirt path to the house. A small man was on his hands and knees, digging in a flower bed beside the front door.

"Adam," Treece said.

Coffin's head snapped around. "Treece!" he said, surprised. With a nimble motion he pushed himself backward and rolled to his feet.

He wore nothing but a tattered pair of denim shorts. His body was tan, lean, and sinewy, without a trace of fat. Strands of aged muscle coursed along his arms and chest as visibly as a drawing in an anatomy text. His eyes were fixed in a permanent squint that had cut deep grooves in the dry brown skin on his cheeks and forehead. A shaggy mane of white hair hung down the back of his neck. He smiled at Treece, displaying abused gums spotted here and there with chipped and yellowed teeth. "It's good to see you; been awhile."

"Aye, it has." Treece enveloped Coffin's bony fingers in his enormous fist and pumped once briskly up and down. "We stopped by to chat you up." He introduced the Sanderses to Coffin.

"Come in, then," said Coffin, leading them into the dark house.

The one-room house was divided by furniture into three sections. On the right there was a hammock, suspended catty-corner by two steel rings embedded in the stone wall. Behind a half-open curtain David saw a toilet and a sink. In the middle of the room was a single stuffed chair, facing a 1950s-vintage television set. On the left were a sink, a hot plate, a refrigerator, a cabinet, and a card table, around which were two chairs and two stools.

"Sit," said Coffin. He opened the cabinet and waved at an array of bottles. "Have a charge? I'm on the tack myself. Old guts can't take the fury of the juniper berries."

Confused, Sanders looked at Treece and saw that he was grinning at Coffin.

"I'll have a spot of rum," Treece said. "How long've you been on the tack?"

"A good while now," Coffin said. "It's not hard if you have a disciplined soul." He looked at Sanders. "For you?"

"A gin and tonic would be fine," Sanders said.

Gail nodded. "The same. Thank you."

"Comin' up." Coffin took four glasses from the cabinet, filled two of them with Bombay gin—no ice, no tonic— and passed them to David and Gail. The other two he filled with dark Barbados rum. He gave one to Treece, took a long swallow from the other, and sat down.

"I thought you were on the tack," Treece said.

"I am. Haven't had a drop of gin in months. Rum isn't drinking; it's survival. Without it, your blood doesn't circulate proper. That's a fact."

Sanders took a sip of the warm gin and suppressed a grimace as the harsh liquid burned his throat.

"So. Tell an old man what brings you by." Coffin smiled. "Or is this just your day to visit the elderly and infirm?"

Treece reached in his pocket and, without a word, placed the two ampules on the table.

Coffin did not touch them; he simply stared at them and

said nothing. He looked up, first at Treece, then at the Sanderses. His face showed no emotion, but there was something different about his eyes, a shininess that Sanders could not diagnose—excitement, perhaps, or fear. Or both.

Coffin jerked his head toward the Sanderses and said to Treece, "How much do they know?"

"All *I* know. They found the pieces." Then Treece told Coffin about Cloche's proposal to the Sanderses.

"Cheeky bastard," Coffin said when Treece had finished. "He should have come to me with his million dollars. They're mine."

"You're supposed to be a fool, Adam. Keep it that way. It's safer. Besides, *Goliath* isn't registered to you any more. I checked. Now—truth. How many were there?"

Coffin hesitated. "Truth is a pain in the ass," he said, holding one of the ampules to the light. "I told the truth once, and damn near got killed for my trouble."

"Cloche may come and finish the job, Adam, if we don't get the stuff up and out of there fast. How many were there?"

Coffin finished his glass of rum, reached for the bottle, and refilled his glass. "They were in cigar boxes. Forty-eight to a box, separated by cardboard grids. The manifest said there were ten thousand boxes, and I believe it. I stacked every one of the bloody things by hand."

"Did the manifest say what was in the glass?"

"No, but we knew. Morphine, mostly. Some raw opium, a bit of Adrenalin. But almost all morphine."

"No heroin?" Sanders asked.

"No. At least—"

Gail interrupted. "It's the same thing."

"What do you mean?" Sanders said.

"It is. I edited a book about drugs once. All heroin is, is morphine heated with acetic acid. As soon as it gets into the body, it's reconverted into morphine."

"Then why don't junkies take morphine?"

"It's not up to them. They take what the pushers push, and the pushers push what the smugglers smuggle. The smugglers smuggle heroin because they make more money from it: a pound of pure morphine converts into more than a pound of heroin, and you don't have to take as much heroin because it's stronger than straight morphine—something to do with the way it gets to the brain. Anyway, if you figure that from that cargo you could make half a million doses of heroin, street value somewhere between ten and twenty dollars a dose, you're talking about a total value of five to ten million dollars. Lord!"

Treece said, "Where was it carried, Adam?"

"Number three hold. The lot of it. Amidships. I had it bagged about with flour."

"Was there anything beneath it?"

"Aye, the ordnance. We chucked our ballast and put the cases of shells down there. It was a dicey sail, I tell you. One of the mates went in irons for three days for sneaking a cigarette. And that was topside."

"She didn't roll over when she went down, did she?"

"Not so far's I know. But I didn't linger to see how she fell."

"So if her guts were ripped out clean, it's likely that the

shells went down first and farthest. The cigar boxes would be atop them."

"Those boxes were wood, remember, and flimsy. They'd be nothing now."

Treece nodded. "Still, they'd not have been crushed by the cases of shells. And the ampules' mass in water is almost nothing, so they'd not have sunk deep in the sand."

"If you ask me, the storms has busted 'em all up by now."

"I'd have thought so, too." Treece fingered one of the ampules. "Until these turned up."

"But they were in a hole, you say, protected. The others is gone, I'll wager."

"Like as not. But we're having a look tonight."

Coffin drained his glass and banged it on the table. "Damn fine. I'll be ready."

Treece smiled. "No. We'll go. If we find some more, then we'll need you."

"But it's my ship!" Coffin hammered his chest with a fist. "You think I'm not fit, is that it?" His eyes were bright, his face flushed from the rum. "I'm fit as a bloody stallion! How old do you think I am?"

Treece said calmly, "I know how old you are, Adam."

"You, then," Coffin said, glaring at Sanders. "How old do you think I am?"

Sanders looked at him, quickly matching dates in his mind. Coffin had to be at least seventy. "I'd say . . . sixty."

"See that, Treece?" Coffin laughed. "Sixty!" He turned back to Sanders. "I'm seventy-bloody-two, my boy! Fit as a stallion!"

"Adam," Treece said, touching Coffin's arm, "no one said

you weren't fit. But I don't want anyone to see you diving on the wreck. You're too well known." Treece warmed to his lie. "You're a bloody celebrity! If people knew you were diving on that wreck, they'd right away spot something was up."

Coffin leaned back in his chair, mollified by the flattery. "There's sense in what you're saying. Wouldn't want to give anything away." He eyed his empty glass. "I say let's drink on it."

"No," Treece said, standing up. "I've got work to do."

Coffin followed Treece and the Sanderses down the path to the road. Treece opened the door of the Hillman and—like an octopus insinuating itself tentacle by tentacle into a crevice in a reef—slowly fit one long limb after another into the driver's compartment.

Coffin said, "Don't breathe too deep, or you'll blow the horn with your chest."

Treece said to Sanders, "You want to follow, or can you find your way?"

"We'll find it. You go ahead."

Treece looked at Gail. He paused, apparently considering his words. "You'll stay at the hotel tonight?"

"I guess so," she said. "Why?"

"Do. And keep your door locked. I don't want to scare you, but Cloche is sure to know you're there."

Gail remembered the sight of the motorbikes that morning. "I know."

Treece started the car, waited for a taxicab to pass, then made a U-turn on the narrow road and chugged off toward St. David's.

After the car had disappeared from view, Coffin stared

down the empty road. The Sanderses mounted their motorbikes and put on their helmets.

"Good-by, Mr. Coffin," Gail said.

Coffin did not respond. "I knew him when he was a boy," he said. "A fine lad."

Gail and David looked at each other. "I'm sure," she said. "He seems to be a fine man."

"Aye. Straight as God Himself. He deserves better."

"Better than what?"

"Loneliness. Sadness. It's one thing for old croaks like me. We're *supposed* to be lonely. But a young fella like him—it ain't right. He should have sons to pass along what he knows."

Sanders said, "Maybe he likes living alone."

Coffin looked at Sanders. His eyes were cicatrices in his bony head. "Likes it, huh?" he said sharply. "Likes it, does he? A lot you know." He turned away.

David and Gail watched Coffin walk up the hill into his house.

Sanders said, "What did I say?"

"I don't know. But whatever it was wasn't the right thing."

Sanders looked at his watch. "Let's go. I've got to get all the way back to St. David's before dark."

VI

The moon had risen well above the horizon, casting an avenue of gold across the still water.

Treece's boat was forty-three feet long, a wooden craft with the name *Corsair* painted on the stern. Standing next to Treece at the wheel, Sanders looked aft. The hull, he guessed, had once been a standard-design fishing boat, but by now Treece had so radically altered it to fit his peculiar needs that it looked eccentric. There were winches on both sides of the cabin, racks for scuba tanks along the gunwales, and, where a fighting chair would be bolted to the deck, an air compressor. An aluminum tube, perhaps twelve feet long and four inches in diameter, was lashed to the starboard gunwale. The lamp in the binnacle threw a faint yellow glow on Treece's face.

Sanders said, "There are so many stars up there, I can't pick out St. David's light."

"Only one that winks regular," said Treece.

The sea was flat calm, and the lights on shore, a mile away, were passing with mechanical smoothness.

"All the lights look the same," Sanders said. "How can you tell where you are?"

"Habit. Once you know the shore line, you can tell by the way lights are clustered. Things like Orange Grove and Coral Beach stick out. You'll see."

"How do you avoid the reefs in the dark? You can't see the rocks."

"A night like this is a bit sticky. There's not enough breeze to raise many breakers. You pick your way through." Treece smiled. "After you make a couple of mistakes, you recess your prop in the hull and put a pair of steel skegs along the bottom so when you hit a rock you get a noisy bong that tells you to back off."

Sanders heard a whine from the bow. He looked through the windshield and saw Charlotte crouched on the pulpit that extended out from the bow. Her haunches were quivering, and her tail twitched excitedly.

"What's her problem?"

"Phosphorescence," said Treece. "Stick your head over the side."

Sanders leaned over the starboard gunwale and looked forward. A mantle of tiny yellow-white lights covered the water displaced by the bow of the boat.

"It's called bioluminescence. The boat disturbs the micro-organisms in the water, and they react by giving off light. Some of them are worms, others are crustaceans. Same as fireflies, basically. The Japs used to rub them on their hands during the war so they could read maps in the jungle at night. Charlotte wants to eat them."

Sanders said, "She's got quite an appetite."

"One day she'll be lunch herself. A while back, she got all hot over a shark that was cruising about; jumped on the bastard's back and tried to take a bite out of him."

"Why didn't it eat her?"

Treece laughed. "The shark was bloody terrified—not exactly accustomed to having some hairy thing jump on him from above. Took a big shit and *zoom!*—off he went. He came back 'round by and by, but by then I had the dumb bitch out of the water."

"Why do you bring her along?"

"She gets lonely if I leave her." Treece swung the wheel a quarter turn to the left. "Besides, she's company."

They fell silent, watching the glassy night water and the twinkling lights on shore. Sanders took a deep breath, exulting in the salty freshness of the air. He could not remember feeling so good, so alive. He felt as if he were living out the dreams of his youth, and, like a child, he was pleased—almost proud—to be alone with Treece. He was mildly ashamed to recognize that he was glad Gail was not with them. This was something special, an experience that would be his alone. He reprimanded himself: Don't be a middle-aged adolescent. The best reason for not bringing Gail along is that this might be dangerous.

He contemplated the possible perils and, as usual, found

himself ambivalent toward them: nervous but excited, afraid of the unknown but impatient to meet it, eager to do things he had never done. As he looked at the dark water, a shiver of anticipation made the hair on his arms rise.

They traveled southwest for another few minutes. "See up ahead," Treece said, pointing. "That's Orange Grove. You can tell by the lights: four in a row close together, that's the dining room. Then a dark spot for the kitchen, then a long thin one—the picture window in the bar."

"What do you do on a foggy night?"

"Stay home."

Treece kept the boat at three-quarters throttle until they were directly off the Orange Grove lights. Then he turned toward shore and slowed to a speed just above idle. He peered through the cabin window at the water ahead. "Could use a bit of wind," he said, "and a bit of cloud cover, too. In that moonlight, we're going to stick out like the cherry on a cream pie."

"How much do you draw?"

"Three feet. We should get through with nothing more than a scratch or two."

"Will I be in your way if I go up forward?"

"No. Sing out if you see anything that wants to dent us."

Sanders walked to the bow. The dog was still blocking the way to the pulpit, and Sanders nudged her aside and went to the end of the pulpit. The bow cut through the water with a *sshhhh* noise that, from where Sanders stood, was as audible as the low chug of the engine. Sanders looked at the streak of moonlight ahead. Something broke water—a flash of silver crossed the moonlight and splashed into the dark. Sanders looked back at Treece, who said, "Barracuda."

They crossed the first line of rocks, and the second. Twenty or thirty yards in front of the boat, Sanders saw rings of water spreading away from a center, as if some unseen hand had thrown a stone from above. "What's that?" he said.

Treece raised up on tiptoes. "Bejesus!" he said, and he swung the wheel hard left. "That bastard would've stove us clean."

"Reef?"

"Aye. We're in the third line now." Treece aimed the bow toward shore and turned off the engine. The boat continued to drift, then finally settled, nearly motionless. Treece jumped up onto the gunwale and walked forward. "No wind, no tide, no nothing. One hook should keep us here." He threw an anchor overboard and let the line run through his hands until it fell slack. He tugged it twice, securing the anchor in the coral, and tied it to a forward cleat. "Let's get dressed."

Followed by the dog, they went aft into the cockpit. As Sanders attached his regulator to the neck of the scuba tank—holding the regulator up to the moon, to make sure he wasn't putting it on backward—Treece went below. He threw two black neoprene wet suits—boots, trousers, jackets, hoods—through the hatch onto the deck.

"Is the water that cold?" Sanders asked.

"No, but the rocks'll flay you at night. Brush up against something you can't see, it'll give you the chills." Treece ducked below again, and returned, carrying in one hand a metal strongbox, in the other a large battery-powered light in an underwater housing. He showed Sanders the on-off switch on the light and said, "We won't use it any more than we have to. It's a bloody beacon down there."

"How will we see?"

"*I'll* see," Treece said, pointing to the strongbox. "You stick next to me." He opened the box. Inside, cushioned with rubber, were a mask and a pistol-grip flashlight. "Infrared stuff. So I can find the rock you left."

When they were dressed, they sat on the starboard gunwale. "Look at your watch," Treece said. "After half an hour, you come up, no matter how much air you've got left. Don't want to run out of breeze at night. There may be a current down there, and it's no fun to swim five hundred yards back sucking a dry tank." Treece reached beneath the gunwale, found a Ping-Pong paddle, and tucked it in his weight belt. The dog wagged her tail and sniffed at Treece's flippers. "Guard the boat, Charlotte," he said.

He looked at Sanders. "Set? We'll go down together. When we hit bottom, turn on the light and have a quick look-around. Make it as short as possible. Soon as you see something familiar, so you know where we are, turn off the light and head for it. If I'm lucky with this"—he held up the infrared light—"we won't have to use that light too much."

"What makes you think anybody'll come out after us?"

"Chances are, nobody will. But there's no sense issuing engraved invitations."

Treece put in his mouthpiece and made a thumbs-up

sign. Sanders answered with the same sign, and they rolled backward into the water.

Beneath the surface was utter darkness. More than an absence of light—it was a thick, enveloping black, a positive nothingness. Sanders' eyes were open, but they did not see—not his bubbles as he breathed, nor the rim around the faceplate of his mask, nor a finger held an inch in front of his face. For a second, he believed he had suddenly been struck blind. Water washed around his nose. He tilted his head to clear his mask, feeling for the top of the faceplate, pressing hard with his fingers, exhaling through his nose, and he saw undulating pinpoints of light—starlight refracted by the water.

As he exhaled and his lungs emptied, Sanders began to sink toward the bottom. He took a breath, and his descent slowed. The water, chilly at first, was warming to body temperature inside his wet suit. He felt warm and helpless and peaceful, as if he were revisiting the womb. He spread his arms and let himself glide softly to the bottom.

His flippers touched sand. There was a gentle current, enough to make standing difficult, so he dropped to his knees. The light hung around his wrist by a rubber thong. He felt for the on-off switch and pushed it with his thumb. A cylinder of yellow stabbed through the black.

Sanders had no idea where he was or which way he was facing. He swung the light left and right over the sand and rocks and was startled by the brilliance of the colors brought out by the incandescent beam. By day, the sand had looked pale blue-gray, the rocks blue-brown, the fish blue-green. But the flashlight brought out the natural colors. He saw the whites and reds and oranges of the coral, the power-pink belly of a slumbering parrot fish. The light hit a line of brown, covered by green, and Sanders recognized it as one of the timbers from the wreck. The head of a small barracuda appeared at the edge of the beam of light. It lingered for only a moment. Sanders looked around. Outside the narrow shaft of yellow, all was black. He wondered if sharks were attracted by light.

Something touched his shoulder. He jerked backward in spasmodic shock and felt fingers tapping him. Then he saw the black figure of Treece move into the beam of light. Treece gestured for Sanders to turn off the light and follow him; he held out his hand. Sanders took the hand, turned off the light, and when he felt a slight tug, began to kick alongside Treece.

Still he saw only black. Without Treece's special mask, the infrared light was invisible. Sanders assumed that Treece was homing in on the cave, for there was no hesitation to his movement: he was swimming fast, in what felt like a relatively straight line.

Treece slowed, then stopped. With his hand, he guided Sanders to a spot on the bottom. He tapped the light, and Sanders pressed the switch. They were at the mouth of the cave.

The light reflected off the white sand and rock walls. Sanders saw the rock marker they had placed in the cave. Treece's hand moved it and set it in the sand next to the infrared light. A finger pointed to the depression in the sand where the rock had been, telling Sanders to train the light there. The finger withdrew, and a hand appeared, holding the Ping-Pong paddle. Treece moved the paddle over the sand in short, swift motions. The sand rose in billows: in seconds, the cave was filled with a cloud. Sanders put his face down beside the light. The hole in the sand grew. It was several inches deep, more than a foot in diameter. Treece brought his face down beside Sanders', and the two heads clustered about the light as the paddle waved the sand away.

Treece stopped fanning. At first, Sanders thought he had given up. Then he saw two fingers reach into the sand hole and withdraw, clutching what looked to Sanders like a brown leaf. There was a faint impression on the leaf, traces of writing or printing. The fanning resumed, and Sanders saw a glint in the sand. The fingers probed again, as delicately as if they were extracting a splinter from a child's foot. An ampule was pulled from the sand.

Soon more leaf appeared—rotten wood, Sanders now assumed, from the cigar boxes that held the ampules; and then another ampule. Then two ampules together. Then, as the hole deepened, the corner of a box, faded and flaking. Sanders backed off a few inches, for most of the box seemed to lie outside the cave. Treece fanned until he had uncovered the box. It lay upside down, a brown square about six inches by eight. He set the paddle down and gently lifted the box bottom, which came away in one mushy piece. Inside, protected by a honeycomb of cardboard partitions, lay forty-eight ampules, all intact.

Treece didn't touch them. He picked up the paddle and began to fan again, moving away from the mouth of the cave. The sand that swirled around the cave was already sifting between the ampules, covering them. Treece fanned until he found the edge of another box, then stopped. He held his left wrist up to the light and rolled back his wetsuit cuff. Sanders saw the dial of his wrist watch: they had been down for thirty-two minutes. Treece's thumb pointed up, and his hand reached to take the light from Sanders.

Sanders rose slowly in the black water, watching the beam of light below him. It would move a few feet, then stop, then move again. Sanders swam without using his arms, kicking smoothly, making as little commotion as possible, for he suddenly felt lonely and vulnerable in the blackness. His senses were useless, and he did not want to attract the attention of anything equipped to prey upon the weak or solitary.

His head broke the surface. He looked around and saw that he had misjudged his ascent; he had risen away from the boat, not toward it. It rested at anchor, a black sculpture in the moonlight, about fifty yards away. He did not want to swim on the surface, where he would make sounds and vibrations that an animal below might determine were being emitted by a wounded fish. So he ducked underwater and kicked in the general direction of the boat. Twice he poked his head out of water, twice discovered that he had strayed way wide of the boat. Since he could see nothing on the bottom against which to measure his progress, he could not maintain a steady course.

He was breathing too fast, too deeply, his lungs gasping for more air than the regulator would give them. Stop it!

he told himself. Stop it, or you'll run out of air. He stopped swimming and lay motionless in the water, forcing himself to breathe more slowly. Gradually, the ache in his lungs subsided. He raised his face from the water, saw the boat, and, with a smooth, deliberate breast stroke, swam toward it.

Sanders reached the boat and held onto the diving platform at the stern that made it possible for divers to board the boat without assistance. He unsnapped his shoulder harness and heaved his tank onto the platform. Then he hauled himself up and sat, breathing heavily, letting his flippered feet dangle in the water. He heard a distant whining from the direction of the bow.

Treece's head popped up beside the platform. He spat out his mouthpiece and said, "Where's Charlotte?"

"Forward. Sounds like she's having a nightmare."

"Not bloody likely." Treece pulled himself, tank and all, onto the platform. With one motion, he shed his tank and stepped over the transom onto the deck. "She doesn't sleep on the boat. She waits for me, so she can lick the salt off my face." He started forward, and Sanders followed.

As they neared the bow, the whining grew louder, more frantic. Sanders saw the outline of Treece ahead of him, a wide, towering figure that moved with certainty and grace even in the dark. He saw Treece stop, then heard him cry, "Bastards!"

"What is it?" As he drew even with Treece, Sanders saw the dog.

She had thrust herself against the port gunwale, where she thrashed in a contorted ball, wildly biting at her flanks.

Something shiny protruded from her rear end, just above the tail, where the dog couldn't reach with her teeth. She had tried to get at whatever it was, and in gnashing at her flanks had torn tufts of hair and flesh from her haunches. Exhausted, whining, she continued to snap at herself.

Treece squatted down and put out a hand to soothe the dog. The dog curled her lip and growled. "It's all right," Treece said softly. "It's all right." He grabbed the dog's neck and forced her head to the deck. With his other hand, he reached around and yanked a piece of steel from the dog's back. Freed from pain, the dog moaned and licked herself.

"What happened?"

Treece strode aft, swung down into the cockpit, and snapped on an overhead light. In his hand was a two-inch-long dart shaped like a feather. "What the Christ do they think they're doing?"

Sanders looked at the dart and said, "Cloche."

"What?"

"Cloche wears a feather exactly like that, only smaller. It must be his calling card. He's already worked on Gail and me. Now he probably wants to force you to deal with him."

"Idiot," Treece said. "Just because he hired some toady to row out here and shoot my dog? That's supposed to make me fall to my knees?" He spat on the deck. "All that does is piss me off."

He looked up and saw the dog hobbling along the gunwale. "Get me the first-aid kit," he said, pointing to a locker on the starboard side. "Got to patch up the old lady."

He lifted the dog off the gunwale and set her on the deck. Gently, he forced her to lie on her good side.

Treece clipped the matted hairs from around the ragged wound, cleaned it with an antiseptic, and poured sulfa powder onto it. As he worked, he cooed lovingly to the dog, soothing, reassuring, treating her, it seemed to Sanders, with paternal tenderness and affection.

The dog responded: she made no sound and did not move.

When he had finished, Treece scratched the dog's ears and said, "I suppose I better bandage you." He reached for a gauze pad and adhesive tape. "Knowing you, you've already got a taste for yourself, and you'll eat yourself right up to the bloody neck." He helped the dog to her feet, and, tail wagging feebly, she tottered to a corner and lay down.

"What do you think they'll do now?" Sanders asked.

"Cloche? No telling. I covered up those ampules, so he'll not be dead sure we found anything. But that just buys us a day or two." Treece shook his head. "Lord, but there's a *Christ* load of stuff down there."

"More than we saw?"

"Aye. That box was just the tip. It looks to me like the number three hold hit the rocks and spilled a little bit. Then maybe she slid backward and busted her guts." Treece made an upside-down V with his hands. "What we saw was up at the top here. The farther down away from the cave I looked, the wider the pattern was, with some of those explosives mixed in."

"Can we get it all up?"

"Not with a Ping-Pong paddle. We'll need the air lift."

He pointed to the aluminum tube lashed to the gunwale. "And we'll have to dive with Desco gear, not air tanks. Can't be coming up every hour for new tanks. That means firing up the compressor, and *that* means noise. It's going to be bad."

"Why?"

"The deep stuff must be all mixed in with the artillery shells."

"They're not armed, are they?"

"Doesn't matter. Brass corrodes. Primers may be weak. And the cordite in those shells is still good as new. Bang 'em together, or drop one on a rock—let alone use a torch —and we'll be playing harp duets for Saint Peter."

"Can we get the government to help?"

"The Bermuda Government?" Treece laughed. "Aye. They'll have the royal scroll-maker draw up a fancy scroll commissioning me to get rid of the nuisance. If it weren't for one thing, I'd be tempted to put a charge down there and blow the whole mess to dust."

Treece fished inside his wet-suit jacket, found what he was looking for, and handed it to Sanders. It was a coin, irregular-shaped and green with tarnish. It looked as if the design on the coin had been impressed off-center, for only about three quarters of the surface of the metal carried any marks at all. Around the rim of the coin Sanders could make out the letters "EI," then a period, then the letter "G," another period and the numerals "170." Closer to the center of the coin was an "M," and in the center was an intricate crest that included two castles, a lion, and a number of bars.

"So?" Sanders said. "You said yourself that one coin doesn't make a treasure."

"True. But *that* coin might."

"Why?"

"After I sent you up, I went along the reef a way and fanned a few pockets around the rocks. I found that coin about six inches under the sand. It was lying up against a piece of iron, which is why it survived and wasn't all oxidized like the one you found."

"Why is it green?"

"That's nothing, it cleans right off. The iron it was lying up against looked to me like the hasp of a padlock. It didn't come loose right away, and I didn't want to spend the time wrestling with it."

"You mean there's a chest down there?"

"Not the way you'd imagine. The wood would have rotted away long since. The coins'd be all clotted together, and a lot of them would be no damn good. There's a clump of them down there, under a rock. I tried to pry one loose, but it wouldn't come. I figure it's stuck to some others."

"There could be more, then. Gold, I mean."

"It's beginning to look like it." Treece held the coin to the light. "Here. The 'M' means it was minted in Mexico City. What does that tell you?"

"That the ship was going east, back to Spain."

"Aye. It was leaving the New World. About a third of the ships that wrecked were on their way *to* the New World, and they didn't carry treasure. They were burdened with wine and cheese and clothing and mining equipment. The numbers are the first three numbers of the date the coin was minted—sometime in the first ten years of the eighteenth century. That jibes with the crest. It's Philip the Fifth's. He took the throne in 1700."

"What do the letters mean?"

"'By the grace of God,'" Treece said. "They're the end of the legend on the obverse of all the coins: *Philippus V*, then *Dei G.*, for *gratia*." Treece turned the coin over. "That's a Jerusalem cross. I can't read the letters, except for that 'M' there, and the 'R,' but it said *Hispaniarum et Indiarum Rex*—King of Spain and the Indies."

"So?"

"In 1715 a big fleet, one of Philip's biggest, went down on the way home."

"I've heard of that fleet. But somebody found it, didn't they?"

"Aye, a diver named Kip Wagner. Ten ships went down, carrying God knows how much in gold and silver, and in the early 1960s Wagner found what he figured was eight of them. He pulled up something like eight million dollars' worth of gold."

Sanders felt excitement surge through his stomach. "And this stuff is from one of the other two ships?"

Treece smiled and shook his head. "Not a chance. *Something's* down there, for sure, but it can't be one of Philip's ten. They all went down off Florida, every one of them. It's been documented over and over again—survivors, eye-witness reports, logs, salvors' records, everything—and no ship's going to move a thousand miles on the bottom of the ocean. No, what we know's no problem; it's what we don't know that's bothersome."

"Like?"

"It's a healthy bet that if there is a ship beneath *Goliath*, it sank between 1710 and 1720. If it was later than that, the coins we've found would have later dates. New World coins didn't stay long in the New World. The Spaniards needed every one of them to keep their country afloat. But there's no record of a Spanish ship sinking on this end of Bermuda between 1710 and 1720."

"It doesn't have to be a Spanish ship, does it, just because it carried Spanish coins?"

"No. Pieces of eight were international currency. Everybody used them. But there's no record of *any* ship sinking off this stretch of beach in the early 1700s."

Sanders said, "That could be good, couldn't it? It means the ship was never salvaged."

"Good and bad. It means we have to start from scratch. Odds are, she went down at night. If there were survivors —and I doubt there were—they'd have no misty notion of where they pranged up. They'd be too concerned with saving their own pelts. So whatever cargo went down with her is probably still there."

"And that could be—"

"No telling. According to the records, between 1520 and 1800 the Spaniards hauled about twelve billion dollars' worth of goodies out of the New World—that's twelve billion dollars' worth in *those* days. About five per cent of that was lost, and about half of what was lost was recovered, which leaves roughly three hundred million dollars on the bottom. Figure a couple of hundred years' inflation of that value, you're well over a billion dollars.

That would be nice and neat—if it were true. The trouble is, everybody was corrupt, and for every dollar's worth of registered treasure on a ship, there was probably another dollar smuggled aboard."

"To avoid taxes?"

"A special tax. By law, the King of Spain got twenty per cent of every treasure, no matter who collected it. A businessman who traded European goods for New World gold still had to pony up the so-called King's Quinto. It was much cheaper to bribe some fellow to overlook a few things than it was to give twenty per cent to the crown."

"That explains the anchor caper," Sanders said. "I ran across something at the *Geographic* about a captain who had his anchor cast in gold and painted black."

"Aye. He was hanged. The point is, there's no way to tell what could be on a ship. There've been a dozen cases of ships sinking and being half-salvaged—and the half that was salvaged toting up to more than was listed for the whole ship. The lead ship of a fleet, the *capitana*, might have had three million dollars in registered treasure on her. But this is no *capitana*: there's no fleet to go with her. It's possible that this ship was taking home some of the survivors of the 1715 fleet. And maybe some of the salvaged treasure. But then there'd be some record—if not here, then in Cádiz or Seville—of the survivors leaving Havana and ending up here. There's nothing." Treece reached inside his wet suit and pulled out an oval of gold. "Here's another bit to the mystery."

"A coin?"

"No." Treece passed it to Sanders. "A medallion."

There was a raised head of a woman on the medallion, and the letters "S.C.O.P.N."

"I think it's Santa Clara," Treece said. "The 'O.P.N.' stands for *ora pro nobis*—Santa Clara, pray for us. Look on the back."

Sanders flipped the medallion. The back was clear, except for the letters "E.F." "Those same initials!"

"Aye. This morning I wasn't able to find any officer or noble or captain with those initials, and I've looked through mounds of papers."

Sanders returned the medallion to Treece. "Maybe it was a present for somebody."

"Not bloody likely. Nobody gave stuff like this away." Treece dropped the medallion and the coin into his wet suit, turned off the overhead light, and started the engine. He sent Sanders forward to raise the anchor, and when he heard the clank of iron on the deck, he swung the wheel hard left and headed seaward.

Sanders returned to the cockpit and said, "What do we do now?"

"We stay away from this place for a couple of days while I try to figure out what the hell's underneath *Goliath*."

"Cloche . . ."

"I know. Now he knows I'm interested, he's bound to raise a ruckus before long. Best thing for you two might be to pack up and go home. Take the risk he'll leave you be."

Sanders didn't reply; Treece was probably right. Maybe he should try to take Gail home on the first plane out in the morning. But if he left, it would mean he had been lying to himself all his life. His dreams and ambitions—of working with Cousteau, of journeying around the world for the *Geographic*—would be stamped as the idle fancies of an armchair buccaneer. Here was a chance to do something he had never done before, a chance to live on the edge rather than slip through existence as an observer. The risks involved were genuine, not gratuitous or self-imposed, and that made them seem somehow more worthwhile.

He looked at Treece, then at the deck, trying to phrase a question. Finally, he said, "What if there is a lot of gold down there?"

"We'll have a royal rumpus getting it up, around those explosives."

"No . . . I mean, what if we do get it up?"

"Why, then . . ." Treece stopped. He grinned at Sanders. "I see the wheels a-whirrin' in the brain. Okay. I'm tempted to lie to you, to convince you to leave, but that's not my way. I figure, if a man wants to put his ass on the line, it's not my place to stop him. So here it is: We go to the Receiver of Wrecks and apply for a license."

"You need a license?"

"Aye, to dive on any wreck. The license is good for a year. We could say we're working *Goliath*, which is an open wreck, and not bother with a license. But I'll apply, to keep things tidy. They've never turned me down yet. The license'll list you and me as equal partners. Normally, the boat counts as a person."

"What's that mean?"

"The boat counts as a shareholder, to take care of wear

and tear and depreciation and expense. All that. But we won't worry about that this time. We'll make some arrangement for expenses. So you and your wife will split half, or however you settle it with her. Whatever we find belongs to Bermuda, technically, but unless they think we're brigands, they'll be reasonable. The stuff the Bermuda Historical Wrecks Authority wants, it'll make us an offer on. If there's something they're really hot to get, we'll have to accept their offer, which is figured out by an arbitrator appointed by—who bloody else?—the government. Whatever they don't want to pay for they'll return to us, and we can do as we damn please with it."

"Sell it?"

"Perhaps." Treece pause. "But I'll tell you now, even though we're daydreaming, that's where we may come to blows."

Sanders was startled. "About selling it?"

"Aye. We've our differences. I don't need money; I imagine you do. I care about preserving finds intact. You don't know enough about wrecks to care."

The remark stung. "I'll learn."

"Maybe." Treece smiled. "Anyway, the way the market is, we probably couldn't sell it. Buggers."

"Who?"

"Back in the late fifties and early sixties, people found a lot of goodies. That's when I found my first, and Wagner found the eight 1715 ships. Everybody wanted Spanish gold, so a few sonsofbitches got cute and started dummying it. It's easy to do and hard to detect. You can't carbon-date gold, and with the technology what it is, a crook can make a right-perfect Spanish coin."

"Can't you spot a phony?"

"Sometimes, but it's hard. Last year, I got a call from the Forrester Museum. A Professor Peabody wanted me to come look at some stuff. He didn't tell me why, but I figured he smelled a rat or he wouldn't be paying me to go all the way to Delaware. I looked at the coins, and I was goddamned if I could find anything wrong. But I knew there had to be *some*thing. I sat in a room staring at the bloody things for a week. They were perfect! I started talking to myself, arguing with myself about every mark on every coin. I argued right into the answer. The coins all carried a 'P.' It was the mint mark, meaning that they were minted at the Potosí mint in Peru. It's Bolivia now. Then I looked at the date on one of the coins: 1627. There it was."

"There what was?"

"The Potosí mint didn't put out any gold coins until the late 1650s. We had the bastard cold. It turned out he'd spent thousands of dollars buying gold in Europe and having coins made."

"What for?"

"Some folks do it for the premium on authentic Spanish gold. You used to be able to get five thousand dollars for a good royal doubloon. I have a bar with only forty-eight ounces of gold on it—even at two hundred an ounce that's less than ten thousand—and I've been offered forty thousand for it. But this lad had a grander scheme. He dummied the coins to convince people he had found a wreck he'd been looking for: the *San Diego*, went down in the 1580s.

He did convince a few, too, and suckered them into investing money in his corporation. He called it Doubloons, Inc. I believe they got him on some fraud charge."

"Did his coins get into circulation?"

"That's the bitch of it. Nobody can be sure. But even if his didn't, someone else will come up with even better coins. You can't hope to sell a coin or a gold bar these days unless you've got papers on it from the Smithsonian and every Christ agency in the world. I've seen coins up for auction that couldn't have cost more than fifteen dollars. Made in the Philippines. Squeeze 'em too hard, you'll rub the date off. It's gotten so bad that some blokes—upright, honest chaps who've got the real thing—are being forced to sell Spanish coins to dentists, who melt them down for fillings. Coins three and four hundred years old, rich with the stink of history. And they're goin' into a hole in some old lady's mouth."

"What can we do with what we find?"

Treece laughed. "*If*," he said. "God knows. One good thing, though: It does look like there's more than coins on this one. Jewelry, too, at least some. There hasn't been too much faking of jewelry yet." He took the medallion from his wet suit and held it in the dim light from the binnacle. "The Indians used to say, 'Gold is the god of the Spaniards.' It buggered up the Indians, buggered up the Spaniards, and it looks like it's going to keep buggering up people till the end of time."

It was after eleven when Treece throttled back and turned *Corsair* into the cove beneath St. David's light. By the glow of the descending moon, Sanders could see that the rickety pier was deserted. Treece's two other boats, a dory and a Boston Whaler, hung limply at their moorings.

They made fast *Corsair*'s lines, put their diving gear away, and walked to the end of the pier. The first few yards of the dirt path leading up the hill were visible in the moonlight. Then the path turned left and vanished in the dark underbrush.

"This'd be a hell of a place to jump somebody," Sanders said, walking with his arms before his face to ward off slapping branches.

"For anyone fool enough to try," said Treece.

Sanders felt a pang of irritation at Treece's manifest faith in his invulnerability. "What are you, bulletproof?"

"I don't imagine. But there's bush about me. A lot of people believe that anyone who mucks with me will be a goner within the day. It's a nice myth to foster."

They reached the top of the hill and walked to the picket fence surrounding Treece's house. The dog, feeling spry again, had already vaulted the fence and was sniffing at something on the front doorstep.

"Tomorrow?" said Sanders.

"I'll be looking through papers all day."

"Should we call you at Kevin's?"

"If you want. Or come out, if you're curious to see how thrilling it is to root around in dusty papers looking for a set of initials." Treece opened the gate and stepped into the yard. "Either way, we'll talk." He walked toward the front door.

Sanders removed the padlock from the front wheel of his motorbike. Like all mobilettes rented to tourists, his had no automatic starter, no gears, and a maximum level speed of 20 mph. He sat on the seat, opened the throttle halfway, and pushed on the pedals. The bike moved slowly; the engine chugged twice and caught.

He heard Treece call, "Hey!" He throttled down and pedaled the bike in a tight circle back to the gate.

"Have a look at this." Treece held something in his hand. It was a Coke bottle, with a white feather inserted in the neck.

"What is it?"

"Bush. To scare me, I guess—though I don't know how they expect voodoo to work on a Mahican Indian brainwashed in Scotch Presbyterian schools." Treece gazed out over the dense underbrush surrounding the yard. "But I'll give 'em this: They've got balls, just to come around here." He cradled the bottle in his hand. Then, angrily, he pegged it high in the air. The bottle spun, catching rays of light and breaking them into shimmering green and yellow fragments, and fell out of sight behind the cliff.

The headlight on Sanders' motorbike was weak, barely adequate to illuminate the potholes on St. David's Road. He traveled slowly, sensing the road rather than seeing it. At the bottom of a short hill, the road bent sharply to the right. Sanders braked on the way down the hill, and by the time he reached the bottom the motorbike was moving so slowly that it wobbled. The road rose again immediately. He opened the throttle and pedaled with his legs, but he could not generate enough momentum. The bike tipped.

Sanders dismounted and began to push the bike up the hill, helping himself with short bursts from the hand throttle.

When at last the road leveled out, Sanders stopped to catch his breath. He sat on the seat and hung his head. When he looked up again, he saw a black shadow standing just beyond the reach of his light.

A voice said, "Have you thought about our offer?"

Sanders didn't know what to say. He looked around, and heard only cicadas, saw only darkness. "We . . . we didn't find anything."

The voice repeated. "Have you thought about our offer?"

"Yes."

"And have you come to a decision?" The accent was lilting, Jamaican. Not Cloche.

"Well . . ." Sanders stalled. "Not . . ."

"Yes or no?"

"Not exactly. There hasn't been much time. I . . ."

"We'll see, then." The shadow moved back into the underbrush. There was a rustle of foliage, and the road was empty.

We'll see, my eye, Sanders thought. If they want to do something to me, why didn't they do it then?

Then a shock went through him: Gail.

VII

He fell twice on South Road. The first time, rounding a
corner, unable to see more than ten yards ahead, he banked
the motorbike too sharply. The rear wheel hit some gravel
and skidded, and Sanders landed on the road on an elbow
and knee, shredding the skin. He fell a second time right
before the turnoff for Orange Grove. He had the throttle
wide open and was moving fast, with too little light to give
him notice of a sudden left turn in the road. He went
straight, plowing into the bushes. Thorns and branches
lashed his face and tore at his clothing. As he righted the
motorbike and pushed it back onto the road, he felt frantic,

almost hysterical. He gunned the engine, and the bike lurched off down the road. He tried to calm himself, arguing that if anything had happened to Gail, he was too late to stop it—nearly an hour had passed since his talk with the man on the road. But what if she was hurt and he could help? What if she was gone?

He turned into the Orange Grove driveway and, through the bushes, saw that there were lights on in his cottage. He dropped the bike, and as he raced for the door, he could see through a window someone in the bedroom. He stopped, feeling the thump of pulse in his temples. The curtains were half-drawn, but Sanders recognized Gail— sitting on the end of the double bed, her hair a mess, her nightgown askew. She was staring, as if hypnotized, at something on the floor.

He threw the door open and saw her recoil, terrified, her arms clutching her breasts. At her feet was a shoe box full of tissue paper.

When she saw Sanders, she let out a gasp and began to sob. For a moment, he looked at her, stunned. Then he shut the door and went to her. He sat on the bed and put his arms around her. She trembled, and the sobs made her back heave.

"Gail," he said. She seemed unhurt; there were no marks on her. Nevertheless, he assumed she had been raped, and when he closed his eyes, he conjured a scene of three or four black men—he thought particularly of the young man with the scar on his chest, Slake—holding her down while, one at a time, they assaulted her. The thought nauseated him, he felt dizzy. He wondered what he would feel the next time they tried to make love. Then anger replaced nausea, and he tried to think how, where, he could get a gun. "Take it easy. It's okay. Tell me what happened."

She nodded. "I'm probably . . ." she said, trying to control the convulsive sobs, ". . . silly. It wasn't . . . that bad."

"What did they do?"

She looked at him and realized what he was thinking. She smiled weakly. "They didn't rape me."

Sanders felt relief, but almost simultaneously he sensed regret at losing the supreme cause for revenge. He still wanted to kill them. "What was it, then?"

"What time is it?" she asked.

"Twelve-fifteen."

"At eleven I went to bed. I locked the door and put the chain on it. I must have gone right to sleep. I don't know how long I was asleep, but I heard a knock on the door. I thought it was you. I called your name, but a voice said: No, you'd been hurt in a motorbike accident, said he was a policeman sent to take me to the hospital. I opened the door. There were three of them."

"Did you recognize anybody?"

"All of them. They were all at Cloche's the other day. One used to be our waiter here, the one with the big scar."

"Slake," Sanders said.

"He was the one who pushed me. He put his hand right here"—she cupped her hand over her mouth—"and shoved me back on the bed. He said if I made a sound, he'd cut my throat. I think he would have."

"I do, too."

"He kept his hand on my throat and asked if we were going to co-operate. I told him . . . I suppose I was a little blunt . . ."

"What?"

"But I was so scared, and I was sure I was going to be raped no matter what. So I said, 'Go fuck yourself.' All he did was laugh and say in that way they have, 'You be careful, missy, or it be you get fucked.' Then he asked me again what we were going to do, and I said something like, you can tell Cloche we wouldn't do what he wants for *ten* million dollars."

"Maybe you should have lied."

"I didn't want to give them the satisfaction."

"So then?"

"One of them said, 'Let's do her.' Then I *knew* I was going to be raped." She shuddered, and he held her shoulders tighter. " 'Do her.' God, what a horrible word. It's like what they used to say: 'Let's waste him.' Slake held my throat with one hand and yanked up my nightgown with the other. He held me so tight I couldn't look down. All I could see was the ceiling. I felt a pair of hands pulling off my underpants." She stopped and began to cry. In a corner, Sanders saw her pants. The fabric was wrapped around the elastic; they had been peeled off her hips and thighs.

"I thought you said they didn't . . ."

She put a hand on his knee and shook her head, sniffling and swallowing. "They didn't. One of them held my legs and spread them apart. I've never felt anything like that in my life . . . helpless, open. It was awful."

134

"But they didn't hurt you?"

"No. The next thing I felt was like a finger running all over me . . . down there . . . from my belly button on down. But it wasn't a finger. It was softer, kind of hairy. I still don't know what it was. A brush, I guess."

"A brush?"

"Look." Gail lifted her nightgown above her hips and lay back on the bed.

Sanders felt panicked and had to force himself to look. He remembered a time, years before, when a doctor friend had invited him to watch an appendectomy. Sanders had worn a surgical mask, and the patient, a teen-age girl, had assumed he was the doctor. Lying there, with her privates exposed and shaven, she had begged him to make the scar as small as possible, so it wouldn't show above her bikini. Sanders found himself fascinated, mildly (and ashamedly) excited, and, finally, when the first incision was made, repulsed.

Gail noticed his discomfort, and she said, "It's okay. Look."

There were six red smears on her groin, rough lines running crosshatched—from pubis to navel, hip to hip, pubis to each hip, and hip to navel. The design, such as it was, looked like a kite.

"What is it?" Sanders asked. "Paint?"

"No. I think it's blood."

"Not yours."

"No. Animal blood of some kind."

"How do you know?"

"I tasted it. It tastes salty, like blood." She sat up and lowered her nightgown.

"Did they say anything?"

"Nothing. Neither did I. I was so scared . . . as long as they weren't hurting me, I didn't dare say anything. The whole thing took less than a minute. Then Slake said, 'Now maybe you think again.' He let me go, but I didn't move. Then one of the others put that thing on my stomach." She pointed to the shoe box. "He said it was a present from Cloche."

Sanders leaned over and unfolded the tissue paper in the shoe box. "Oh, Christ," he said.

"I don't ever want to see it again." Gail stood and walked to the bathroom.

Sanders put the shoe box on his lap and removed the doll. It was crude—linen wrapped around straw—but its meaning was clear: the hair on the doll's head was human, exactly the color of Gail's. Her appendectomy scar was stitched to the right of the silver sequin that represented the navel. And there were six red streaks on the doll's groin, in the same pattern the men had painted on Gail. But the streaks on the doll had been slashed with a knife, and from them tufts of red and blue cotton hung grotesquely down the legs.

Sanders stared. His fingers felt cold; his mouth was dry and cottony. He had never known a fear like this. Threats to himself he thought he could handle, but this was beyond his control—which, he was sure, was what Cloche had in mind. He heard water running in the bathroom.

"It's blood," Gail called. "It comes off easily."

"Do you think they really would . . ." Sanders started to ask.

"What?"

"Nothing." Sanders pitched the doll across the room. He went to the telephone and, when the hotel operator answered, said, "Get me Pan American, please."

Gail came out of the bathroom. Her hair was combed, and she held a glass of whiskey in her hand. "This should help," she said. "It's . . ." She stopped when she saw Sanders on the phone.

"Oh, for . . ." Sanders said into the phone. "Okay, thanks." He hung up.

"What were you doing?"

"Trying to get us the hell out of here. The airlines don't open until nine in the morning."

"You mean home?"

"Damn right."

"But he'll follow us."

"Let him."

"I'm all right." She saw that the hand holding the glass of scotch was shaking, and she smiled. "I'll *be* all right."

Sanders paused. "I don't think they're kidding. Neither do you."

"No, I don't."

"Then what's the argument? It's not worth the risk, not even the smallest chance that somebody really would rip your guts out. Treece said it: We're here on holiday, our *honeymoon*, for God's sake. We're not here to get murdered by a maniac."

"It's not *us* you're worried about, is it? It's me."

137

"Well, not—"

"You think you can take care of yourself."

When he said nothing, she continued. "Don't worry about me. We can't spend the rest of our lives terrified. Besides, we *have* to stop Cloche from getting those drugs. He'll use them to ruin lives, to kill innocent people; he doesn't care. Well, I do. I'm going to do what I should have done all along: go to the government. I have to."

"What do you mean? Treece told you: It won't do any good."

"Maybe not, but I can't walk away from it." Her hand still trembled, but there was a look of fierce intensity on her face. "It wasn't you they threw on the bed; it wasn't your crotch they painted. I'm staying, at least until I talk to the government."

Sanders looked away.

She went to him and touched his face. He put his arms around her and kissed her forehead.

"What did you find tonight?" she asked, her head against his chest.

"Ampules. Boxes of the damn things. They're there, no question."

"Any Spanish stuff?"

"A silver coin and a gold medallion."

"What did Treece think about them?"

"He thinks there might be another ship. *Underneath Goliath.*"

Sanders recounted his conversation with Treece, and as he spoke, the enthusiasm he had felt on the boat returned.

Watching him, seeing his excitement at the prospect of a

treasure, his delight in the newly learned minutiae of Spanish ships, she felt like smiling. But, out of the corner of her eye, she could see the doll.

Treece looked tired; his eyes were red, and the skin beneath them was lined and puffy. He seemed subdued. He led the Sanderses into the kitchen, where the dog lay curled by the stove, occasionally licking the bandage on her flank. On the kitchen table was a neat stack of papers —some old and yellow, some photostats.

Gail told Treece about the visit from Cloche's men and showed him the doll.

"He's trying to spook you," Treece said, "show you how powerful he is. Not that he'd hesitate to kill you. But at the moment it wouldn't accomplish anything for him. All it'd do is raise a storm and seal it good you wouldn't help him. But if he ever decides for himself that you really won't go along, beware. The bastard'd cut your throat as soon as shake your hand."

"We almost left," Sanders said.

Treece nodded. "It's not sure he'd get at you in New York."

"Not sure?" Sanders said. "You think he's serious about following us to New York?"

"Wouldn't have to follow you. A phone call'd suffice. He's a vengeful bugger and well connected. But no question, you'd be safer there."

Gail said, "It seems like we're safer *here*—at least as long as he thinks we'll help." She turned to Sanders. "You were right. I should have lied."

139

"Sounds to me like you haven't made up your minds yet," said Treece. "Before you do, you might want to hear what I found out last night, or I should say this morning. I think I know—now hear me; I say I *think*—what ship is under *Goliath*."

"You found E.F.," Sanders said.

"No." Treece pointed to the papers on the table. "These are just the beginning, but they've got a couple of clues in 'em. You remember we talked about that 1715 fleet?"

"Sure."

"This may have something to do with that fleet. Try to follow." He picked up a piece of paper. "The 1715 fleet was commanded by a general named Don Juan Esteban de Ubilla. He had wanted to set sail for Spain in late 1714, but there were delays, as there always were. Ships were late coming from the Far East, the Manila galleons that carried K'ang Hsi porcelain, ivory, jade, silk, spices, all manner of stuff. He waited in Vera Cruz for over a year for the cargo to arrive, be lugged across the jungle, and loaded onto his ships. He set off for Havana, where all fleets gathered for last-minute preparations. There were more delays in Havana: ships had to be repaired, more cargo loaded, manifests made up. The early spring of 1715 slipped by, then late spring, then early summer. Pretty soon, it was the middle of July. Ubilla must have been going berserk."

"Why?" Gail asked.

"Hurricanes. There's a West Indian jingle that goes, 'June, too soon; July, stand by; August, come they must; September, remember; October, all over.' A hurricane was

140

the worst thing that could happen to one of those fleets. The ships were pigs. They couldn't point closer than about ninety degrees to the wind, so in a big breeze they were helpless. They were always overloaded, wormy, and rotten. They leaked all day every day.

"Anyway, while Ubilla was waiting, he was approached by a fellow named Daré, master of a vessel that had once been French but now flew the Spanish flag and carried a Spanish name—*El Grifón*. Daré wanted to join Ubilla's fleet, and with bloody good reason: His manifest listed more than fifty thousand dollars in gold and silver, and if he sailed alone there wasn't a chance he'd get by the Straits of Florida. Jamaican pirates would get him. They had spies everywhere, and they'd know exactly when he left Havana. But Ubilla said no. He was all hot about the delays and the weather, and he didn't want the headache of shepherding another vessel; ten ships was plenty to keep tabs on. Daré pressed; he hinted that there was something special about his cargo, something other than what the manifest said. Ubilla wouldn't budge."

"All that's in there?" Gail said, indicating the papers on the table.

"Most of it. Everybody kept diaries in those days, and Spanish bureaucrats were fanatics about keeping detailed records, usually for self-protection. Anyway, under normal circumstances Ubilla's word would have been law. He was responsible for the fleet, and it was up to him to say who sailed with him and who didn't. But evidently there was more to *El Grifón* than Daré was willing to tell. He went over Ubilla's head, to the highest royal representative in Havana, and in jig time Ubilla was ordered to take *El Grifón* with him. So now there were eleven ships in the fleet."

Sanders broke in. "You said last night there were ten ships in the fleet, and they all sank off Florida."

"That's what I thought. That's what *everybody* thought." Treece held up a sheet of paper. "This is Ubilla's manifest. It lists ten ships and all their cargo. What must have happened is that Ubilla had made up his manifest, had done all his paper work, and he was impatient as hell to set sail. If he had gone by the book and presented his manifest for revision, to take into account the eleventh ship—one he didn't want to bother with anyway—the bloody bureaucrats would have kept him in Havana for another month. They insisted on listing every farthing that went with a fleet, or at least every farthing they weren't bribed to ignore—and that would have delayed the fleet's departure until the middle of the hurricane season."

Gail said, "How did you find out about *El Grifón?*"

Treece picked through the pile of documents and found a frayed, cracked, yellow piece of paper. He pushed it across the table to her. "Don't bother to read it. It's in Old Spanish, and the fellow couldn't spell worth a damn. It's a survivor's account. About four lines from the bottom, there's a word spelled *o-n-c-e*—the number eleven. I must have read that bastard a hundred times before, and I never picked it up. He says there were eleven ships in the fleet." He riffled the stack of paper. "It was easy enough to check, or double-check once I had that clue. The King's flunky kept a meticulous diary, and he mentioned *El Grifón* as leaving with Ubilla. Reading him kept me up half the night. He was a pompous bastard, and I had to wade through a pile of self-serving crap. When Ubilla got the order to take Daré with him, he apparently told Daré to join up with the fleet a few hours out, so as to avoid the bureaucrats knowing—they'd have forced him to wait till he could revise his manifest." Treece coughed, stood up, and, without asking, poured three glasses half full of rum.

"The fleet of ten, plus one, left Havana on Wednesday, July 24, 1715," he said, sitting down. "It carried two thousand men and, officially, fourteen million dollars' worth of treasure. The real value was likely something over thirty million. The weather stayed fine for five days. You'd think they'd be well out to sea by then, but those hogs only made seven knots, so they'd barely got to Florida, somewhere between where Sebastian and Vero Beach are today. They had no way of knowing it, but ever since they'd left Havana there had been a hurricane brewing down south, and it had been gaining on them every day.

"It caught up with them on the sixth day out, a Monday night, and by two in the morning it was beating the bejesus out of them: forty-, fifty-foot seas, hundred-mile winds blowing out of the east and driving them west, toward the rocks. Ubilla gave one course correction after another, and most of the ships tried to follow him, but it was hopeless. Daré must have been the only one who consciously disobeyed. Maybe he didn't trust Ubilla; maybe he was just a royal fine sailor. Either way, he kept *El Grifón* half a point farther to the northeast than the other ships, and, by Christ, he survived."

"He made it alone?" Sanders said.

"No. He went back to Havana. He was still worried about pirates. That, or his ship might have been so beat up that he didn't dare try the crossing without making repairs. And now," Treece said with a mischievous smile, "the plot thickens. There is no record at all of what happened to Daré and *El Grifón* once he got back to Havana. For all practical purposes, he disappeared. So did his ship."

"He could have tried to make it alone," Sanders said. "Later on."

"He could have. Or perhaps he laid low for a while, changed his ship's name, and joined another fleet."

"Why would he do that?" Gail asked.

"There are reasons. But a caution: What I've been telling you is fact, close as I can get it. From here on, it's pure speculation." He took a drink. "We know that Daré was carrying goodies worth a hell of a lot more than his manifest said, else he never would have been foisted off on Ubilla. It's a good bet that only a couple people knew what Daré had on board—Daré himself and the King's man in Cuba. Suppose Daré went back to Havana and reported to the officials that the fleet was lost. Then suppose he went to the King's man and made a deal. Say, in return for a portion of Daré's goodies, whatever they were, the King's man would report that *Grifón* had gone down with the fleet. Daré would then disguise the ship and sail away again, scot-free. He could keep what was on board, because everyone thought it had all been lost."

Sanders said, "That's an awful lot of 'supposes.'"

"Aye," Treece conceded. "I told you, I don't *know* anything yet. The only decent evidence we have is time. For instance, the date on the coin fits. Most of the other evidence is negative: no one ever heard of Daré or *El Grifón* again; no other ships were reported sunk around here in those years. And I can't find a likely candidate for ownership of the E.F. pieces, which means they were part of a secret cargo—or at least an unregistered one."

"But Bermuda's only one island," Sanders said. "*Grifón* could have gone down anywhere. Florida, the Bahamas . . ."

"Possible, but not probable. In the deep, maybe, but that was rare. We know Daré was a bloody good sailor. He'd not mess with Florida in bad season again. And the Bahamas channel was abandoned long before then as too dangerous. If he went down—and I'll grant you, it's an 'if' —he went down here."

"Why would he even come here?"

"As you'll learn if you take the trouble," Treece said, "he had no choice. The route to the New World was southerly, down the coast of Spain, across to the Azores, then over the ocean on the easterly trades. The route home was northerly, up the coast of the States, then a turn to the east. It was mostly eyesight navigation. They didn't have proper instruments for determining longitude, so they used Bermuda as a signpost to tell them when to turn east. The weather didn't have to be too bad for them not to be able to see Bermuda until they were on it. Christ, man, there are more than three hundred wrecks on this island. They didn't all happen by coincidence."

"What are the chances of getting it up?" Gail asked. "I mean, if it is *El Grifón*."

"Getting the ship up? Not the faintest prayer. There's

145

nothing left of her. It's getting what was on her that's possible."

"But nobody knows what that was."

"True, but we're a step beyond daydreams now. There is *something* down there." Treece looked happy, excited. "By rights, you found her. Whatever she is, you were the first to find her. You didn't know it, and you still wouldn't if I hadn't told you, but that doesn't alter the facts. What I'm telling you is, I don't want you to go away from here and then get all hot later on if I find something. What's there—a lot or a little—is half yours."

Sanders was grateful, and he started to say so, but Gail cut him off.

"You should know one thing," she said. "I'm going to the government about the drugs."

"Oh Christ!" Treece smacked his hand on the table. "Don't be stupid. The government won't do a goddamn thing."

Sanders was surprised at Treece's sudden vehemence, confused as to whether Treece's anger came from annoyance at the change of subject, the break of mood, or from genuine contempt for the government. Treece was glaring at Gail, and Sanders wished he knew how to help her.

But she seemed to need no help. She looked back at Treece and said evenly, "Mr. Treece, I'm sorry if I annoy you. But we're not Bermudians; we're tourists, guests of your government. I don't know what you have against them, but I do know that we—David and I, anyway—have *got* to tell them about the drugs."

146

"Girl, I can get those drugs, and I mean to. I don't want Cloche to get 'em any more than you do. I've no love for that filth. I've seen what it can do."

Gail's expression did not change.

Treece stood up. "Tell 'em, then! Learn your own fool lesson."

Sanders felt that Treece was ordering them to leave. "What will you do?" he said.

"What I told you I'd do, and not a damn thing more. I'll register the Spanish ship."

"What'll you call it?"

"Spanish ship. That's all the bastards need to know."

They had lunch sent to their room. While they waited for the food to arrive, Gail studied the Bermuda telephone directory. The listings for the various departments and agencies of the government took up nearly a whole column. "I don't even know what I'm looking for," she said. "There's nothing like a bureau of narcotics control."

"Narcotics is probably handled by the police," said Sanders, "which is just where you don't want to go." He paused. "I can't figure it: What the hell do you think Treece has against the government?"

"I don't know. But something. Maybe it's what the bell captain said—St. David's Islanders don't think of themselves as Bermudians."

"It seems more than that. He was *mad*."

"What about customs?"

"What?"

"The customs department."

"Nobody's trying to smuggle them in."

"No, but Cloche wants to smuggle them out." She asked the hotel operator to connect her to the customs bureau. When a voice answered, she said, "I'd like to make an appointment to speak to someone, please."

The voice said, "May I ask what this is in reference to?"

"It's . . ." Gail chastised herself for not having a ready answer. "It's about . . . smuggling."

"I see. Something is being smuggled?"

"Yes. Well, not exactly. Not yet. But it will be."

The voice became skeptical. "Exactly what? And when?"

"I'd rather not say over the telephone. Is there someone I can see?"

"May I ask who's calling, please?"

"Yes." Gail was about to say her name, when she remembered what Treece had said about Cloche: He has friends in many strange places. Quickly, she tried to determine whether the voice on the other end of the line belonged to a black woman. "I'd . . . rather not say."

Now the voice was impatient. "Yes, madam. May I ask, are you a Bermuda resident?"

"No."

"Then I suggest you contact the Department of Tourism." There was a click as the phone was hung up.

"That was a big success," Gail said, running her finger down the list of government agencies. "I should have asked Treece who to go to."

"I don't think he'd have told you," Sanders said.

She called two other agencies, but because she declined

to give specifics over the telephone, at the end of each call she was again referred to the Department of Tourism. Finally, she called the Department of Tourism and asked to speak to the director.

"May I ask what this is in reference to?" said the woman who answered the phone.

"Yes. My husband and I are here on our honeymoon, and we have had an unfortunate experience. We'd like to discuss it with the director."

"Does it have to do with money?"

"I beg your pardon?"

"Money. Have you run short of funds?"

"Of course not. Why?"

"Oh. Good. I'm sorry, but I've been instructed to ask. We do get those calls."

"No. It's not that at all."

"One moment, please." The woman put her on hold for a moment, then came back on the line and said, "Would four o'clock be all right?"

"Fine."

"May I have your name, please?"

"We'll let you know when we get there. Thank you." Gail hung up.

They rode their motorbikes along South Road toward Hamilton. The rush hour had not yet begun, but, even so, the traffic leaving Hamilton was much heavier than the traffic going into town. Businessmen, dressed in knee socks, shorts, short-sleeved shirts, and neckties, sat sedately on their 125-cc. motorcycles, briefcases strapped behind them. Women, finishing the day's shopping, carried their children in wire baskets on the rear fenders of their motorbikes. Wicker baskets hung down both sides of the rear wheel, full of groceries.

The Department of Tourism shared offices with the Bermuda News Bureau on the second floor of a pink building on Front Street, overlooking Hamilton Harbour. A cruise liner was moored at the Front Street dock, and the milling tourists choked the traffic to a standstill. The Sanderses parked their motorbikes between two cars on the left side of the street, locked the front wheels, and waited for a break in the traffic to let them cross the street.

"I wonder . . . ," Gail said.

"What?"

"I'm ashamed to say it. But it's true. What if this man turns out to be black?"

"I know. I thought of that, too."

"I feel like I'm getting to be a racial paranoid. Every time I see a black face, I'm convinced Cloche has sent someone to get me."

The receptionist was a pretty, young black woman. As they approached her desk, Gail said, "I'm the one who called before." She looked at a clock on the wall: it was 4:10. "I'm sorry we're a little late. The traffic was terrible."

"May I have your name . . . now?" said the receptionist.

"Of course. Sanders. Mr. and Mrs. Sanders."

"The director is unavailable. There's a convention of travel agents at the Princess, and he's in meetings all day. I made an appointment for you with his assistant." She rose and said, "Follow me, please." She went to an office in the rear of the room and spoke through the open door. "Mr. and Mrs. Sanders." She showed the Sanderses through the door and said, "Mr. Hall."

The man stood to shake hands. He was white, about forty, tan, and lean. "Mason Hall," he said. "Please come in."

Sanders shut the door behind him, and he and Gail sat in chairs facing the desk.

Hall smiled and said, "What's the problem?" His accent was East Coast American.

Sanders said, "What do you know about a shipwreck off Orange Grove—*Goliath*?"

Hall thought for a moment. "*Goliath*. Mid-forties, right? British ship, I think."

They told Hall their story, eliminating both the clinical details of the assault on Gail and Treece's suspicions about the existence of a Spanish ship. As they were finishing, Gail looked at David and said, "Treece was against our coming to the government."

"I'm not surprised," Hall said. "He's had some run-ins with the government."

"What kind?" Sanders asked.

"Nothing serious. And it's all pretty long ago. Anyway, I'm glad you did come. Even if nothing else happens, you've had more than your share of unpleasantness. I'm sorry, and I know the director would want me to extend his apologies, too."

"Mr. Hall," Sanders said, "that's very nice. But we didn't come here for apologies."

"No, of course."

"What can you do?"

"I'll talk to the director this evening. I'm sure he'll want to confer with the Minister, when he returns."

"Where is he?"

"Jamaica . . . a regional conference. But he'll be back in a few days. Meanwhile, we'll check with the police and see if they know anything about this fellow Cloche."

"The police?" Sanders said. "I told you, Cloche said he has friends in the police. I know he does."

"We'll do it all very quietly. I'll call you as soon as we know anything." Hall stood up. "I do want to thank you for coming by. How long will you be here?"

"Why?"

"Because if it will make you more comfortable, I'll be happy to have a policeman assigned to you."

"No," Sanders said. "Thanks. We'll be all right."

They shook hands, and the Sanderses left Hall's office.

Outside, they walked along Front Street. The sidewalk was crowded with window shoppers from the *Sea Venture*, who peered at the Irish linen and Scottish cashmere and French perfume in the window of Trimingham's, and calculated the savings on the duty-free liquor advertised in the spirit shops.

"Do you think he believed us?" Gail said.

"I think so, but I think if we wait for him to do anything, we'll die of old age."

A few doors ahead, Sanders saw the Pan American ticket office. When they were abreast of the door, he touched Gail's arm and pointed.

She stopped and looked at the foot-high blue letters "Pan Am" painted on the window. "We're damned if we do and damned if we don't," she said. "I don't know if I could live with the pressure at home; the threat, the not knowing, always wondering: What if . . . ?"

David gazed at the lettering for a few seconds more, then said, "Let's go see Treece."

"I'll not say 'I told you so,'" Treece said. "Bloody fools have to be scorched before they'll admit there's a fire."

Sanders said, "Did you register the Spanish ship?"

"Aye. You didn't tell the noble Mr. Hall about it, did you?"

"No."

"He was pretty . . . reserved . . . about you," said Gail.

"Reserved?" Treece laughed. "That's not the word for it. Paper-pushers can't figure me out. All they understand is bullshit and politics, which amount to the same thing."

"You think they'll do anything?"

"Maybe, around the turn of the century." Treece shook his head, as if to dismiss the government from his mind. "So," he said, "now that you've a half interest in what may turn out to be nothing, what are you going to do?"

"Stay," Gail said, "we don't really have a choice."

"You've figured your risks?"

Sanders said, "We have."

"All right. A few ground rules, then. From this moment on, you're to do what I tell you. You can question all you want, when there's time. But when there's not, you jump first and ask questions later."

Gail looked at David. "Leader of the pack."

"What's that?" Treece said.

"Nothing, really. When we were diving, David got annoyed at me for not obeying him."

"And rightly, too. We could get through without a bruise, but there'll be times when getting through at all may depend on how quick you respond. Any time you're tempted to buck me, know this: I'll kick your ass out of here in a trice. I'll not have you getting killed on my account."

"We're not out to fight you," Sanders said.

"Fine. Now"—Treece smiled—"bad-ass decision number one: Go back to Orange Grove and turn in your mobilettes. Pack your gear, check out, and call a cab to bring you out here."

"What?"

"See? You're bucking me already. If we're going to get into this mess, I want you where I can keep an eye on you, and where Cloche's people can't. Back there, Christ knows who-all will have you in their sights."

"But . . . ," Gail protested. "This is your—"

"It may not have all the amenities of your hundred-dollar-a-day bungalow, but it'll do. And you won't have to worry about some tomcat planting voodoo dolls in your bed."

VIII

When the taxi had departed, leaving the Sanderses and their luggage outside Treece's house, Gail said, "You think we'll sleep in the kitchen?"

"What do you mean?"

"That's the only room in the house we've ever seen. He's never even let us in the front door."

The screen door flew open, and the dog bounded down the path toward them. She stood inside the gate, wagging her tail and whining.

Treece appeared in the doorway. "It's okay, Charlotte." The dog backed away a few feet and sat down. "Need any help?"

"We can manage." Sanders opened the gate, hefted the two large suitcases, and, with Gail following him, walked along the path to the door. Gail had an air tank slung over each shoulder.

"You have meat on you," Treece told her. "Those aren't light."

He held the screen door for them and ushered them into the house. The doorway opened onto a narrow hall. The floor was bare—wide, polished cedar boards. An old Spanish map of Bermuda, the parchment cracked and yellow-brown, hung in a frame on the wall. Beneath the map was a mahogany case with glass doors, full of antique bottles, musket balls, silver coins, and shoe buckles.

"In there," Treece said, pointing to a door at the end of the hall. "Here, give me those bottles. Are they empty or full?"

"Empty," Gail said.

"I'll set 'em out by the compressor."

Sanders said, "You have your own compressor?"

"Sure. Can't dash into Hamilton every time I need a tank of breeze."

David and Gail went into the bedroom. It was small, nearly filled by a chest of drawers and an oversize double bed. The bed was at least seven feet square, and obviously handmade: cedar boards pegged together and rubbed with an oil that gave them a deep, rich shine.

"This is his room," Gail whispered.

"Looks like it. What do you think that was?" Sanders pointed to a spot on the wall above the bed. A painting or photograph had hung there until recently: a rectangle of clean white was clearly visible against the aged white of the wall. They heard Treece's footsteps in the hall. Sanders dropped their suitcases on the bed.

"We can't take your room," Gail said to Treece, who stood in the doorway. "Where will you sleep?"

"In there," Treece said, cocking his head toward the living room. "I made a couch big enough for monsters like me."

"But . . ."

"It's better I sleep there. I'm a fitful sleeper. Besides, I was told I snore like a grizzly bear." He led them toward the kitchen.

As they passed through the living room, Gail decided that a woman had lived in the house and had decorated it, though how recently she couldn't tell. Most of the decor reflected Treece: gimbaled lanterns from a ship, brass shell casings, old weapons, maps, and stacks of books. But there were feminine touches, such as a needlepoint rug and a gay, flower-pattern fabric on the couch and chairs.

The paintings on the walls were mostly sea scenes. There were two empty spots, from which pictures had been removed.

In the kitchen, Treece said, "I might's well show you where things are." He looked out the window. "It's that time of day." He opened a cabinet filled with liquor bottles. "Make yourself a charge if you like. I'll have a spot of rum."

Sanders made drinks, while Treece guided Gail through the other cabinets.

"Can't we contribute something?" Gail said.

"By and by. Food's not much of a burden." Treece smiled. "Feel you've been asked to a house party?"

"Sort of. Show me what you want to have for dinner, and I'll get to work."

"Supper'll be along. I'll take care of it." Treece took a glass of rum from Sanders. "We'll start tomorrow; pick Adam up on the beach."

"Coffin?" Sanders said. "He's going to dive?"

"Aye. I tried to put him off, but he wouldn't have it. He still thinks it's his ship, and he's hot to stick it to Cloche."

"Is he good?"

"Good enough. He's a pair of hands, and we'll need all the hands we can get. We'll have to work like bloody lightning, 'cause Cloche will get on to what we're doing fast, and then it'll be dicey as hell. Another thing about Adam: He has a zipper on his mouth. Once he shuts it, nobody'll open it. He learned a lesson from that beating."

"Once we have the drugs," Gail said, "what will you do with them? Destroy them?"

"Aye, but not till we've got every last ampule. If we were to destroy the ampules bit by bit, as we recover them, and Cloche were to find that's what we're doing, we'd be finished. There'd be no reason for him not to have us killed on the spot. Same if we started turning them over to the government lot by lot. Cloche'd see his whole plan going up in smithereens, and he'd kill us just to keep his options open. But if we accumulate them . . . The best way for us to stay healthy is to keep Cloche hoping, let him think we're doing all his work for him, gathering them up and saving them—and when we've got the lot he'll try to pirate them from us."

Sanders noticed that Gail was eying him quizzically. At first he didn't know why; then he realized that he had been smiling as Treece spoke—an unconscious grin that betrayed the strange excitement Sanders felt. He had felt it before: he had a particularly vivid recollection of the sensation as he was about to parachute for the first time. It was a potpourri of feelings—fear made his arms and fingers tingle and his neck and ears flush hot; excitement made his breath come too fast, bringing on lightheadedness; and anticipation (probably at the thrill of being able to say he had actually jumped out of an airplane) made him smile. The fact that he proceeded to sprain his ankle during the jump in no way diminished his glee, nor the fact that he had never jumped again.

Gail frowned at him, and he forced himself to stop smiling.

They heard a muffled thump outside the kitchen door. Treece stood and said, "That'll be supper." He opened the door and retrieved a newspaper-wrapped package from the stoop.

"Supper?" Gail said.

"Aye." Treece set the package on the counter and unwrapped it. Within, still wet and glistening, was a two-foot-long barracuda. "It's a beauty," he said.

Gail looked at the fish, and remembering the barracuda that patrolled the reef and stared at her with vacant menace, her stomach churned. "You *eat* those things?"

"Why not?"

Sanders said, "I thought they were poisonous."

"You mean ciguatera?"

"I don't know. What's that?"

"A neurotoxin, a nasty bastard. Nobody knows much about it, except that it can make you sick as hell and, now and again, put you under."

"Barracudas have it?"

"Some, but so do about three hundred other kinds of fish. In the Bahamas they throw a silver coin in the pot when they boil a barracuda. They say if the coin turns black, the fish is poisonous. But here in civilization we have a much more scientific test." Treece picked up the fish, held out his right arm, and measured the fish against it. "We say, 'If it's longer than your arm, it'll do you harm.' I got a full hand on this one, so it's obviously safe."

"That's a comfort," Gail said.

"It's not as stupid as it sounds. Ciguatoxin is more common in bigger fish, and the bigger the fish, the more of the stuff he's bound to absorb. We figure that in a little brute like this one, even if he is ciguatoxic, chances are pretty good of getting away with nothing more than a bellyache." Treece reached in a drawer and found a filleting knife and a sharpening stone. "Don't be put off," he said. He spat on the stone and rubbed the slim blade in tight circles in the pool of saliva. "I've been eating beasts like that for the better part of forty years, and I've never been stabbed yet." With quick, sure sweeps, he began to scale the fish. The silvery scales flew from the knife blade and floated to the floor.

"Where did he come from?" Sanders asked.

"The reef, I imagine."

"No, I mean how did he get here? I've never heard of a fish that rolls itself in newspaper and deposits itself on your doorstep." Sanders chuckled at his little joke.

"Somebody brought him. They do that. A person catches a few fish, has more than he needs, he'll drop one by."

Gail said, "Is this what you mentioned before? Looking after the keeper of the light?"

"Not really." Treece flipped the barracuda over and scaled the other side. "We take care of our own. Kids' mother gets sick, neighbors'll feed 'em and look after 'em. Ever since . . ." He seemed to hesitate. "They know I don't have time to go fishing and have to cook for myself, so they leave a little something." With two sharp strokes, Treece severed the head and tail. He tossed the tail in the garbage. "You want the head?"

David and Gail shook their heads, looking—with undisguised revulsion—at the fish head impaled through the eye by the point of Treece's knife.

"It's not bad, if you don't have anything else," Treece said, flipping the head into the garbage. "But this fellow has a generous carcass." He slit the barracuda's belly from tail to throat and scooped out the innards. Then he turned the fish around and made a slit along its backbone. The whole side of meat came free.

"You might heat me up some oil," he said to Gail.

"What kind?"

"Olive oil. It's over there by the burner. Dump half a bottle in a pan and fire her up."

Treece sliced the two fillets in half and dropped them in the pan of hot oil, where they bubbled and spat and quickly turned from gray-white to golden.

Gail made a simple salad—Bermuda onions and lettuce—and asked Treece where the dressing was.

"Here," he said, handing her an unlabeled bottle.

"What is it?"

"Wine, they say. I don't know what's in it, but it goes in most everything—salads, cooking, your stomach. Don't want to drink too much of it, though. Give you a fearsome head."

Gail poured an inch of the liquid in a glass and drank it. It tasted bitter, like vermouth.

The sun had dropped below the horizon when they sat down to eat, and rays of pink, reflected off the clouds, streamed in the window and washed the kitchen with a warm, soft glow.

Treece saw Gail toying with her fish, reluctant to eat it. "I'll risk my mortal bones," he said, smiling. "If he's cigua-toxic, you'll know it in a few seconds. One fellow was lugged off to hospital with the poisonous morsel still in his craw."

He didn't use a fork, but broke off a big piece of barra-cuda with his fingers and put it in his mouth. He cocked his head, feigning dread at the possible onset of crippling cramps. "Nope," he said. "Clean as a Sunday shirt."

The Sanderses ate the fish. It was delicious, moist and flaky with a crisp coating of fried oil.

At 9:30, Treece yawned and announced, "Time to put it away. We'll want to be up early. Have to fuel the compressor on the boat and show you how the air lift works. Ever used a Desco?"

"No," Sanders said.

"Have to give you practice, then. There's no trick to it, once you learn how to watch your air line. If it fouls on something, or kinks, you'll think the beast from twenty thousand fathoms has grabbed you by the throat."

"We won't dive with tanks?" Gail said.

"We'll take some, just in case. That's another thing: We'll have to fill them in the morning. That compressor out back makes a God-awful din. But you should try to use a Desco. You never run out of air, unless the compressor on the boat runs out of gas. You use a tank for five hours and you'll think you've been kissing prickly pears. The mouthpiece begins to smart after a while."

"There's no mouthpiece on a Desco?"

"No. It's a full-face mask. You can talk to yourself all you like—sing, make a speech, give yourself a royal cussing. You can talk back and forth, too, if you read lips worth a damn."

They were in bed by ten. The wind whistled outside, swooping up from the sea and over the cliff. As Sanders leaned over to turn off the bedside light, he saw the dog standing, tentatively, in the doorway.

"Hi," Sanders said.

The dog wagged her tail and leaped onto the bed. She curled up and lay between Gail and David.

"Shoo her off," said Gail.

"Not me. I need all my fingers."

They heard Treece call, "Charlotte!" and the dog's ears

stiffened. Treece appeared in the doorway. "Forgive her. That's her rightful place. It'll take her a day or two." He said to the dog, "Come along," and the dog raised her head, stretched, and went to Treece, who said, "Sleep well," and shut the door.

The first bark seemed to be part of Sanders' dream. The second, loud and prolonged, woke him. He looked at the radium dial on his watch: It was 12:10. A faint yellow light seeped around the edges of the closed window shade and flickered on the walls. The dog barked again. Gail stirred, and Sanders shook her awake.

"What is it?" she said.

"I don't know." He heard Treece walking in the hall. "It might be a fire."

"What? In here?"

"No, outside." He rolled off the bed and pulled on his boxer shorts. "Stay here." He walked toward the door. "If there's trouble . . ."

"If there's trouble, what?" Gail reached for her bathrobe. "Hide under the bed?"

Sanders opened the bedroom door and saw Treece standing at the front door, naked except for a brief bathing suit. The dog stood beside him. Though Treece filled the doorway, beyond him Sanders could see a glow of firelight and some dark forms.

"What is it?" he whispered.

Treece turned at the sound. "Not sure. Nobody's said anything."

Sanders approached Treece and stood beside him,

slightly to the side. By the gate there were two men, dressed in black and holding oil torches that sent streams of thick black smoke into the night air.

"Well?" Treece said aloud. He put his left hand on the doorjamb and shifted his weight. Sanders saw that the apparently casual change of position put Treece's hand within easy reach of a sawed-off shotgun that stood in the corner behind the door.

The two torchbearers stepped apart, and between them, walking slowly toward the gate, was Cloche. He was dressed entirely in white, against which his black skin shone like graphite. The firelight sparkled on the gold feather at his neck and on the round panes in his spectacles.

Sanders heard Gail's barefoot steps on the wooden floor and smelled her hair as she came next to him.

"What do you want?" Treece said, his tone a blend of anger and disdain. "If you've business here, state it. Else, be on your way. I'm in no mood for silly games in the middle of the night."

"Game?" Cloche raised his right hand to his waist and dipped the index finger.

Sanders heard a buzz. Instinctively, he ducked, and there was a thunk against the wooden door frame. A featherless arrow quivered in the wood, six inches from Treece's head.

Treece had not flinched. He pulled the arrow from the wood and tossed it on the ground. "A crossbow?" he said. "Put feathers on it; it'll fly truer."

"Your . . . friends . . . are not very prudent," Cloche said. "They paid a visit to the government. I told them not to. Now the police are asking about me."

"And?"

"You know what I want. I know they're down there—ten thousand boxes of them."

"That's myth."

"Your friends do not think so. They seemed quite convinced when they spoke to Mason Hall."

Still looking at Cloche, Treece whispered to Sanders, "Go 'round back and make sure nobody's there."

As Sanders padded down the hall, he heard Treece say, "You know tourists. They hear stories. . . ."

The kitchen was dark, and the door and windows were closed. Sanders found the handle of a drawer, opened it, and fumbled with his fingers for a knife. He found a long heavy blade of carbon steel and slipped it into the waistband of his shorts. The cold metal against his thigh made him feel secure, though he knew it was a delusion: he didn't know how to fight with a knife. But he was quick and strong, and he knew the house. In the dark, against a man unfamiliar with the house, he thought he would be able to handle himself.

He opened the kitchen door. There was no movement outside, no sound except the wind. He closed the door and locked it, then locked both windows. Now, he told himself, if somebody tries to get in, we'll hear the sound of breaking glass. He went back to the front hall—pleased with himself—and stood beside Gail, his left hand resting on the hilt of the knife.

". . . a mystery to me," Cloche was saying. "Why you should be willing to help the British swine. After what they did to you."

"That's not your affair!" Treece snapped.

"Yes, it is. You have as much reason as I to hate them. Look what you lost."

Sanders saw Treece glance quickly at him and Gail. Treece looked uncomfortable, eager to change the subject.

"Leave it be, Cloche. All you need know is that I'll not let you get those drugs."

"What a pity," Cloche said. "The enemy is there and you will not fight him. Are you worried about your little kingdom on St. David's? I have no designs on that."

Treece said nothing.

"Very well," Cloche said at last. "With you or without you, the result will be the same."

Two men moved out of the darkness and stood behind Cloche. Each carried a crossbow, loaded and cocked and pointed at the door. Cloche took a small bag from one of the men behind him. He held the bag by the bottom and flung its contents toward the door. Three linen dolls, each with a steel feather-dart in its chest, rolled in the dust.

Treece did not look down.

The crossbowmen fired.

Sanders slammed Gail against the wall and shielded her with his body. Treece dropped onto one knee and, in the same motion, reached for the shotgun. Sanders heard the arrows buzz through the doorway and clatter against the stone fireplace.

Treece fired three times, holding the trigger down and pumping the action. In the narrow hallway, the sound of the explosions was thunderous and painful.

When the echo of the last explosion had died, and all

that remained was a ringing in Sanders' ears, he turned and looked at Treece. He was still on his knee, the gun cocked and ready to fire.

Where Cloche and his men had stood, now there was nothing but the two torches—abandoned, burning scattered pools of spilled oil.

"Hit anybody?" Sanders asked.

"I doubt it. They broke and ran when they saw this." Treece patted the gun. "I don't think they expected it."

Sanders felt Gail trembling and heard her teeth chattering. "Cold?" he said, putting an arm around her shoulders.

"Cold? Terrified! Aren't you?"

"I don't know," Sanders said honestly. "I didn't have time to think about it."

Gail touched the knife in Sanders' undershorts. "What's that for?"

"I had it . . . just in case."

Gail said to Treece, "Will the police come?"

"The Bermuda police?" Treece stood up. "Hardly. I told you, they don't muck about with St. David's. If they heard anything—and I don't imagine they did—they'll pay it no mind. Just the half-breeds shooting each other up. It's the Islanders that concern me."

"Why?"

"They'll have seen, and heard. They're a superstitious lot. I venture that was part of the purpose of Cloche's visit, to throw the fear into them."

"Fear of what?"

"Of him. They see a coal-black man, dressed all in white —that's what they dress 'em in when they die—coming up a hill in the dark of night with two torchbearers and two crossbowmen: that's powerful bush. If he comes again, there's nothing short of holocaust that'll bring people out of their houses."

Sanders said, "Should we set watches?"

Treece looked at him. "Watches?"

"You know: four hours on, four hours off . . . in case he comes back."

"He won't be back tonight."

"How do you know? Christ, you didn't think he'd dare come up here in the first place!" Sanders was surprised at the harsh sound of his own words. He was challenging Treece, which was not what he had intended, and from the look on Treece's face, a challenge was not what he had expected. Sanders knew he was right, but he didn't care. He wanted to expunge his words. "I didn't mean . . ."

"If he comes back," Treece said evenly, "I'll hear him. Or Charlotte will."

"Fine."

"It's late. There's a lot to be done tomorrow." Treece nodded to Gail, turned, and walked down the hall toward the living room.

David and Gail went into the bedroom and closed the door.

"Bite your tongue," she said.

"I know."

"Never mind. There's no harm in letting him know we're scared."

"It wasn't that. It's just better to be prepared." Sanders pulled off his shorts and climbed into bed.

169

Gail sat on the edge of the bed and hugged her bathrobe around her. "I can't go back to sleep."

"Sure you can." Sanders stroked her back. He smiled, wondering if the sudden, surprising flood of ardor had anything to do with the danger they had just been through.

When they awoke in the morning, they heard voices in the kitchen. Sanders put on a pair of trousers and left the room.

Treece was sitting at the kitchen table, cradling a cup of tea. Across from him, dressed in a stained sleeveless T-shirt, his mouth full of dark bread, was Kevin. They looked up when Sanders entered the kitchen. Kevin's face conveyed no sign of recognition, even when Treece said, "You've met."

"Sure," Sanders said. "Hello."

Kevin said nothing, but Sanders thought he saw him blink in his direction. He poured himself a cup of coffee and took a seat at the table.

Treece said to Kevin, "Does he have anybody who can use the equipment?"

Kevin shrugged.

"Does he have an air lift?"

"Papers didn't say."

"What's this?" Sanders asked.

"You remember Basil Tupper, the jewelry-store fellow who paid you a visit? Two crates of diving gear came in on the Eastern flight from Kennedy this morning, addressed to him."

"How do you know?"

"A friend in customs. There were bottles, regulators, suits—six of everything."

"Didn't the government ask questions?"

"Nothing illegal about it. He paid the duty—in cash. Besides, he imports so much crap for his jewelry business that most of the customs people are his chums. He could say he was starting a dive shop."

Treece cocked his head, listening, and for the first time Sanders noticed the low, muffled chugging sound of an engine, coming from somewhere outside the kitchen.

"Compressor's running out of juice." Treece stood and said to Kevin, "Call Adam Coffin for me. Tell him to be on the beach at high noon." Then he said to Sanders, "You better rouse your lady. If Cloche is training divers, we've just lost our practice time. You'll have to settle for on-the-job training."

"She's up," Sanders said.

They went outside. Kevin left, and Sanders followed Treece to a small shed behind the house. Inside the shed, a gasoline-powered air compressor was coughing and sputtering as it used up the last of its fuel. Two scuba tanks were connected by hoses to the compressor. Treece checked the gauges atop each tank. "Twenty-two hundred," he said. "Want to top them off at twenty-five." He stopped the compressor, filled it with gasoline from a jerry can, and restarted it. "Gonna get me an electric system one of these days. Gasoline's a mean hazard."

"Fumes?"

"Aye. That's why you see that hose there." He pointed to a metal exhaust pipe that led from the compressor down to the dirt floor and out through a hole in the wall of the shed. "When I first got the thing, I left it outside, just covered over by a lean-to affair. The wind swirled all around it, but I paid it no mind—till one day it swirled the exhaust fumes right back into the air intake. That was a memorable dive; almost bought me a one-way ticket to the glooms."

"How did you find out?"

"Started to doze off at fifteen fathoms. I figured pretty quick that was what was happening, so I chucked the tank and let her rip for the surface. I made it, but barely."

Gail appeared at the door of the shed, a piece of toast in her hand. "Good morning," she said.

"That's about all I'd eat if I was you," Treece said. "Got a hell of a lot of work to do, and you don't want to be puking in your mask."

They left Treece's dock a few minutes before eleven. In the cockpit of *Corsair* there were three coils of yellow rubber hose. One end of each hose was screwed into the compressor; the other was attached to a full-face mask. Six scuba tanks were arranged in the racks along the gunwales. The aluminum tube lashed to the starboard gunwale had been rigged to a coil of pink rubber tubing, and it, too, was connected to the compressor. On a ledge in front of the steering wheel Treece had placed the sawed-off shotgun. The dog rode on the pulpit, swaying slightly with each swell but never stumbling. David and Gail flanked Treece at the steering console.

"You really think they'll come for us?" Sanders said, gesturing at the shotgun.

"Never know." He looked at Gail. "Ever use a gun?"

"No."

"Adam'll take the first shift aboard, then. It's better, anyway. He knows how to turn off the compressor, and he won't have any second thoughts."

"Turn it off?"

"Aye. That's the only way to let us know if something's cooking topside. We'll get the message pretty quick when we start sucking nothing. Long as you don't hold your breath on the way up, there's no problem. Of course," Treece smiled, "if things are really hopping up here, we might be better off staying down there breathing sand."

Treece throttled back and began to pick his way through the reefs. The offshore breeze was strong enough to cause foam to roil around the rocks, so he had no trouble finding the slim passages between the reefs. As they neared the Orange Grove beach, they could see Coffin standing in the wave wash, a rawhide figure in torn denim shorts.

There were no swimmers in the water, so, once inside the reefs, Treece opened the throttle and sped toward shore. When the boat was within ten yards of the line of gentle surf, he shifted into neutral, and the boat glided to a stop. Coffin ducked under a wave and swam to the boat. Treece put a hand over the side and, with one heave, brought Coffin into the cockpit.

"I'm glad you dressed formal for your trip to Orange Grove," Treece said.

Coffin spat sea water over the side and wiped his nose. "Buggers. Told me not to use their elevator; told me it was private property. I told 'em to call my solicitor." He laughed. "Rode down with the nicest piece of flesh I've seen in years. I fell deeply in love; almost got engaged."

Treece swung the boat seaward. On the way to the reef, he briefed Coffin about Cloche's threat and about the diving gear that had cleared customs that morning. When he told Coffin that he wanted him to stay aboard, Coffin protested, but Treece convinced him, praising his supposed skills with firearms and his rapport with complex machinery.

They anchored behind the second line of reef. "Once we get everything fired up," Treece said to the Sanderses, "we'll go down. I'll take the air gun. David, stay on my left. You ever see an air lift work?"

"No."

"There's a tube alongside it that forces compressed air up through it. Creates a kind of vacuum and sucks up the sand. It can buck like a bastard, so stay clear, and don't get your hands too close to the mouth or it could drag your fingers up inside and cut the crap out of them. It'll clean sand off the bottom faster'n you can believe. When we uncover ampules, you pick them out as quick as you see them. I'll have to be bloody careful not to let 'em get sucked up with the sand, or they'll smash in the gun. And you," he said to Gail, "stay on *his* left. You won't be able to see a damn thing down there beyond about two feet, so don't wander. Here." He gave her a canvas tote bag. "He'll pass you the ampules as he gathers them; you put 'em in there. When the bag's full, you tap him, he'll tap me, and you'll lug it up. Don't come up without telling me;

I need time to move the gun. If I get too far ahead of you, the sand'll cover the ampules before you can gather 'em. If anything goes wrong, Adam'll shut off the compressor. It'll get hard to breathe right away, but you can probably get one more breath out of it. Come up as close to the bow as you can and hug the boat. You're hard to see up there, and if there's anybody aboard wants to do you dirt, you'll have at least a couple breaths before you have to go down again. Okay?"

"Okay," said Sanders.

"I . . ." Gail hesitated.

"Say it," Treece told her. "Get it out now. I don't want you springing surprises on me."

"I don't like that . . ." She pointed at the Desco masks and coils of yellow tubing. "It scares me."

"Why?"

"I don't know. Claustrophobia, I guess. I can't stand the thought of being . . . tethered. If someone turned off the compressor, I think I'd have a stroke."

"C'mon," Sanders said.

"It's the truth," she said. "I can't help it."

Treece said, "No problem. Rather have you comfortable than all jeebly and upset. Use a tank. We've got plenty."

"Thanks."

"Anybody got anything else to say, say it now. Once I fire up that beast, you won't be able to hear yourselves think."

"You want wet suits?" Sanders asked.

"Aye. We'll be down a long time. The water's warm, but not that warm. After an hour, you'll be shedding body heat like feathers." Treece took a screw driver from a tool box, primed the compressor, and touched the screw driver to two contact points on the starter motor. Sparks jumped from the contacts, and the compressor roared to life.

Sanders went below. The cabin of *Corsair* looked like a divers' flea market. Coils of rope and chain hung from the overhead. Two salt-spotted fishing rods rested on bulkhead brackets. In one corner there was a tangle of old regulator hoses, the rubber cracked and rotten. Tools—hammers, chisels, screw drivers, wrenches—littered the bunks. There was no door on the compartment that housed the head; for toilet paper, a Sunday newspaper supplement had been shredded and tacked to the bulkhead. Sanders found a heap of wet suits, masks, and flippers. He sorted wet-suit tops and bottoms, trying to make matches for himself and Gail. Beneath the pile, he saw a rusty knife and a rubber sheath with straps designed to bind it to a diver's calf. He put the knife in the sheath and took it and the wet suits topside.

Gail was threading two-pound weights onto her belt. He gave her a wet suit and said, "What do you normally use, six pounds?"

"Yes."

"The suit'll double your buoyancy. You might dump those twos and load up with three or four fours."

Gail nodded. She saw the knife in his hand. "What're you planning to do with that?"

"I don't know. Dig in the sand. I found it below."

Treece threw the aluminum tube overboard. It lay on the water for a moment, churning the surface, then slowly sank, trailing the coil of pink tubing behind it. A stream of bubbles popped to the surface.

Treece yelled to Sanders. "Throw that coil over to port. I'll put mine over starboard. Keep 'em from snarling right off."

Sanders threw the yellow coil over. It floated, and air bubbled from the face mask. He mounted a harness on a scuba tank, checked the regulator, and helped Gail into the straps. Then he strapped the knife onto his right leg, added ten pounds to his own weight belt, and buckled it around his middle. He wiggled his feet into his flippers and said, "I guess I'm ready. It feels strange: no tank, no mask."

Gail said, "Throw me the sack when I get myself together, okay?"

"Sure."

Gail rolled backward off the gunwale. She cleared her mask and held up a hand. Sanders leaned over the side, gave her the handles of the canvas bag; she waved and dove toward the bottom.

Treece went over next, then Sanders—jumping beside the coil of hose, retrieving the mask, and slipping it over his head.

As Sanders kicked downward, he sorted out his feelings about diving with the Desco apparatus. His field of vision was much greater than with an ordinary mask; he could see his nose. The air hissing in front of the opening above his right eye felt cool. It was nice not to have a rubber mouth-piece in his mouth; he found he could talk to himself. But he was also aware of a faint tug at his head. He looked up and saw the rubber coil snaking down behind him. He saw

Treece's air hose leading across the bottom toward the reef, and he followed it.

Treece was waiting at the mouth of the cave, holding the aluminum air lift well above the bottom. Even underwater, it emitted a loud noise, like a strong wind rushing between buildings.

When David and Gail joined him, Treece positioned them beside the cave. He made a circle of thumb and forefinger and looked at them. He said, "Okay?" The word was thick and indistinct, but the meaning was clear. They responded with the "okay" sign. Treece touched the mouth of the air lift to the sand.

Instantly, sand vanished from the bottom. It looked to Sanders like a speeded-up film of a vacuum cleaner working on a pile of cigar ashes. In seconds there was a hole a foot wide and half a foot deep. Sand and pebbles were blown out the back end of the tube, causing a dense, blossoming cloud. The tide was running to the right, tending to carry the cloud away from them, but the wave action on the reef fought the tide, and soon Sanders found he had to lie on the sand to see the hole.

The tip of an ampule showed through the sand, quivering against the force of the suction. Sanders grabbed the ampule and passed it to Gail. She set it on the bottom of the bag.

The hole was deeper now, and suddenly a side gave way. Sand rose in Sanders' face. Through the fog he saw a shower of glimmers; he reached into the hole and closed his hand around several ampules. Treece raised the air lift, letting the sand settle so Sanders could see to collect the ampules. Then Treece moved the tube a few feet to the right and started another hole. Right away, he was in a field of ampules, some clear, some yellow, and a few amber.

Gail moved closer to Sanders, taking the ampules from his hand as carefully as possible, setting them, one by one, in the canvas bag. It felt good to move around. The water inside her wet suit was warming to body temperature, and when she moved her arms or legs, pockets of water were squeezed from one part of the suit to another. She tried to count the ampules in the bag, but there were too many. She worried that if she kept adding more and more ampules, they might be crushed when she took them out of the water. Here they weighed almost nothing; out of water the liquid might be dense enough to cause the ampules on the bottom of the bag to crack. She tapped Sanders on the shoulder and pointed to Treece, a hazy gray figure only three or four feet away. Sanders tapped Treece, who raised the air lift off the sand. Gail kicked over to him and showed him the bag. He nodded and pointed upward.

As she surfaced, the bag acted as a sea anchor, holding her back. She had to struggle to make way, kicking as hard as she could and using her hand to force herself upward. She looked down and saw Treece tap Sanders and beckon him toward the reef.

Coffin had seen her bubbles, and he was waiting on the diving platform. He took the bag from her, and as he looked into it, his eyes glazed in recollection. All he said was "Aye."

Gail hauled herself onto the platform and lay on her stomach, panting.

"Next time," Coffin said, "leave your weights on the bottom. Makes it easier."

Gail said, "Yes," and chided herself for not having thought of it.

"I'll have this bag emptied for you in a jiff; just want to stow the glass."

She pushed herself into a sitting position. "No rush."

Coffin walked forward, and Gail could hear a tinkling sound as he removed the ampules from the bag.

"No trouble?" she called.

"Not a peep. I don't guess the bastard'll try anything with all them folks on the beach. He's a piece of work underwater, ain't he?"

"Treece? I suppose. Is the air lift hard to handle?"

"For most men. It can buck like a goat. But Treece'll hold it steady as a tree for five and six hours at a go. I think he'd stay down there all his life if he could. He's been happiest down there, away from people, for a long time." Coffin's voice trailed off.

"What do you mean, a long time?"

"You don't know?"

"I guess not."

"Well, it ain't my place to tell tales."

"Mr. Coffin," Gail said, controlling her annoyance, "I'm not asking you to tell tales. But there's something about Treece that everybody but us seems to know, and nobody will say. We're living in the man's house, sleeping in his bed. I think we have a right to know *some*thing."

Coffin picked the last of the ampules from the bag. "Maybe you do. All I'll tell you is this: He was married." He walked aft.

180

"Where's his wife?"

"Dead." He handed her the bag. "Two hundred and forty-six. Got a long way to go."

Gail looked at Coffin, debating whether to press him for more information. She decided not to try: If he wanted to talk, he would—when he close to. Pressing might anger him. She lowered her mask over her face, bit down on her mouthpiece, and slipped off the diving platform into the water.

Underwater, she rolled the bag into a ball to keep it from dragging. She looked down and saw Treece and Sanders working in the reef, several yards to the left of the cave. Through the cloud of sand that billowed above them she could not tell which man was which. She started down, and the water that seeped into her wet suit felt cold. She wondered how much air she had left, looking forward to the interlude that would come when she had to change tanks. The sun would feel good, and perhaps she could coax Coffin into sharing a few more facts about Treece's wife.

She swam through the floating sand and felt dusty motes cling to her hair. She heard a hammering sound, as though someone were working on an anvil. Blinded by the sand, she was suddenly rammed in the chest by a blast of air and pebbles; she had swum to within inches of the discharge from the air lift. She recoiled and let herself fall to the bottom. Debris rained around her as she crawled forward.

Treece was banging the end of the air lift against the coral, trying to break off a piece so he could put his hand in a hole. A fist-size chunk of coral broke loose and rattled up the tube. Treece felt with his fingers, then shook his head: his hand was too large. He pointed to Sanders, who worked his fingers into the hole and withdrew them, clutching a green crusty piece of metal, which he passed to Treece.

Gail tapped Treece, to let him know she was there. He turned and gestured for her to open the bag. She unfolded it, and he dropped the relic inside. Then he led them back toward the cave.

Sand had drifted into the hole Treece had made, and now there was a barely perceptible dent in the bottom. Treece positioned the Sanderses as they had been before and touched the air gun to the sand.

For the first six inches, as Treece redug the hole, there was nothing but sand. But soon he found the carpet of ampules, and Sanders plucked them, in twos and threes, from the shifting bottom and passed them to Gail.

Lying prone on the bottom, moving nothing but her hands, Gail felt a deep, unpleasant chill. The water in her suit was still and clammy. Her body, needing to generate heat, sent a shiver into her arms, then her shoulders, then her neck. She hoped she would run out of air soon.

Sanders picked the last two ampules from the hole. Treece backed up a foot or two, touched the gun to fresh sand, and, in half a minute, exposed countless new ampules.

A lump appeared in the bottom of the hole, a hard cone. Sand slipped away from it until Sanders could see a metallic green peak. Suddenly he knew what it was: an artillery shell. He reached for it, and quickly Treece hit his hand with the air lift, then raised the air lift over his head and looked at Sanders. He held up the index finger of his left hand: Pay attention, he was saying. He pointed to the green cone and shook his finger, then pointed at himself: You stay clear; I'll handle it. He pointed at Sanders, at the air lift, at the cone: Take this and train it on that thing. Sanders nodded and reached for the tube. There was a circular grip near the mouth. Treece kept his hand on the grip until Sanders seemed to have firm grasp, and then Treece let go.

Watching Treece use the gun—his hand on the grip, the tube tucked snugly under his arm—Sanders had concluded that the air lift was a docile beast, so he held the grip loosely. The mouth of the tube drifted across the bottom, sucking up sand and stones. Suddenly the tube inhaled a stone it couldn't pass, and, clogged, it jumped from Sanders' hand and slammed into his armpit. Whipped by a hundred feet of hose full of compressed air, the tube bounced Sanders along the bottom like a Yo-Yo. Sanders wrapped his arms around the tube and tried to dig his heels into the sand, but the tube snapped him upward and swung him back and forth. He saw flashes of the surface and streaks of gray and brown as he was swept past the reef. He relaxed his hold, trying to free himself from the tube, and it cracked him across the ribs.

Then the tube fell still. Gasping, peering through a swirl of sand and bubbles, Sanders saw Treece holding the bottom of the jumping air lift against the reef, banging it on a rock. He slammed it down again and again until, finally, the stone was disgorged. The tube swayed slowly in the tide.

Treece made the "okay" sign and raised his eyebrows,

questioning. Sanders touched his ribs and nodded. Treece gestured at the grip: Hold it steady, and it'll behave. He led Sanders back to the hole.

Gail touched his shoulder and looked worriedly into his eyes. He made the "okay" sign and dropped to his knees. Treece handed him the grip and fit the tube under his arm. Sanders held the grip so tightly that his knuckles whitened. When he was sure he was in control, he nodded at Treece and dipped the gun to the sand. It twitched and hummed against his body, but held firm.

Treece swam to the other side of the hole, facing Sanders, guiding him around the green cone, directing that he dig the hole wide enough so that it wouldn't collapse on itself.

The shell was standing on end, and it widened—as sand was stripped from it—to a diameter of about six inches. It was coated with marine growths, but, judging by the way Treece was handling it, it was still very much alive.

When the shell was almost free of sand, Treece wrapped his hands around its middle and gingerly lifted it from the bottom. He inspected it, then set it on the sand at the base of the reef. He took the air lift from Sanders and scoured the ragged hole for more ampules.

The bag filled quickly. Gail was marrow-cold, longing for the sun's warmth but unwilling to admit it to the men. She would force herself to wait the last few minutes until the bag was full enough. Then, to her delight, she felt the tightness of breath that signaled a nearly empty tank. She tapped Treece, ran her finger across her throat, and pointed to the surface. Treece gestured at the bag and

raised his left hand, with two, then three, fingers extended
—telling her to bring down more bags. She nodded. As she
rose toward the surface, she saw that Treece and Sanders
were staying at the hole instead of moving to the reef.
They were going to dig as many ampules as they could, as
fast as they could.

Ten or fifteen feet above the bottom, the weight of the
bag reminded her to drop her weight belt. She unsnapped
the belt buckle and watched the twelve pounds of lead
drop to the sand.

Again Coffin was waiting for her at the surface. As she
passed him the bag, she said, "There's something in the
bottom."

"What?"

"I don't know. They found it on the reef." Gail took off
her tank and passed it to Coffin.

"You want a fresh one?" Coffin asked.

"Yes. He wants more bags."

"Shouldn't wonder. If what's supposed to be down there
is down there, it'll take a bleeding eon to get it up with one
bag."

Gail pulled herself onto the diving platform and unzipped her wet-suit jacket. She leaned back against the stern
of the boat, letting the sun warm her cold, wet skin. There
were tender spots on her face, at the pressure points from
the mask, and her mouth felt stretched and sore from the
mouthpiece—as if a dentist had been working on a back
tooth and hyperextended her lips. She wiped her nose and
saw blood on her hand.

"Tired?" Coffin said as he unloaded the ampules.

"Exhausted."

"I'll take a trip, then. There's nothing going on up here."

"No, it's all right," she said, not sure why she was rejecting his offer. "I'll take one more. If something does happen, better to have you here."

"At least we'll rig up something to make it easier."

Gail rested for a few more minutes, then climbed into the boat and disconnected her regulator from the empty air tank. As she prepared a new tank, she tried to think of a subtle way to get Coffin talking about Treece's wife. There was no subtle way, so finally she said, "What did Treece's wife die of?"

Coffin glanced at her, then concentrated on the bag. "I'm counting," he said, dropping ampules into plastic sandwich bags. "There. Fifty." He tied off the sandwich bag and started to fill another one.

Gail was silent until she had finished working on her tank. Coffin dropped the last ampule in the plastic bag and tied it off.

"Has she been dead long?"

Coffin ignored her. "Two-ten," he said. "That's four fifty-six altogether." He reached into the bottom of the canvas bag and removed the piece of green metal. "Hello."

"What is it?"

"An escutcheon plate." He held it up. The plate was shaped like a fleur-de-lis. In each of the leaves there was a keyhole. Around the edges were six holes where nails had been. "Covered the lock on a box or chest. What's he want with that?"

"He didn't say."

Coffin set the escutcheon plate on the shelf in front of the steering wheel. "It's just brass."

Gail paused. "If you won't tell me," she said, "I'll ask him."

Coffin opened a locker and took out two canvas bags and a coil of three-eighths-inch hemp. "That would be a cruel thing to do." Coffin fed an end of the rope through the handles of one of the bags and tied a bowline. He paid out twenty or thirty yards of rope, cut it, and tied the cut end to a cleat on the stern. He repeated the procedure with the other bag, securing the rope to a cleat amidships.

When he was finished, he stared at the knife for a moment, thinking. Then he stabbed it into the gunwale and turned to Gail. "All right. I don't want you asking him. I don't want you giving him pain. He's had his fill of that."

Embarrassed, Gail started to say something, but Coffin cut her off.

"When he was a lad, he raised his share of hell on Bermuda. No more than most boys, I guess, but his hell-raising seemed to have a direction, as if he was trying to say something. He never shoplifted or robbed anything from common folks. Everything he did was against authority—the police or the British. I remember, the British tried to confiscate some common land on St. David's to build an installation of some kind. The Islanders got all hot about it, claiming the land was theirs by rights. 'Course, the British took it anyway, but they had the devil's own time building anything. Treece and his cronies tore things down as fast as they were built, sugared the gas tanks of all the construction equipment, things like that.

"Anyway, when he was about twenty-three, he met a British girl, Priscilla. I forget her last name. She was here on holiday, and she met Treece in St. David's, pretty much by accident. Lordy, she was a gorgeous girl! And nice. A kinder, sweeter lass never drew breath. Treece taught her how to dive, how to look for wrecks—Christ, how to do everything but talk to fish. She taught him how to handle people, how to handle himself. Calmed him down like an oil slick on a wave. She went home to England but came back the next summer and took a job in Hamilton working with kids. A year after that, Treece and her got married— that must have been about 1958, thereabouts. The proper Brits on Bermuda didn't take kindly to the marriage. They never did know what to make of St. David's people. Sometimes they called 'em red niggers; most often they pretended St. David's didn't exist. But once Priscilla moved in with Treece on St. David's—rather than the other way around, bringing him out into civilization where he could embarrass someone—they forgot about it. She kept her job in Hamilton, and he stayed on the island.

"It was like Treece was all of a sudden a new person. There was no more anger in him, no room for it. There was too much happiness.

"For two, maybe three years, everything was fine. They raised wrecks together. To keep the larder full, Treece did salvage work. His father was still alive then, so he didn't have the job with the light. One spring in the early sixties, Treece found his first treasure wreck, the *Trinidad*. It didn't yield much as treasures go—a gold bar, an emerald ring, a few other things—but it was enough to give him a

188

fair poke. Right away, Priscilla got pregnant. Nobody knew it at the time; it didn't come out till after. But they should've known: she had the glow of life about her. She wore that emerald ring so proud, and she was near bursting with love and . . . well, I guess goodness is about the only word.

"Like I said, she worked with kids, troubled kids, the ones who hadn't done enough to merit a stay in the brig but who couldn't quite handle everything society said they should handle. She loved those kids like they was her own.

"This was around the time the drug thing was just getting big in the States. Not here; it's never amounted to much here. But there was talk about Bermuda being used as a halfway station for smugglers. A ship arriving in Florida or Norfolk with a European cargo raises eyebrows, especially if it's stopped at, say, Haiti or the other islands on the way. But sailboats on a round trip from the States to Bermuda, or businessmen down here for long weekends—nobody paid them no mind.

"One day, one of Priscilla's kids got loose-lipped and spilled something about a schooner due from down south with a load of drugs. She thought it was just talk, but she mentioned it to Treece. Treasure-divers are wired into everywhere, every bar and fish market. They have to be, to pick up clues: so-and-so saw a pile of egg-rock ballast here; somebody else spotted a strange timber there; 'Hey, look at the coin I found off Spanish Rock.' That kind of thing. So it wasn't hard for Treece to check the rumor, and it was true. A private yacht was due into St. George's with ten kilos of heroin. Part of it would be moved aboard a cruise ship in loaves of bread; the rest would be stowed here and taken up north little by little by 'businessmen.'

"In those days, Treece still had some trust in the government. Priscilla had taught him that all authority wasn't necessarily out to get him. So they went to the government, right to the top, and told what they knew. Well, the government didn't believe them, and, to be fair, there wasn't much evidence for them to believe—fair, that is, considering that they were pigheaded about Treece from the start. They didn't have *any* idea how much he knew. As far as they were concerned, this was all rumor started by a kid.

"That got Treece pretty riled, partly out of pride. Here he had the bloody goods on some people smuggling heroin, and the government wouldn't take his word. He decided to stop them himself and present the drugs to the government on a platter. He didn't know what he was getting into, and he did a couple of foolish things, like tell one too many people what he was up to. He was threatened a few times, and that got him still hotter. Priscilla tried to calm him down, but it was hard 'cause she agreed with him.

"Not to burden you with all the details, Treece and some chums met the yacht outside St. George's harbor and tried to board her. There was a bloody great rumpus, and the yacht steamed away."

"With the drugs?" Gail asked.

"Aye, but their plan was a wreck. Four days later, Priscilla was found dead at her desk in her office. The medical examiner said she had died of an overdose of drugs, and the case was closed. What people figure happened, one of the smugglers' contacts here—his operation ruined—waited for her in her office one morning and, before anybody else got there, stuck a needle in her. There were track marks on her arms, but they were all fresh, put there to make it look like she was a user.

"Treece near went crazy, with grief and guilt and fury. He half-blamed himself, half-blamed the government."

"Did he ever find the man who killed her?"

"No one knows . . . for sure. But about a week after she died, a man was found in St. George's, high in the top branches of a tree. Every bone in his body had been broken at the joints. His fingers were all bent upward, his arms bent backward, same with his knees and his toes. His head was turned full around, like someone had tried to unscrew it. He was a bartender, mostly unemployed but always with ready cash. Nobody was ever prosecuted, and the only reason anybody connects it with Treece is that it had to have been some powerful man who splintered that fellow and hauled him fifty feet off the ground.

"For about a month, Treece stayed drunk, morning, noon, and night, guzzling anything that had a charge to it. He sat in his house, and the only people who dared go near it were the folks delivering booze and food. Then one day he came out and started diving, did all manner of crazy-ass things: dove alone, in foul weather, went too deep and stayed too long. It was like he was trying to purge himself, or kill himself, and he damn near did that: got bent up like a pretzel and had to spend three days in a decompression chamber. A fisherman found him floating on the surface."

"What brought him down?"

"Down? You mean back to normal? Time, I guess. But what's normal? He's never been the same as he was before she died. I doubt he ever will."

"Was Cloche involved?"

Coffin paused. "I'd bet on it, but there's no proof. Anyway, the important thing is, Treece sees the same thing happening again."

After a moment's silence, Gail said, "Thank you." She felt a sadness, a vicarious pain for Treece. She tried to form a mental picture of his wife, but the only image that fit was herself.

Coffin held the scuba tank for her while she put on the harness and straightened the straps. He handed her the canvas bag she had brought up and said, "When you're in, I'll give you the other two. Take 'em down and set a rock on 'em so they won't drift away. When they're full, give three tugs on the line, and I'll haul 'em up. Follow 'em, though, to make sure they don't tip."

"Okay." She stepped over the transom onto the diving platform, checked tank and mask, and jumped into the water.

Pulling the ropes behind her, she swam for the bottom. Without weights, she tended to float, and she had to use both arms to aid her descent. She found her weight belt on the bottom, strapped it on, and made her way toward the cloud of sand.

She had been gone longer than she thought. A mound of ampules more than a foot high and two feet wide rose in the sand beside David. She kneeled on two bags and opened the third. She found she could scoop handfuls of ampules off the mound and drop them in the bag; they floated safely to the bottom. She filled one bag, then another, then the third. She tapped Sanders to let him know she was going up, and tugged three times on the two ropes. As she unbuckled her weight belt, the two ropes tightened and the bags rose. She grabbed the ropes with one hand and, holding the untethered bag with the other, let herself be dragged to the surface.

"You're bleeding," Coffin said.

Gail crossed her eyes and saw bloody water washing around her nose. She tilted her head back and blew her mask clear. "I know. It's nothing."

"Sure you don't want me to take a trip?"

"I'll do one more."

Carefully, Coffin pushed the ampules out of the bags onto a tarpaulin he had spread on the deck. "I'll count 'em while you're down," he said, passing the bags to Gail.

She went down again, and this time she felt pain—a tight ache in the sinus cavities above her eyes. She stopped a few feet below the surface, struggling to maintain depth, and waited for the pain to subside. She descended farther, until the pain stopped her and forced her to wait. This is the last one, she thought: too many ups and downs.

There was pressure now on her ears, too, and she made herself yawn. She felt two squeaky pops, and the pressure was gone. As she started down again, she saw something move—a grayish blur at the edge of the gloom beyond the reef.

She looked harder, straining to see through the haze. Nothing. Then, farther to the left, another flicker of movement. She turned her head, trying to anticipate where it might appear next. Behind her, away from the cloud of sand, the water was clearer, and as she turned, she saw it: gliding out of the fog as if from behind a curtain was a shark. It moved with sure, unhurried grace, thrust through the water by smooth strokes of its crescent tail.

A knot of panic struck Gail's stomach. She was more than halfway to the bottom, and she remembered David's warning about not fleeing for the surface. She could not tell how big the shark was, for, in open water, there was nothing against which to measure it. Nor could she tell how far away it was; it cruised at the outer limit of her vision. But how far could she see? Fifty feet? Sixty?

The shark swam in a wide circle, and as streaks of sunlight caught its back, Gail could see faint stripes along its sides, light brown slashes against the gray-brown skin. One black eye seemed to be watching her, but it registered no interest, no curiosity.

Still holding the ropes, she continued down toward the belching air lift. She found her weights, strapped them on, and tapped Treece. When he looked at her, with her right hand she made a sinuous swimming motion, then, with her fingers, a biting motion. She pointed off to the right, where she guessed the shark would be by now. Treece looked in the direction she was pointing, but, surrounded by drifting sand, he saw nothing. He looked back at her, shook his head, and, with a curt wave of his hand, dismissed the danger.

Sanders was not sure he understood what Gail had told Treece. He recalled her nervousness in the company of a barracuda and assumed she had seen another one. But seeing the wide-eyed fear on her face, he wondered. He put the heels of his hands together, spread his fingers, then slammed them closed—a fair approximation of a big mouth. He looked at her, raised his eyebrows, and spread his arms, asking, How big? She shrugged: Can't tell. But she spread her arms as wide as she could: At least this big. Sanders noticed that half an inch of bloody water was washing around in her mask. He pointed to it and shook his finger, telling her not to clear the mask, not to put blood in the water.

She nodded, but misunderstood. Before he could stop her, she pressed the top of her faceplate and exhaled through her nose. A stream of green, mucous water flushed from her mask and drifted off in the tide.

Sanders smacked himself on the forehead and shook his head. He pointed to the drifting threads of blood.

Gail's eyes looked stricken. She touched his arm and pointed to the surface, asking if she should go up. He held her wrist and shook his head firmly: No. He pointed to an empty canvas bag, picked up a handful of ampules, and dropped them into the bag.

The ditch Treece had excavated contained a major lode. There were ampules everywhere, poking up through the sand like raisins in a rice pudding. Picking carefully with the air lift among the artillery shells, Treece would touch a leaf of rotten wood and let the suction peel the leaf away, revealing forty-eight ampules, in eight neat rows of six.

Sanders could not keep up with Treece. He plucked four, six, ten ampules from the sand at a time and passed them back to Gail, but always Treece would have un-covered more. He tried to lift a full box, but though it looked intact, it had no bottom, and the ampules fell away in the sand. He cupped his hands, scooped fifteen or twenty ampules, and turned to give them to Gail. Her hands weren't there. He turned, angrily, to face her, and saw her staring at the reef.

The shark was no more than ten feet away, moving from right to left between them and the coral. It was six or seven feet long, a sleek torpedo of muscle. It watched them, but made no move toward them, and Sanders won-dered if it was seeking the source of the blood in the water. He reached to his calf and unsheathed the knife. He saw that Treece had not noticed the shark. He tapped him and pointed, as the shark swam away to the left, keeping a steady ten or twelve feet from the divers and four or five feet from the reef.

Treece watched the shark pass Gail and turn, perhaps twenty feet away, diasppearing behind the cloud of sand. He rapped his knuckles on the air lift and shook his head. He seemed to be saying, Stay calm.

With the knife in his right hand, Sanders had only his left free to gather ampules, and that hand couldn't accom-plish much because Gail wouldn't take any more ampules from him; she stayed rigid on her knees, clutching a half-full bag and waiting, panicked, for the shark to reappear.

He saw it first. As before, it came from the right, still keeping its distance but, Sanders thought, slightly closer than on its previous pass. It approached the preoccupied Treece and moved toward Sanders, who crouched, holding the knife in front of him. Then Gail saw it, and, shocked, she flailed her arms. The shark saw the movement, and its head twitched, dipping toward Gail.

Gail's arm touched Sanders' side, and the sensation was a trigger that snapped him forward. His right hand was extended, the knife blade pointing up.

The shark saw him coming and dodged, its head jerking to the right, its tail thrashing twice. But instinct told it to avoid the reef, and, apparently confused, it slowed enough to let Sanders jab the knife into its underside, a foot ahead of the tail.

Sanders' only conscious thought was how soft the flesh was; the knife went in up to the hilt. Then the body convulsed and tore the knife from his hand. Blood spurted from the wound in a thick green cloud.

The shark darted away, swimming erratically, its body shuddering, tail twitching. The head turned and the jaws snapped at the bleeding belly. The shark was trying to eat itself.

The knife had fallen a few feet away, and Sanders swam to retrieve it, worried that the shark would return and, in anger, attack.

But it was not the shark that attacked. Sanders felt a hand grip his ankle and drag him backward. Lying on his back, he gazed into Treece's furious eyes. He saw Treece's lips moving, and he heard sounds, but no words.

Treece grabbed Sanders' arm and yanked him to his feet. His fingers completely circled Sanders' upper arm and, on the inside of the arm where they met, pinched painfully.

Scared and confused, Sanders didn't know what he had

done to enrage Treece, and as he looked into the shouting face, he was genuinely afraid that Treece might kill him.

Treece grabbed the knife from Sanders' hand and rammed it into the air-lift intake. It rattled up the tube. Then Treece pointed at the surface and started up. He stopped, returned, and gathered up one of the artillery shells.

Gail still crouched on the bottom. Sanders took her arm and helped her to her feet, pulled three times on one of the ropes, and guided her hand to it when the rope was tightened by Coffin's pull.

As he swam with Gail to the surface, Sanders saw a gray shadow moving in the distance. Hazy as it was, Sanders could see that it was big, much bigger than a man.

When he neared the boat, he looked down and saw the wounded shark, twisting and rolling on the reef. Then the air stopped flowing into his mask.

He kicked to the surface, exhaling the last of his air. He grabbed the diving platform with one hand, removed his mask, and said, "Hey, what . . ." The sound of Treece's voice silenced him.

". . . dumb, goddamned, idiotic, crazy thing to do I ever saw in my life!" Treece was already in the boat, railing, Sanders assumed, at Coffin, who had turned off the compressor.

Sanders dipped his face in the water to clean his nose, so he didn't see the hand that reached for him. He heard the word "You!" and felt himself grabbed under one arm and hoisted out of the water and over the transom. His feet slammed onto the deck.

Gail, hanging off the platform, watched Sanders fly out of the water, and a picture struck her: a man, wedged high in a tree, with his limbs splayed backward.

Treece held Sanders by the arm and shook him, snapping his head back and forth. "What in the name of the gentle Jesus do you think you're doing? You think you're goddamned Tarzan? You're a goddamned hazard, that's what!"

"What . . ."

"Bugger up a day's work . . . Jesus Christ!" Treece pushed Sanders away and turned to take Gail's tank off the platform.

Sanders rubbed the welts on his arm. "She was bleeding!"

"Cat shit!"

"She was! In her mask. She cleared it into the water."

Treece looked at Coffin and said, "Christ, spare me from idiots." He turned back to Sanders and opened his mouth to shout, but apparently changed his mind. "All right," he said, struggling against his temper. "First off, that little fish wasn't about to eat us."

"Little!" Sanders said. "That thing was at least seven feet long." Confident now that Treece was not going to hurt him, he felt embarrassed, aggressively resentful. He wanted to question Treece's declarative cockiness.

"If it was five feet, I'm the King of Spain. Water magnifies everything."

Sanders felt himself blush. "Even so . . ."

"Second," Treece said, "there wasn't enough blood in the water to make him more than a little nosy. He was having a look-see. If he'd have got serious, you'd have seen the excitement ripple along his body; he'd've got real agitated. And soon as I spotted that, all we had to do is gather together in the air-lift cloud. Sharks won't go in it, or if they do, they'll get the hell out in a hurry without waiting to bite anything. The sand clogs their gills, and they hate that: it can kill 'em. I had his grandfather try to eat me once—a *big* bastard of a tiger shark, all of fifteen feet long —and I just waited him out in the cloud. But sticking him with a knife is the last bloody thing in the world you want to do. The *last!* When you've got no other choice, when it's either stick him or be dinner, then you stick him. But not before."

"Why?"

"He's liable to bite you. They're not supposed to have enough brains to get angry, but I tell you, I've seen 'em do a right fancy imitation of being pissed off. You want to see another reason, get in the water."

"What? Where?"

Treece tossed him a face mask. "Put this on and hang off the platform." He said to Gail, "You, too. But for Christ's sake, don't go tooting off somewhere."

Tentatively, not knowing what to expect, David and Gail slipped off the platform and clung to the chains that attached it to the boat. They held their breaths and put their faces in the water.

The scene thirty feet away, on the reef, looked like a gang fight. All that remained of the shark Sanders had stabbed were a few mutilated pieces, and those were being fought over, with savage frenzy, by countless other sharks. Half a dozen large tiger sharks flailed in a blurred ball around a piece of offal. A smaller shark chased a shred of flesh to the bottom, took it in his mouth, and sped away, pursued by two others. There were sharks everywhere, swimming in frantic bursts, responding to smells and sounds and commotion in the water, searching for prey. Some were gray, some brown, some striped. Large sharks took random swipes at smaller ones, who darted out of reach—or, when they were not quick enough, were wounded and set upon by the mob.

As the Sanderses watched, more and more dark, sinuous shapes glided out of the twilight blue. One cruised directly beneath the boat, and, seeing something on the surface, rose toward them. They hoisted themselves onto the platform and climbed into the boat.

Treece and Coffin were counting ampules on the deck. Treece did not look up. "See what you did?" He was not gloating; his tone of voice said simply: Now you understand.

"I see."

Gail said, "How long will they stay around?"

"Till the food runs out. But if they're beating up on each other like they usually do, the food won't run out. They'll be there a good long while."

"So today's wiped," Sanders said. "I'm sorry."

"Aye." Treece relented. "It's no great tragedy. We got a fair load for today, and one thing about those beasts: They'll keep anybody else from messing around down there."

Gail shivered. She removed her wet-suit top and dried herself. "How many have you got?"

"Four thousand"—Treece looked at Coffin—"eight hundred and seventy," Coffin said, wrapping the last plastic bag of ampules.

"Not enough." Treece looked at the shore. "And not much bloody time. I imagine Cloche has had people on the bluffs all day."

Coffin said, "He can't make 'em into good divers in two days. And he'll have to build an air lift. Can't send a bunch of bunnies out here to pick around in the sand with their fingers."

"Two days, no. But not much more than that, to make 'em middling competent. And when he's ready, they're going to come fast. I think maybe we'll be working nights, too." He saw a look of chagrin on Gail's face, and he said, "Not tonight. We'll give your bugle a rest."

"What will you do with this?" Sanders rested his hand on the artillery shell.

"Nothing, for now. I just wanted to get it out of there. Later on, I'll clean it up and sell the brass."

"Is it really live, after thirty years?"

"Aye." Treece said. He set the shell in a vise bolted to the starboard gunwale. From a locker he took a huge wrench which he fit to the bottom of the shell. He tugged on the handle, but the wrench didn't budge. "Corroded into a bloody weld." He braced his foot against the bulkhead, wrapped both hands around the wrench, and leaned back. His biceps balled into tight knots; the sinews in his neck strained against the skin, and a red hue suffused his face.

There was a metallic squeak, then the sound of a crack, and the wrench handle moved. Treece heaved again and broke the seal. He unscrewed the bottom of the shell and dropped it on the deck. "Look here."

The interior of the shell was filled with stiff, gray, spaghettilike strands, bunched tightly together.

Coffin handed Treece a pair of pliers and a box of matches. Treece fished one of the strands from the shell casing and, holding it with the pliers, gave Sanders the matches. "Light it."

"What is it?"

"Cordite. That's what makes everything explode."

Sanders held a match to the end of the cordite strand. There was a flash, and the strand burned with the brilliance of magnesium.

Gail said, "That's all there is to a shell that big?"

"All? Christ, girl, pack a hundred of 'em together and touch a primer charge to 'em, and you can blow Bermuda to pieces."

"How many are there?"

"No way to know," Coffin said. "There was about ten ton when we started, but some of it's been salvaged."

Treece tossed the cordite overboard. It hissed as it hit the water, and, sinking, emitted a stream of bubbles.

They fetched the air hoses from the water and coiled them on the deck. Treece fastened the air-lift tube to the gunwale, then started the engine. Charlotte, who had been sleeping on the bow, lurched to her feet and—like a soldier reluctantly assuming a midnight watch—took her post on the pulpit.

Coffin hoisted the anchor, and Treece eased the boat through the reefs and headed for shore.

"What time tomorrow?" Coffin said.

"Early. Say eight o'clock. We'll do four or five hours in the morning, dry off for the afternoon, and start again around six." He teased Coffin. "I know you old folks need your afternoon nap."

"The hell you say!" The boat was still seventy-five yards from shore. "I'll outlast 'em all." Coffin hopped onto the gunwale and dove overboard.

Treece watched, grinning, until he saw Coffin surface and start to swim toward shore. Then he swung the boat seaward.

As the boat rose and fell in the gentle swells, something slid off the steering console and clattered to the deck: the escutcheon plate. Gail picked it up and handed it to Treece.

"Lordy, I almost forgot about that," he said, adding, with a smile at Sanders, "what with all the excitement caused by the daredevil shark hunter."

"Adam said it was a plate that went around a lock."

"Aye, but not just any lock. I've heard of these, but I've never seen one. I don't know that any others still exist. It was called a three-lock box. See the three keyholes; it took three keys to open the lock."

Sanders said, "What was the point of that?"

"To keep one or two people from making off with the goodies inside. Three partners, three keys. Say someone was sending something from the New World back to Spain. The King had a master set, all three keys. The man in wherever it was—Havana—probably had two, the captain of the ship one. They locked the box in Havana, and the captain took it aboard ship. He couldn't open it with only one key. When he got to Spain, he presented the box to the King."

"Wouldn't be hard to pry open."

"No, but they didn't usually. The Spaniards took locks as . . . well, not holy, but special. The British and Dutch sent documents and what-all back and forth in regular boxes; if a ship was pirated, that was that. No lock would do any good. The Spaniards locked everything, almost symbolically. But a three-lock box!" Treece ran his fingers over the escutcheon plate. "Aye, that is interesting."

"Why?"

"It means there was something very damned important in that box. More'n likely, something very damned important to the King of Spain."

IX

By the time they tied up to Treece's dock, the sun was resting on the western horizon, a swollen ball of orange.

Treece sniffed the evening air and said, "Going to get messy tomorrow."

Sanders' impulse was to ask Treece how he knew the weather would change, but by now he could anticipate the answer, something like "Got a feeling" or "You can smell a breeze coming." So he said instead, "How bad?"

"Maybe twenty knots, out of the south. It'll bounce us around a fair amount."

"Can we work?"

"Got no choice. Cloche'll be working, you can bet on that. It'll be all right; we'll weight-up heavy."

Sanders began to peel off his wet-suit pants, but Treece stopped him.

"We're not done yet."

"We're not?"

"Got to put away the ampules. Can't leave 'em lying around on the boat."

"I know, but I figured . . ." He stopped when he saw Treece pointing overboard at the dark water. "Oh."

"I want you to know where they are, in case something happens to me."

"What's going to happen to you?"

"Who knows? Maybe a terminal case of the ague, or a sudden onset of heebie-jeebies. Maybe nothing. It's just insurance. There's a cave underwater at the base of the cliff. Tide washes it, but if we put 'em way back and bury 'em, they'll stay." He turned to Gail. "You don't need to come."

"I can," she said, "if you want me to."

"No. You'll be more use up here, passing bags to us."

They rigged two scuba tanks and brought the bags of ampules up from below. Treece half-filled the canvas bags, then handed Sanders a flashlight. "Overweight yourself," he said. "That bag'll want to come to the surface. Adam squeezed all the air he could out of the plastic bags, but you can't get every last bit. If you're way heavy, you can let your weights drag you and the bag to the bottom. When you get down, follow my light."

"Okay."

Treece pointed to a rectangular wooden box on the dock and said to Gail, "Fetch me a fish out of that box."

"A fish?"

"Aye. It's full of salted fish. I keep 'em there for Percy. He lives in the cave."

Gail climbed onto the dock and opened the lid of the wooden box. The smell of fish made her step backward and hold her breath.

"Pick a big one," Treece called. "Want to keep him occupied so he doesn't take a shine to us."

"What's Percy?" Sanders asked.

"A frightful big moray eel, a green. He's lived in that cave long as I can remember. We get along all right, but he's a hungry bastard, and I like to keep on his good side by giving him dinner now and again."

Gail reached into the fish box and grabbed the largest tail she saw. She swallowed, to keep from gagging. "Don't you keep ice?"

"No need. Salt keeps 'em fine." Treece took the fish from her. "That ought to keep him busy for a while." He said to Sanders, "Let me go in first. I want to see him, make sure he knows what's going on. Let a bastard like that blind-side you, it'll be a nasty evening. And don't go sticking your hands in any holes. For all I know, he's got relatives in there sharing the rent with him." He lowered his mask over his face, rolled off the gunwale, resurfaced, and reached for bag, fish, and light.

Sanders followed immediately and found, as Treece had said, that the extra weight and the air trapped in the plastic bags roughly counterbalanced each other, so he sank without effort.

The cove was not deep—fifteen or, at most, twenty feet, Sanders estimated as he watched the beam from his light move between the sandy bottom and the boat above. The canvas bag was cumbersome: it tugged at his left arm, so Sanders pressed it against his stomach and followed Treece's receding light.

Treece waited at the entrance to the cave—a dark hole, taller than a man, in the craggy face of the cliff. When Sanders joined him, Treece shined his light into the cave and swung it from side to side. At first, the cave seemed to be empty—pocked gray limestone walls extending thirty feet into the darkness. Then Treece fixed his light on a back corner of the cave and pointed with his finger, and Sanders saw something move.

Slowly, Treece swam into the cave, holding the fish in front of him. Sanders trailed a few feet behind.

At the base of one wall there was a heap of rocks, the result of a partial collapse of the wall ages ago. Treece held the fish up to the wall.

The snout of the moray emerged from a crevice between the rocks and the wall. Sanders had seen morays in aquariums, but never anything to rival the size of the green body that now slithered out of the crevice. It was more than a foot thick, top to bottom, and at least six inches wide.

The moray writhed and twisted until it had extricated as much of itself—about four feet—as it intended to. Then it hung suspended from the rocks, glancing, with its cold pig eyes, at Sanders, at Treece, at the fish. The mouth opened and closed rhythmically, exposing the long needle teeth joined by viscid, mucous strands that glittered in the light.

The head tilted slightly and—so quickly that, afterward, Sanders would not recall having seen it move—seized the fish.

Treece did not let go; he held the fish just forward of the tail. The moray pulled, then stopped, then suddenly began to spin its body, like a rug unrolling, until a chunk of fish belly tore away. The eel backed off, swallowing, its teeth forcing the flesh back into its throat, green skin rippling with the effort. Then it struck again, this time grabbing the fish's backbone, and yanked the fish from Treece's grasp. It tried to retreat into its hole, but the fish was too big to fit sideways through the crevice, so the moray contented itself with jamming its prey into the narrow opening and dismembering it from below.

Treece motioned for Sanders to follow him, and, reluctant as he was to turn his back, in darkness, on the moray, Sanders obeyed.

The roof of the cave was about eight feet high, and Sanders saw the beam from Treece's light shine on it, then saw Treece's canvas bag floating upward to it. The bag nudged the roof and rested against it. Sanders reached up and placed his own bag next to Treece's, then joined Treece on the bottom.

They dug a wide, deep hole in the sand and dumped the bags of ampules into it. They leveled off the hole with sand, to keep the bags from floating free, then returned to the boat.

They made three more trips, each time digging a new hole. When they left the cave at the end of the last trip, the moray had devoured all but the last few inches of the fish: the tail still protruded from the crevice, quivering as it was bitten from beneath.

"How big is that thing?" Sanders asked when they were aboard the boat.

"Percy? Never seen the whole of him, but I bet he's all of ten feet. Soon as it gets full dark, he'll come out and prowl around. Some night we can go down and see him when he comes out."

"No, thanks. He looks mean enough in his hole. I don't want to meet him in the open."

"What? I thought you shark killers didn't know the meaning of fear."

"Look, dammit . . ." Sanders was annoyed at Treece's needling, wanted him to stop, but was not eager to provoke a confrontation, nor to beg.

"Don't get all fired up," Treece said. He snapped his fingers at the dog, and she jumped from the boat onto the dock. "Lead the way, Charlotte. See if there's any brigands lurking." The dog trotted happily toward the path, sniffing at the underbrush.

Treece pulled the two empty air tanks from the rack and set them on the dock. "Best fill these tonight."

When they reached the house, they saw a paper-wrapped package outside the kitchen door. Treece picked it up, smelled it, and said, "Supper."

"Fish?" Gail asked, queasy from the recollection of the fish box on the dock.

"No. Meat." Treece opened the door and held it for them.

Gail said, "Don't you ever lock your door?"

"No. Like I told you, only the Spanish have faith in locks."

Inside, Treece said to Sanders, "Fix me a bit of rum while I throw this beast on the fire."

"Sure." Sanders said to Gail, "You want anything?"

"Not yet. I'd like to take a shower. I feel like a week-old bass."

"Know how to work the heater?" Treece said.

"Heater?"

"There's a gas heater next to the stall. Turn the valve half a turn clockwise and wait about two minutes. That'll start warming it, and by the time you're finished showering, it'll be nice and hot."

"Thanks." Gail left the kitchen.

Sanders handed Treece a glass of rum and sipped at his scotch. "Anything I can do?"

"No. Rest your bones."

Sanders sat at the table and watched Treece light the stove, pour oil into a frying pan, drop in the meat, and dust it with herbs.

When he was satisfied that the meat was cooking properly, Treece turned away from the stove and looked at Sanders. "What's pecking at your shell?"

"What?" Sanders didn't understand.

"With the shark business. What are you looking for?"

Sanders thought: Oh Christ, here we go again. "Nothing. It was stupid. I know that." He hoped his admission would end the conversation.

"I think there's more," Treece said. "I think, inside you, you think you did something ballsy."

Sanders blushed, for Treece was right. Beneath the knowledge that he had acted stupidly, impetuously, dangerously, there was a little-boy's pride at having stabbed a shark. Though he would not say so, he had even fantasized about how he would shape the story for telling to friends. He said nothing.

"It's natural enough," Treece said. "A lot of people want to prove something to themselves, and when they do something they think's impressive, then they're impressed themselves. The mistake is, what you *do* isn't the same as what you *are*. You like to do things just to see if you can. Right?"

Though there was no reproach in Treece's voice, Sanders was embarrassed. "Sometimes. I guess . . ."

"What I'm getting at . . ." Treece paused. "The feeling's a lot richer when you do something right, when you know something has to be done and you know what you're doing, and *then* you do something hairy. Life's full of chances to hurt yourself or someone else." Treece took a drink. "In the next few days, you'll have more chances to hurt yourself than most men get in a lifetime. It's learning things and doing things right that make it worthwhile, make a man easy with himself. When I was young, nobody could tell me anything. I knew it all. It took a lot of mistakes to teach me that I didn't know goose shit from tapioca. How old are you?"

"Thirty-seven."

"That's not young, but it's not next door to the grave. You could start now, and spend another forty years learning about the sea without running out of new things to know. That's the only hitch in learning: it's humbling. The more you learn, the more you realize how little you know." Treece drained his glass and stood to refill it. "Anyway, all that's a long way around saying that it's crazy to do things just to prove you can do 'em. The more you learn, the more you'll find yourself doing things you never thought you could do in a million years."

Sanders nodded. He didn't know whether Treece's attitude toward him had changed, or his interpretation of Treece's attitude had changed. He felt curiously privileged, and he said, "Thank you."

Treece seemed flustered by the remark. He snapped his fingers and said, "The tanks. I almost forgot. Better get that monster fired up now, or she'll be chugging away all night."

Sanders followed him out the door and stood with him while he started the compressor and attached the two scuba tanks.

When they returned to the kitchen, Gail was making herself a drink. Her feet were bare and she wore a cotton bathrobe. Sanders kissed her neck; it smelled of soap.

"You taste good," he said.

"I feel good, all but my sinuses."

"Headache?" Treece asked.

"Not a real headache. Up here." She touched the bones above her eyes. "They feel stuffed up. It hurts to touch them."

"Aye, they're abused. Adam'll dive tomorrow. You can tan yourself." Treece turned the meat in the frying pan, reached into a bin beneath the sink, and took out an assortment of vegetables: beans, cucumbers, squash, onions, and tomatoes. He sliced them over a mixing bowl, added a dose of dressing, and stirred the brew with a fork.

The meat was dark red, almost purple, and it tasted strong.

"Do you hang your beef here?" Gail asked, dipping a piece of meat into the salad dressing, to mellow the flavor.

"I don't know. Why?"

"I just wondered."

"Like it?"

"It's . . . interesting."

"It's not beef, y'know."

"Oh?" she said uneasily. "What is it?"

"Goat." Treece cut a chunk of meat, put it in his mouth, and chewed happily.

"Oh." Gail's stomach churned, and she looked at Sanders. He had been about to take a bite of meat, but now his fork was stopped a few inches from his mouth.

He saw her looking at him, and he held his breath, put the meat in his mouth, and swallowed it whole.

After supper, Treece put his plate in the sink and said, "I'm going for a stroll; probably see Kevin for a while. No need for you to wait up."

"Anything we can do?" Gail asked.

"No. Enjoy yourselves." He wiped his hands on his pants and took a bottle of rum from the cabinet. "Kevin drinks palm wine, home brew. Rot your insides faster'n naval jelly." He clucked at the dog, who was sleeping under the table, and said, "Let's go." The dog struggled to her feet, stretched, yawned, and followed Treece out the kitchen door.

When the gate had closed, and the sound of Treece's footsteps had faded away, Sanders said, "Nice of him."

"What?"

"To leave us alone." He reached across the table and took her hand.

She neither withdrew her hand nor responded to his touch. "Treece was married," she said, and then she told him the story Coffin had told her.

As he listened, Sanders remembered his conversation with Treece, and he realized that what had seemed like friendly advice had been genuine, heartfelt concern, that Treece had been trying to guide him away from a course that he, Treece, had taken and that had deprived him, forever, of the promise of joy. Realizing this, Sanders felt a cold fear unalloyed by the thrill of adventure.

"I love you," he said.

She nodded. There were tears in her eyes.

"Let's go to bed." He rose and put the dishes in the sink, then returned and led her to the bedroom.

For the first time, she was unmoved by his love-making, and after a few moments he stopped trying and said, "What's the matter?"

"I'm sorry . . . I can't . . ." She rolled away from him and faced the wall.

He lay awake for a long time, listening to the chug of the compressor outside. Gradually, the sound of her breathing beside him grew more even, and soon she was breathing in the rhythm of deep sleep.

Sanders' sexual longing was not pure desire; he felt a need to impress his love upon her, as if to comfort her. But she did not want him—at least did not want what he wanted to give her—and Sanders suddenly found himself annoyed at Treece. Treece had not told them about his wife, didn't even know they knew, but somehow he, his past, his grief, had come between them. Sanders knew his annoyance was irrational, but he could not control it.

Finally, he slept. He could not awake at the new sounds that intruded on the still night, the sound of an automobile engine, in different cadence from the compressor motor; the sound of tires crunching on gravel.

It was the wind that woke him in the morning, whistling through the screen and rattling the shutters, blowing straight off the sea and gathering force as it swept over the cliff.

Treece sat in the kitchen, leafing through old papers.

Sanders did not ask if he had found anything new; by now he knew that Treece would speak when he had something to say. So all he said, with a flip of his hand toward the window, was "You were right."

"Aye. She's blowing pretty good. But it's worse up here than below. We'll be all right."

Sanders looked at his watch; it was 6:30. "What time do you want to go?"

"Half an hour, forty minutes. If your girl wants to eat, you better rouse her."

"Okay." Sanders couldn't contain his curiosity. "Anything new?"

"Bits and pieces; nothing that amounts to much. Diaries —Christ, to hear some of those sailors' myths, you'd think bloody Fort Knox was on every ship that sailed."

The ride along the south shore was rough. *Corsair* slammed into quartering seas, lurching and shuddering and leaving a yawing wake; spray flew over the port bow and splashed against the windows. The dog, who had made a futile attempt to ride on the bow, lay in a dry corner of the stern and complained every time her body thudded against the heaving deck.

David and Gail stood in the cockpit beside Treece, bracing themselves against the bulkheads.

"We can dive in this?" Sanders said.

"Sure. It's all of twenty knots, but we'll anchor in the lee of the reef and go along the bottom."

"What if the anchors don't hold?"

"Then Orange Grove'll be the owner of a brand-new pile of wreckage."

When they were abeam of Orange Grove, Treece turned the boat toward shore. Waves crashed on the reef and burst in plumes of foam.

Sanders had expected that, as always, Treece would pick his way carefully through the reefs. Instead, he lingered seaward of the reefs for a few moments, examining the currents and the patterns of the waves, then pushed the throttle forward and aimed for a spot in the first reef.

"Hold tight," Treece said. "She's gonna buck."

The boat lunged toward the line of rocks. Caught in the surge of a wave, the stern swung around to the right; Treece spun the wheel hard right, and the boat straightened. He throttled back for a second or two, then gunned the engine and headed for the second reef.

By the time they had cleared all the reefs and were cruising in the relatively calm lee, Sanders felt sweat running down his temples into the neck of his wet suit.

"Roller coaster," Treece said. He saw one of Gail's hands, still clenched around a handle on the console, and he patted it. "It's done."

She relaxed her grip and smiled wanly. "Wow!"

"I should've warned you. That's the only way to clear the bastards in a sea like this. If you time it right, there's enough water to get over the rocks. But if you try to gentle your way through, the waves'll bang you into them for sure."

They did not have to idle in the chop, waiting for Coffin. As soon as he saw the boat cross the reefs, he hurdled the low line of breakers and began to swim.

"Sorry we're late," Treece said as he hauled Coffin aboard. "Did a bit of bouncing out there."

"I 'magine. Anchor in the lee?"

"Aye. You willing to get wet today? Girl's head's messed."

"Like to."

Treece turned the boat toward the reefs. Coffin went forward and examined the anchor lines. "Port and starboard?" he called.

"Aye, with a Christ lot of scope. I'll give a yell." Treece gunned the boat through the first two lines of reef, then slowed as he neared the third line. The boat pitched and rolled wildly, with no rhythm, but Coffin—using his thick brown toes as stabilizers, bending and unbending his knees to absorb the shock of the boat's motion—kept his footing on the bow.

Watching Coffin keep his balance, Sanders smiled and shook his head.

"What?" Gail said.

"I was just remembering. When Treece first said Coffin was going to dive, I asked him if Coffin was any good. Look at him up there. If that was me, I'd have been overboard a dozen times already."

Gail took his hand.

"Starboard!" yelled Treece.

Coffin threw an anchor at the reef; the coil of rope at his feet whipped overboard.

Treece shifted into neutral and let the boat slide backward until the rope sprang taut.

Coffin put a hand on the quivering rope and said, "She's bitin' good."

Treece put the boat in forward gear and ran up the anchor line. He called "Port!" and Coffin threw the other anchor.

When both anchor lines were taut, Treece turned the key, and the engine died, leaving the sounds of the waves banging on the rocks, the wind hissing over the water, and the slapping of the hull on the surface.

Treece said to Coffin, "You'll want a Desco."

"Aye. Don't want a bottle bangin' around, not in this surge."

Treece rigged three air hoses to the compressor, checked the fuel level and oil pressure, and started it.

As they dressed, Treece said to Gail, "Not that you'll need it, but you might's well learn." He took the shotgun from the steering console, pumped it until all five rounds had ejected into his hand, and passed it to Gail. "It'll be all ready to go. All you do is pull back on the forward grip and press the trigger."

Gail held the gun gingerly, as if it were a snake. Unconsciously, the corners of her mouth turned down, and she frowned. She worked the action and pulled the trigger; there was a metallic click. "What do I aim at?"

"You don't aim. You hold it at your hip. If you put it to your shoulder, it's like to tear your arm off. Fire it in the general direction of what you want to hit, and if it's close enough to you, it'll come to pieces." Treece took the gun and replaced the five shells in the chamber.

"I couldn't," said Gail.

"We'll see. One of Cloche's maniacs comes at you waving a butcher knife, you'll find you can do the damnedest things." Treece saw the distress in her face. "Like I said, you won't have to use it. Likely your biggest concern'll be keeping your breakfast down."

Treece went below and returned with six old, unmatched wet-suit gloves, which he tossed on the transom. "Find some that fit you," he said to the others. "Gonna be grasping for rocks just to stay in one place. And make sure you got enough weight; want to head for the bottom like a stone to get out of this topside trash."

They went over the side. Sanders started to rise to the surface to clear his mask, but quickly changed his mind: the waves wrenched his body from side to side, sweeping him to within inches of the bouncing hull. He exhaled and dropped swiftly to the bottom. He could not stand on the sand; the current was less severe than on the surface, but still strong enough to cast him forward and back, like hay in a windstorm. He fell to his knees and crawled toward the reef. Above him, Treece descended fast, dragging two canvas bags and the air-lift tube.

The surge near the reef was worse: waves washing overhead caused bottom eddies that pushed the divers onto the rocks. Sanders tried to stop before the reef, but couldn't. His hip struck a rock, and he tumbled toward sharp outcroppings of coral. He swung an arm blindly, hit something, and grabbed it: a coral ledge. Without the rubber glove, his hand would have been torn. His body hung horizontally in the current; he saw Treece and Coffin, lying face down in the sand, apparently free from the surge, already digging with the air lift.

Sanders dragged himself forward, hand over hand, until he reached the bottom of the reef. He flattened himself beside Coffin. Though his legs still tended to swing toward the reef, he found that by jamming his knees into the sand he could remain fairly steady. Coffin passed him a bag, then the first few handfuls of ampules.

In an hour, they filled all three bags six times. Sanders made six trips to the surface, there to struggle to hold onto the heaving diving platform and to avoid being swept under the boat while Gail emptied the bags. He was cold and tired, and his sinuses ached. Each descent was more difficult, took longer, for his ears resisted clearing and the sinus cavities above his eyes squeaked in protest.

With hand signals, Sanders asked Coffin to change places with him, to take the next few trips; Coffin agreed. Sanders lay prone at the lip of the hole Treece was digging, and, as the air lift exposed the ampules, snared them before they could be carried away.

Another hour passed—seven trips this time—and Coffin and Sanders changed places again. Rising with the bags, Sanders looked at his watch: almost eleven o'clock.

He clung to the platform and waited for the bags. When Gail handed them to him, he lifted the bottom of his mask and said, "How many?"

"I can't count them all. Six, eight thousand, maybe ten. I stopped counting at five thousand; you're bringing them up too fast."

Sanders made five more trips with the bags, and by now he felt a physical misery more profound than anything he had ever experienced. No specific pain or discomfort was worse than any other: everything felt terrible, even his toes, which were wracked with periodic cramps that forced him to kick in an awkward, inefficient fashion. Hanging on the surface, he looked down and wondered how long it would take him to get to the bottom this time; his last descent had taken so long that by the time he arrived at the reef, enough ampules had been excavated to refill the bags immediately.

He forced himself down through the layers of pain and crawled to the reef. He was settling beside the heap of ampules when a surge hit him. He flailed with his legs, reaching for the bottom, but his legs wouldn't touch; he was thrust at the wall of coral. In the last seconds before he hit the reef, he raised his gloved hands in front of his face and brought up his knees, hoping to take the impact with his flippers or his arms.

His right knee hit first, and whatever it hit gave way and broke. Then he was spun around and his buttocks hit the rocks, jerking his head backward. The muscles in his neck resisted, but his head hit—not hard, for something cushioned it: a sea fan. He scrambled for a handhold and found a rock, which pulled free and tumbled down the face of the reef, knocking other rocks loose as it fell.

The surge passed, and Sanders lay against the reef, breathing hard, assessing the damage done to his aching body. There were new pains, but none seemed more wretched than those he had had before.

He inched down the reef face, making sure of each handhold before he moved to the next. Glancing to his left, he saw something shine within the bowels of the reef, a twinkle that dulled as soon as the shaft of sunlight moved away. It was in a hole at least two feet deep. Another ray of light coursed into the hole; again a twinkle.

Sanders leaned back against the reef, one leg wrapped around a boulder, one hand clutching a piece of coral. He waved, to attract Treece's attention, but Treece was intent on the ditch full of ampules. He waited, knowing that Coffin would look up when he noticed that the ampules he was passing back to Sanders weren't being collected, and a moment later he saw Coffin's eyes. He pointed at Treece and at the hole in the reef.

Coffin tapped Treece; Treece looked up, set the air lift against the reef, and swam to Sanders.

A cloud passed before the sun, and the shadow crept along the bottom, darkening the water and turning the sand gray. Treece looked at Sanders, raised his eyebrows, and mouthed the word "what."

Sanders raised his palm to Treece, then pointed to the surface, saying: Wait till the light returns. The shadow moved over the reef and away; arrows of light darted into the hole.

Treece looked, waited, looked again. He nodded his head, made the "okay" sign to Sanders, and plunged his arm into the hole.

Sanders watched Treece's face as his fingers probed the bottom of the hole; Treece's eyes narrowed in concentration, brow furrowed.

Suddenly Treece's eyes snapped wide, his mouth opened, and he yelled in pain and shock. He tried to pull his arm out of the hole, but something was holding it. His shoulder was banged onto the coral, and Sanders saw it twitch. Then, gritting his teeth and bracing his other arm against a rock, he hauled back: The arm came free, dragging with it the writhing, curling body of a moray eel, jaws clamped tight on the soft, fleshy juncture of his right thumb and forefinger.

Treece yelled again, incoherently, and reached with his left hand to grab the moray behind the head. But the eel's body, no longer anchored in the reef, waved in frantic spasms and pulled itself out of reach. The eel trembled and, in a blur of green, coiled itself into a knot; using the body as its own anchor, the head was pulling Treece's hand through the knot.

Treece could not get at the head, so he pounded the body aimlessly with his left hand. But the eel did not respond: bit by bit, the back-slanted teeth were drawing his hand into the mouth.

Backed against the reef, reflexively retreating, Sanders recalled the size of the moray they had seen the night before. The head was twice, three times, the size of the one attached to Treece. Then Sanders saw the flesh tear away —a crescent rip in the rubber glove, tattered green-tinged skin waving in strips, billowing blood.

The eel unknotted itself, swallowed, and lashed at Treece's midsection. Treece dodged, snapped his left hand onto the eel's body, four or five inches behind the head. The head turned, jaws gnashing the water, searching for something to bite. Treece put his injured hand in front of his left hand and squeezed, the pressure pumping blood from the wound. Ignoring the flailing body, he forced the eel's head onto a rock and crushed it. The body jerked twice and was still. Treece released his grip, and the eel fell slowly to the sand.

Treece pointed at Sanders, then at the hole in the reef, telling him to reach in and find the object. Without thinking, scared, Sanders shook his head: No. Treece jammed his left index finger into Sanders' chest and again pointing to the hole: Do it!

Sanders reached into the hole. He closed his eyes, listening to his rapid pulse, his labored breathing, anticipating— imagining—a sudden stab of pain. His fingers walked down the coral and felt the softness of sand. Nothing. In its thrashing, the eel could have knocked the object deeper into the hole, or buried it in the sand. His shoulder was tight against the coral; he could go no farther. His fingers moved left and right, scraping over the bottom, sensing pebbles and bits of coral; then, at the limit of his reach, something hard. He strained against the coral, trying for another half inch, and managed to grasp the object between the tips of his fingers. He pulled it closer, dropped it, recovered it in a solid grip.

He withdrew his arm and opened his eyes. He was alone. The air lift rolled against the reef, bubbling; the pile of ampules lay untouched in the sand. Looking up, he saw Treece and Coffin at the surface. Treece kicked and disappeared onto the boat.

Sanders opened his fist and looked at the object in his palm. It was a gold figure of a crucified Christ, five inches high. The nails in the hands and feet were red gem stones, the eyes blue. Sanders tipped the figure on its side and saw, engraved on the base of the cross, the letters "E.F."

Treece leaned against the gunwale, while Coffin wrapped gauze around his wounded hand.

Sanders stood on the platform and removed his mask. "Bad?"

"No. Thank the gentle Jesus for that glove, though. Main problem with those bastards is infection."

"Did you put anything on it?"

"Aye. Sulfa. Forget that: What'd you find?"

Sanders climbed over the transom and handed Treece the crucifix.

Treece examined it, noticed the initials, then held it a

few inches from his face. "My God, that's a piece of work."

Gail leaned over, careful not to impede Coffin, and stared at the figure. "It's beautiful."

"It's more than just beautiful. See the rubies in the hands and feet? The Spaniards almost never used rubies. They liked emeralds; green was the color representing the Inquisition. They argued about the rubies for a hundred years or more. They began to use 'em late, in the beginning of the eighteenth century, but only for the King. Another special thing is, there are no fixings."

"Fixings?"

"Holding it together. It wasn't cast in one piece; they didn't have the equipment. And there aren't any pins or nails or pegs. It's like one of those Chinese puzzles: a lot of pieces that fit together only if you assemble 'em in the right order. Look close, you can see little hairlines where the pieces join. Our friend E.F. was either very rich or very dear to someone very rich."

Coffin split the end of the strip of gauze and tied a knot. Treece flexed his hand, grimaced. "Cumbersome bugger."

"Shouldn't you see a doctor?" Gail asked.

"Only if I see the red horrors creeping up my arm." Treece pushed off the gunwale and stood up. He raised his bandaged hand and said to Sanders, "Guess you're not the only stupid sonofabitch on this vessel. If that'd been Percy, he'd be munching on my neck by now."

Sanders said, "I thought of that."

"Adam," Treece said, "you and David go get the last of the glass and the gun. We'll take a holiday till nighttime."

"You're gonna dive again?" Coffin said. "With that hand?"

Treece nodded. "I'll go home and rig up something to keep it dry. It'll do to hold the gun; that's all it was doing down there anyway."

They brought up three more bags of ampules, raised the anchor, and crossed the reefs to take Coffin to the beach.

"I'll stay if you want," Coffin said to Treece. "You can't put the glass in the cave with her head messed and your hand messed."

"No. Get your rest. I'll call Kevin and have him help."

"Kevin! You'd trust him?"

"Aye. He'll take the pennies off the eyes of the dead, but he's loyal to me."

"He is, is he?"

"Don't you start, too. It's enough I've got to worry about old David challenging me every time I draw bloody breath." Treece saw that Sanders had overheard him, and he smiled. "Sorry. But you are a contentious bugger. Getting better every day, though, I'll give you that."

Treece stopped the boat about fifty yards off the beach. "That's it, Adam. Don't want to beach her in the surf."

"No problem." Coffin looked at the waves. "Still blowin' pretty good."

"Aye, but she's swinging around to the west. Ought to be a right nice evening to take a plunge."

"What time?"

"Say seven. This time we'll be punctual."

"Okay." Coffin peeled off the wet suit and dove into the water.

On the way back to St. David's, David and Gail counted ampules. She had already bagged a hundred lots of fifty, but two or three times that amount remained, piled on the bunks, wrapped in towels, filling the rusty sink. To keep the ampules from smashing, Treece drove slowly, letting the boat wallow in the rolling seas.

They were still counting and bagging ampules an hour and a half later when Treece nosed *Corsair* up to the dock.

When they had tied off the last bag, Sanders said, "That's it: twenty-three thousand two hundred and seventy."

"So about twenty-eight thousand, all told." Treece looked at the heaps of plastic bags on the deck. "We're going to make the Baggie company rich."

Gail calculated figures in her head. "At this rate, even if we up it to fifty thousand a day, we've got nine or ten days to go."

"Aye, and that time we do not have."

After lunch, Treece left the house and walked down the hill. Gail stood at the sink, washing the dishes. Sanders came up behind her, wrapped his arms around her waist, and nuzzled her neck. "It'll take him at least twenty minutes, down and back," he said. "We could accomplish a lot in twenty minutes."

She leaned back against him. "You think?"

"Come on." He took her arm and led her to the bedroom.

They made love, with quiet, gentle passion. When they were finished, Gail saw that David's eyes were moist. "What's the matter?" she said.

"Nothing."

"Then why are you crying?"

"I'm not crying."

"All right, you're not crying. Why are your eyes wet?"

Sanders started to deny that his eyes were wet, but, instead, he rolled onto his back and said, "I was thinking how lucky I am . . . what it would be like if you died and I knew I'd never ever be able to hold you again. I wonder how he can live with that."

Gail touched his lips. "I guess you live with memories."

They heard the kitchen door open. Sanders got out of bed and pulled on his bathing suit.

Kevin stood in the kitchen with Treece. His huge brown belly spilled over his tight tank suit, concealing it almost entirely. The only other clothing he wore was a pair of dusty old wing-tipped brown shoes without laces. The look on his face radiated intense dislike for everything.

Treece patted Kevin's fleshy shoulder and said to Sanders, "He can't wait to plunge all this lard into the briny. A regular sea horse. When was your last dip, Kevin? Fifty-five, was it?"

Kevin grunted sullenly.

They walked down the path to the dock. When he saw the ampules in the boat, Kevin's eyes widened. "Shit," he said. "That the lot?"

"No. That's what we got so far. There's a whole pisspot left."

"How many?"

"Who knows?" Treece said, smiling. "This here's all concerns you." He started the compressor.

Sanders put on his wet suit. It was clammy and cold. "What about your friend down there . . . Percy?"

"He'll be in his hole asleep, probably. But you might drop him a fish anyway."

Sanders looked at Treece's bandaged hand. "I don't have to feed it to him, do I?"

"No, just lay it over his hole, or nearby. He'll smell it out."

It took Sanders and Kevin two hours to place the ampules in the cave. Sanders was cold and tired, but Kevin, who wore nothing but bathing suit and weight belt—no wet suit, no flippers—seemed unaffected by the water or the work.

Gripping the diving platform and resting on the surface for a moment before hauling himself aboard the boat, Sanders saw Kevin take the last bag of ampules from Treece and, without a word, submerge.

"I thought he didn't like the water. He's a machine."

"Hates it," Treece said, "but you give him a task to do and that's what he is, a machine. If I have heavy salvage work, he's the one I take; got about ten horsepower inside him, and so much lard that he never gets cold. He's something of a paradox: greedy as hell, but so surly he can't work with the people who've got the money to pay him."

"You'll pay him for this?"

"Aye. He'll want a hundred dollars, I'll offer twenty, and we'll settle for fifty."

"Not bad wages."

"No, but he's good. I could get all manner of idiots for five an hour, but they'd take all bloody day at it, then go drink up the proceeds and blab all over the island about what they've been doing. Besides, Kevin doesn't get much work. I like to do what I can."

Sanders climbed into the boat and unzipped his wet suit. His chest and arms were goose flesh.

"Go on up and have a shower," Treece said. "Kevin and I'll finish up."

Sanders shivered. "Okay."

Treece took Sanders' wet-suit jacket and hung it from a corner of the deckhouse roof. "Sun'll bake it warm before tonight."

The walk up the hill warmed Sanders some, but not enough; he was still shivering when he reached the house. He poured himself a scotch and took it with him to the shower.

When he finished showering, he went to the bedroom. On the way, he caught a glimpse of Treece in the kitchen. He opened the bedroom door quietly—Gail was asleep— pulled on a pair of trousers, and put his wallet in a hip pocket.

Treece sat at the kitchen table, a glass of rum to his right, a pile of papers to his left, and the gold crucifix in front of him.

Sanders poured himself another drink. "Was it what you said? Fifty?"

"Aye."

Sanders took two tens and a five from his wallet and put them on the table. "Our share."

Treece contemplated the bills and said, "All right." He tapped the crucifix with his finger. "You've got that and a hell of a lot more, from your share of this."

"What's it worth?" Sanders had no idea of the value of

Spanish gold. In metal value alone, there were probably seven or eight ounces of gold—maybe twelve hundred dollars' worth. The gems were tiny.

"Roughly? If we wanted to sell it, if we *could* sell it, if we had an open market for it—roughly a hundred thousand dollars."

"Jesus Christ!" Sanders' hand jumped, and he spilled scotch on the table.

"Don't go spending it, 'cause more'n likely you'll never see it. Before there's a farthing, we'll have to get the lot up, have it appraised, report it to the bloody government, decide if we want to sell any or all of it, negotiate with the bastards—which can take months—and then, maybe . . ."

"Still, a hundred thousand! Where's the value?"

"Premium, mostly, and that's another problem. Premium's hard to set; it's subjective. What's workmanship worth?" Treece cradled the crucifix in his palm. "Damn, but those Dutch Jews were craftsmen!"

"Dutch Jews? I thought this came from South America."

"It did. But most of the fine jewelry—the stuff for royalty—was made by Dutch Jews hired by the Spaniards and shipped over to the New World. The Spaniards and the Indians couldn't do this kind of work. The other thing you pay for is provenance. That's what I've got to keep looking for, the bloody provenance."

"Why?"

"Like I told you before, folks are manufacturing stuff left and right and passing it off as Spanish. You have to be able to prove, really *prove*, where it came from." Treece slapped the pile of papers. "So it's back to the bloody documents."

"E.F. is a name, right? It has to be."

Treece looked at Sanders as if he had uttered a remark of monumental stupidity.

Sanders flushed. "I mean . . . it's not like the 'D.G.' on the coin, or the other stuff, 'King of Spain and the Indies.' E.F. is a person."

"Aye, it's a name. And in here I have the names of all the Spanish nobility in the late seventeenth and early eighteenth centuries. It's not much help, but it's a start."

"Can I help?"

"No. It takes a practiced eye to know what to look for." Treece handed the crucifix to Sanders. "Here's a task for you: Figure out how Mr. Jesus comes apart."

Sanders held the crucifix close to his face. There was a faint hairline between the Christ's neck and shoulders, and Sanders tried to turn the head. It didn't budge. "I don't know where to begin." He took a sip of scotch, then failed to disguise a yawn.

"Best thing you could do," Treece said, "is go fall down for a couple of hours. Three-thirty now; we should leave the dock by six. Earlier, if the breeze hasn't slacked off some."

"You're right." Sanders finished his drink and went into the bedroom.

Gail was curled, like a baby, on her side of the bed, snoring thickly through clogged sinuses.

Sanders stepped out of his trousers and crawled into bed. He considered putting his hand over Gail's nose, to make her change position and, perhaps, stop snoring long enough for him to fall asleep. But suppose he woke her . . .

The next thing he knew, Treece was tapping him on the shoulder and saying, "Time to get wet again."

The wind had shifted to the west and dropped to a pleasant breeze, and as they cruised along the south shore in the low sunlight, they could easily see the lines of reef.

Treece gave Sanders the wheel and said, "Just point her straight." He went below, rooted around in some boxes, and reappeared with a thin rubber kitchen glove and some elastic bands.

"You can't get that fist of yours in that glove," Sanders said.

"No." Treece put the glove on the gunwale, took a knife from a sheath tacked to the bulkhead, and sliced the fingers off the glove. He handed Gail the glove, and she held it for him as he worked his hand into it. He slipped an elastic band around his wrist, sealing the top of the glove, then put on a wet-suit jacket and a rubber diving glove.

"You're diving?" Gail said.

"How does your head feel?"

"Fair to poor."

"I'm diving. I don't think I could suffer being topside with all you experts below, anyway. My imagination'd drive me crazy." Treece flexed his fingers; he could not close his fist. "Little water won't hurt. This'll keep the stink away from the gobblers."

The lights in the Orange Grove Club shone brightly in the twilight. The setting sun made the surf line glow pink-white, but the beach itself was in shadow cast by the high cliffs. The calm sea permitted Treece to bring the boat to within twenty yards of shore. The beach was empty.

"Where is he?" Sanders asked.

"He'll be along." Treece looked at his watch. "We're five minutes early."

They waited, rocking softly. Every couple of minutes, Treece gave the engine a brief burst of power, to keep the boat from being swept ashore. The sky blue was darkening quickly.

At 7:15, Treece said, "It's not like him to be late."

"Want me to go check?" said Sanders.

"Check what? If he's late, he's late."

"Maybe the hotel people are giving him grief . . . about using the elevator or something."

"All right."

Sanders zipped up his wet-suit jacket and put on his flippers.

Gail said, "Be careful."

"Of what? There's nothing on that beach but crabs."

"I don't know, but . . . please."

"I will." Sanders put on his mask and fell into the water.

Five yards from shore, Sanders found that he could touch bottom. He took off his flippers and mask and trudged through the small waves. Standing on the beach, he looked left and right; he could see for at least a mile in both directions, and although the light was dim, he could tell that the beach was deserted. He dropped flippers and mask above the high-water mark and started for the cliffs, dark rock curtains looming into the indigo sky. Behind him, to his right, a sliver of yellow was rising over the horizon: a new moon. He heard the muffled thuds and hisses of the waves on the sand and the whisper of wind through the foliage atop the cliffs.

As he stepped into the shadows, he looked up; he could see the rectangular elevator cage outlined against the sky. He walked toward the base of the elevator pole, intending to summon the cage to the bottom of the cliff. He could not see the pole, so he used the cage above him as a guide. In full stride, he tripped on something and tumbled to his knees.

He couldn't see anything. Still on his knees, he turned and felt with his hand. The smell of ordure filled his nostrils, and for a moment he thought he had fallen over a defecating animal. Then his fingers touched flesh, cooling: an arm. He drew a quick, shocked breath, felt a rush of fear, and probed with his fingers.

He leaned closer and saw Coffin's glazed, lifeless eyes staring at the sky. Drying blood trickled from his mouth.

Sanders put his fingers to the base of Coffin's neck and felt for a pulse: nothing. Then he sprang to his feet and ran.

He stopped at the water's edge, just long enough to pull his flippers on his feet, then dove over a small wave and swam frantically toward the boat.

"He's dead!" Sanders gasped as Treece dragged him aboard. "They must've thrown him off the cliff."

Treece squeezed Sanders' wrist. "You're sure?"

"Positive! No breathing, no pulse, no nothing."

"*Shit!*" Roughly, Treece cast Sanders' hand away.

238

Sanders thought: That's a strange elegy—shit. But what more was there to say? The expletive was eloquent enough, conveying anger and dismay.

He looked at Gail. Her whole body was shivering, and her breaths were short, almost sobs. She stared fixedly at the water. He went to her and put his arms around her. She did not react to his touch, did not recoil from the cold clamminess of his wet suit. He breathed on her hair and whispered, "Okay . . . okay."

She looked up at him and said flatly, "I want to go home."

"I know," he said.

"I want to go home now. It can't be worse than this."

Sanders started to speak, but Treece, gazing at the cliffs, spoke first: "No goin' home now. He's ready to make his move."

Sanders said, "What move?"

"I imagine he thinks his divers are ready; doesn't need us any more. I thought we had a bit of time, but we have got no bloody time at all." He slammed the gear lever all the way forward. The engine growled, the propeller cavitated, then bit into the sea, and the boat lunged toward the reefs.

When they had reached the reef and set the anchor, Treece said to Sanders, "Can she dive?"

"I'm not sure. I'll . . ."

"I can dive," said Gail. "I can't be alone up here. I'll get down all right, if I take my time."

"I hate like hell to leave us empty topside," said Treece. "Charlotte's not too handy with a shotgun. But I don't see we have a choice. He may not try anything else tonight, figure he shook us good enough for one day."

They dressed, and Gail mounted her regulator on an air tank.

"You two take the lights," Treece said. "Keep 'em trained on the nozzle of the gun. Use your free hands to collect the glass. I'll try not to get ahead of you." Treece started the compressor and tossed the air-lift hose overboard. "Christ, that monster makes a din. If it weren't for the bloody gun, we could leave her quiet and use bottles."

They went into the water and switched on the lights. Treece looked at David and Gail, nodded his head, and dove for the bottom.

The dog stood on the bow, watching the lights recede into the darkness, sniffing the warm night air.

Sanders and Treece reached the bottom first. Gail lingered behind, descending as fast as her ears and sinuses would permit. There was something different about the air she was breathing; it seemed to have a faint taste, mildly sweet, but it was having no ill effect, so she continued to the bottom.

They were working away from the reef, perhaps ten yards from the little cave, in a new field of ampules. Sanders' light was steady on the mouth of the air lift, and he picked the ampules out of the hole one by one.

Gail settled across the hole from Treece and lay on her stomach, a canvas bag at her side. She felt no tenseness at all, no worry; she was surprised, in fact, at how relaxed she felt. Even when the air lift uncovered an artillery shell, her mind registered it as a thing, not a concern.

Treece did not bother to remove the artillery shell. He dug around it, and when the air lift exposed another piece of ordnance—a long, thicker brass canister—he simply avoided it, too. Soon, however, he could not avoid the shells; they were everywhere, mixed in with thousands of ampules. Treece signaled for a move to the right, and pushing off the bottom with his left hand, he floated six or eight feet away. Sanders followed directly behind him.

It took Gail several seconds to realize they were gone. She stared at the hole in the sand, thinking vague, dreamy thoughts, enjoying the pretty yellow air hose that snaked through the water after David. Her eyes followed the hose, and when at last she saw the two men, she ambled casually along the sand, letting her light play on the colors in the reef.

She didn't want to shine the light in the new hole Treece was digging; she preferred to watch two yellow fish that cruised around the reef and glowed when the light struck them. But she saw Sanders look at her and point insistently at the air lift, so she swung her body around and drifted to the bottom. She yawned, feeling wonderful—warm and cozy in the black water.

Sanders worked within the beam of his own light, intent on gathering the ampules as fast as he could, face pressed close to the bottom.

It was Treece who first noticed that the radius of light was too small. He raised his head from the hole and saw Gail's light bobbing aimlessly in the water, beam swinging from surface to bottom and side to side.

By the time Sanders thought to look up, Treece had al-

241

ready sprung. He kicked violently toward Gail's light, tearing the Desco mask off his face as he moved. He wrenched the light from Gail's hand and shone it on her face; her eyes were closed, her head hung limply. Treece dropped the light and reached for her head, pulled the regulator out of her mouth, and knocked off her mask. Then he put a hand behind her head and forced her face into the Desco mask. He raised his knee and, carefully, shoved it into her stomach.

Sanders didn't know what was happening; all he saw was the beam of the other light, lying in the sand. He swung his light upward and found motion, fixed on it, and pushed off the bottom. Treece's hands surrounded Gail's head. Weak streams of bubbles—from the mask, from Gail's regulator, and from Treece's mouth—shepherded them to the surface.

Treece reached the diving platform, exhaled the last of his breath, and let his mask fall from Gail's face. He pushed her onto the platform, face down, and, while he hauled himself after her, began to press rhythmically on her back.

Sanders' head broke water. He saw Treece kneeling, heard him saying, "Come on . . . give me a hearty one . . . come on . . . there we go . . . there we go . . . whups!" There was a gagging sound, a splash, then Treece's voice again, "There we go . . . one more time . . . there we go . . . okay . . . there's the girl . . . one more time . . . that's a good one." Treece sat back on his heels. "Sonofa*bitch!* That was frightful close."

Through a fog of semiconsciousness, Gail felt a scratchy

pain in her throat and tasted acid, watery vomit. She was nauseous; a heavy, throbbing ache filled her skull. She groaned feebly and heard Sanders say, "What happened?" Then she felt herself being lifted, and Treece's voice saying, "Know in a minute."

Treece lay her on the deck, on her side. He bent over and opened one of her eyes with his thumb. "Okay?"

The other eye felt heavy, but she forced it open and whispered, "Yes."

Treece picked up her regulator hose and held the mouthpiece under his nose. He pushed the purge valve, and air from the tank squirted up his nostrils. "Lordy." He grimaced. "By rights, you should be having tea with the Angel Gabriel."

"What is it?"

"Carbon monoxide."

"Exhaust?" Sanders said. "From the compressor?"

"Not from the compressor. I told you, it's vented right."

"From what then?"

"Someone knew what he was doing, probably backed a car up to the air intake."

"Tried to kill her?"

"Her or you or me. I don't imagine they cared which."

Sanders looked down at Gail. She had propped herself on one elbow and her head hung limply, as if she expected to vomit.

He turned to Treece and snapped, "That is *it!*"

"That's what?"

"The end! It's finished! We've lost, and that's too damn

bad! You turn this goddamn thing around and get us out of here!"

"We can't," Gail said weakly. "There's no . . ."

"Oh yes, we can! Let him have it all. The gold too. Who gives a shit? It's better than . . ."

Treece said, "Calm down."

"I *won't* calm down! Suppose they *had* killed her. What then? Calm down? Too bad?" Sanders felt his hands shaking, and he clenched his fists. "No thanks. Not again. He's not gonna get another shot at her. We're getting out of here!"

Sanders walked forward to the wheel and searched the instrument panel for the starter button. He had seen Treece start the boat a dozen times but had never paid attention to the mechanics. He pushed one button after another, and nothing happened.

"You have to turn the key," said Treece. His voice was toneless, matter-of-fact.

Sanders reached for the key, but he did not turn it. He looked at Treece standing placidly in the stern.

"There really is no way out, is there?"

"No."

The two men faced each other for a few seconds. Then Treece bent down and touched Gail's shoulder and said, "How you feeling?"

"Better."

"Stay topside; breathe deep. The shotgun's by the wheel. Let me show you something." He helped her to her feet, led her to the compressor, and pointed to a wing nut on the side of the machine. "See that? If you see a boat coming or you hear something—if *any*thing happens you don't like—turn that nut half a turn to the right. It'll shut off the compressor. We'll be on the surface in a fine hurry, I promise you."

"Okay." Gail hesitated. "I meant to ask you . . ."

"What?"

"What will you do with Adam?"

"Leave him where he lays. Nothing we can do for him; he's gone where he's going."

"What about the police?"

"Look, girl . . ." There was a hint of testiness in Treece's voice. "Forget all the law-and-order nonsense. There's no one going to help us. We survive, it's thanks to us; we don't, it's our own fault. Tomorrow morning, somebody'll find Adam and call the police, and they'll come, all efficiency, and cart him away and write in their little pads that Adam went wandering out to the cliffs at night—drunk, they'll say—and fell overboard. We go to the police, they'll come to the same damn conclusion, only —for appearances—they'll make us spend days answering dumb-ass questions from the paper-pushers. Police are a waste of time." Treece motioned Sanders aft to the diving platform.

When the two men had assembled their gear, Sanders said to Gail, "You'll feel better if you lie down."

"I'm okay. You be careful." She smiled.

Treece made the thumbs-up sign, Sanders responded, and they jumped backward into the water.

Gail watched Sanders' light as it descended toward the light that lay on the bottom, her light. That light was

245

picked up, and the two beams moved together across the bottom, stopped and fuzzed as the mist of sand permeated the water.

She shivered and raised her eyes to the dark cliffs. She tried to envision what Coffin's body looked like, crumpled in the sand. She shook her head to rid herself of the thought, walked forward, and took the shotgun from the shelf in front of the wheel. She sat on the transom, cradling the gun in her lap—hating it, afraid of it, but grateful for it.

A noise behind her: splash, bump. She jumped off the transom and spun, cocking the gun and aiming it at the water. A hand broke the surface and reached for her; it held a canvas bag full of ampules. Gail put the gun down and, trembling, reached for the bag.

Sanders lifted the bottom of his mask. "You all right?"

"Yes." She emptied the bag onto the tarpaulin on the deck. "I almost shot you, that's all."

"If they come, I don't think it'll be in a submarine," Sanders said. He took the empty bag from her and dropped below the surface.

Gail knelt on the deck and began to count ampules, groping for them in the dark.

With only two divers working, the collecting went slowly. Each time Sanders surfaced, Treece stopped digging in the hole, for fear of unearthing ampules that would be swept away in the tide. Waiting for Sanders to return, he moved to the reef and probed with the air lift. He dug at random, finding ampules in one spot, artillery shells in another, nothing in another. He came to a small pocket in the reef, where the coral receded about five feet from the reef face and formed a kind of cove. He concentrated on the cove, touching the air lift to the bottom and watching the sand vanish up the tube.

Sanders returned and tapped Treece on the shoulder. Treece nodded, intending to return to the field of ampules, and routinely checked his watch. The wet-suit sleeve covered the dial, so, to read it, Treece had to cradle the air lift under his right arm and use the fingers of his right hand to peel back the left sleeve. It was eleven o'clock. Treece let the sleeve fall back into place and moved his right arm away from his side, to drop the air lift into his hand. He missed it; his bandaged, rubber-covered hand did not respond quickly enough, and the air lift fell to the bottom. It hit the sand and bucked; Treece lunged for it with his left hand, caught it, and wrestled it under control. Then he saw a gleam.

As it bounced on the bottom, the tube had moved to the right side of the little cove and, always hungry for sand, had gouged a hole on its own. The gleam was at the bottom of the hole.

Treece gave Sanders his light and motioned for him to train both lights on the hole. Then, like a surgeon exploring an incision, Treece lowered the air lift to the gleam. His left hand hovered near the sand, to catch the object if it was wrenched free and flew toward the tube; his right held the tube a foot off the bottom, diluting its power to a point where it barely disturbed the grains of sand.

It was a pine cone, about the size of a tennis ball, per-

247

fectly shaped of gold. Each of the countless ridges on the pine cone was topped with a tiny pearl.

Delicately, Treece plucked the pine cone from the sand and held it beneath the lights. Motes of sand passing between the pine cone and the light made the gold shimmer.

A canvas bag hung off Sanders' wrist. Treece reached into the bag, set the pine cone gently on the canvas bottom, and resumed digging.

Another gleam: a half-inch circle of gold. Treece pinched it between his fingers and pulled; it would not come. He stripped more sand away and saw that the circle was connected to another circle, and that one to still another: a chain of gold.

When twenty links where exposed, Treece was able to pull the rest of the chain free with his hand. It was seven or eight feet long. Treece pointed to a clasp at the end of the chain. Sanders looked closely and saw the engraved letters "E.F."

Treece dug for a few more minutes and found nothing. He put the gold chain in the canvas bag and pointed upward.

"Careful with that," Sanders said as he handed the bag to Gail. He passed her one of the lights. He heard Treece surface beside him and said, "How come we're quitting? Maybe there's more."

"Maybe, but it's too late to get it all now, and I don't want to do a half-ass job and leave a bloody great ditch down there for someone else to spot."

"It's incredible!" Gail said, shining the light on the pine cone in her palm.

"Turn off that damn light!" Treece said. The light snapped off. "Someone on the cliffs with glasses could pick that out clear as day."

Treece climbed aboard, turned off the compressor, told Sanders to haul in the air hoses, and started the engine. He looked back at Sanders, who was coiling the hoses neatly on the deck.

"Don't bother with that. Just throw it on board. Soon's you're done, take the wheel."

Treece stepped onto the gunwale and walked forward, impatiently nudging the dog out of the way.

Sanders brought the air lift aboard and hauled on the hose.

"Take the wheel," Treece called.

"Just a sec."

"Now, dammit!"

Sanders looked at Gail and handed her the hose. "Here. You finish it." He took the wheel.

"Put her in gear," Treece said, "and give me a bit of throttle. Want to run her up the anchor line."

Sanders obeyed. Treece hauled the anchor aboard and came aft. As he dropped into the cockpit, Sanders said, "What's the rush?"

Treece did not reply. He relieved Sanders of the wheel and pushed the throttle full ahead.

There was no conversation on the way back to St. David's. Treece stood at the wheel, preoccupied. David and Gail coiled hoses and counted ampules.

Nor did Treece say anything when they reached the house a few minutes before one o'clock. He poured himself a glass of rum, put the pine cone and chain on the kitchen table, and pulled a box of documents out of a closet. He nodded when the Sanderses said good night.

At four o'clock that morning, Treece identified E.F.

X

He refused to accept the first shred of evidence. He sat at the kitchen table for almost two more hours, cross-checking documents and making notes. When finally he had removed all doubt, he rose, poured himself another glass of rum, and went to wake the Sanderses.

Gail came into the kitchen first, and Treece said, "How you feeling?"

"Okay. No one tried to murder me in my bed. I'm grateful for that."

"Feeling rich?"

"What do you mean? Should I?"

Treece smiled mischievously. "Wait till David gets here."

Gail looked at his face, at his red eyes and the pouches beneath them. "Have you had any sleep?"

"No. Been reading."

Then she knew. "You found E.F.!"

In the bedroom Sanders stepped into a pair of bathing trunks. A polo shirt hung over the back of a chair. He reached for it, then stopped and thought: The hell with it; I'll just be taking it off in an hour. He looked at himself in the mirror and, pleased, slapped his flat stomach. He was brown and lean, and he felt good. Even his feet felt good, tough and callous; he couldn't remember when he had last worn shoes. He went into the kitchen.

Gail and Treece were sitting at the table, cradling cups. As he walked toward the stove to pour some coffee, Sanders said, "Morning." They didn't answer him, and passing the table, he saw them exchange a glance. Annoyed, he thought: *Now* what?

He sat at the table and said, "Well?"

"Feeling rich?" Treece said.

"What?"

Gail could not contain herself. "He found E.F.!"

Now Sanders understood, and he smiled. "Who is he?"

"She," Treece said. "You remember, a while back, when you found the medallion, you said, 'Maybe it was a present for somebody.'"

"Sure. And you said, Not a chance."

"Aye, but then other things didn't make any sense. A man might have worn the medallion, but he wouldn't have worn the cameo you found; that was a lady's piece. And certainly the pine cone was. Perhaps it was being carted home to a wife or lady friend; what you said made me think of that. I went through all the papers again, and I came up dry; there's not a bloody E.F. among them. A captain of one of the *naos*, a cargo ship, was a Fernández, but he went down off Florida."

"So who was it?"

Treece ignored the question, sipped his tea. "The pine cone got me thinking, that and the crucifix. It wasn't possible for goodies like that to go unrecorded—the man who made 'em, the man who sent 'em, the man who commissioned 'em, *some*body would have made a note of them. I figured I was nosing around the wrong alley, so I put all the New World papers aside for a while and went back to the history books. That's where I found the first hint."

"What?" Gail said. "The name?"

"Aye, and a shopping list. If I'm right"—Treece looked at Sanders—"and by now I know I'm right, what's down there—flush up against enough live explosives to make angels out of half the human race—is a treasure the likes of which no man has ever seen. It's beyond price. Men have been looking for it for two hundred and sixty years; people have been hung over it; and a King of Spain stayed randy all his life for lack of it."

Sanders said, "Is it *El Grifón?*"

"Aye. It has to be. Listen. In 1714 King Philip the Fifth's wife died. She wasn't half stiff before Philip took a fancy to the duchess of Parma. He'd probably fancied her for quite a while, but now that his wife was gone he could bring the good duchess out of the closet. He asked her to marry him. She agreed, but she wouldn't sleep with him until he had decked her out with jewels—quote—unique in the world. Philip must have had a fearsome lust, because he snapped off a letter to his man in Havana. The chap copied it in his diary, which was included in the appendix of a ratty old book about the decline of Spain in the New World in the eighteenth century. Anyway, Philip's letter was a shopping list of jewels to be made in the New World and shipped back to Spain. Below the copy of the letter, the fellow listed what he had assembled." Treece recited from memory. "Item: two ropes of gold with thirty-eight pearls on each. Item: a gold cross with five emeralds. And so on and so on. It spills over to the next page of the book, which some idiot tore out a hundred years ago."

"No pine cone?"

"No, and no crucifix like ours, at least not on the page that's still there. But there is a reference to a three-lock box."

Sanders said, "That isn't conclusive, is it? You said yourself that they used those boxes all the time."

"For real high-priority goods. But you're right; it isn't special to *El Grifón*. So it was back to the papers." He sipped his tea. "The usual way for the King's treasure to be transported was in a chest in a strong room near the captain's cabin aboard the *capitana*. For some reason, Philip didn't trust Ubilla, the commander. The King's letter to Havana said that the jewels were to be shipped with the most trustworthy of all the fleet's captains, and no one else—no one—was to be aware of their existence. Philip didn't realize it at the time, but that last provision was a bad mistake."

"Why?" Gail asked.

"Think, girl. It's what we were talking about before, about *Grifón*. Up comes a storm; most of the ships go down. Only two people in the world know who had the jewels, the captain who had them and the man in Havana who assigned them to him. The captain survives, makes a deal with the man in Havana, who writes the King that he assigned the jewels to one of the captains who went down and was—poor chap—killed. Then he and the captain split the goodies. The captain waits awhile, rechristens his wreck of a ship, loads it with a relatively worthless cargo, and sets sail for home. If he makes it, he'll never have to sail again. He'll have enough to keep himself and his family and two or three small countries afloat. I don't have even half the list of jewels, but the bit I do have lists more than fifty pieces. The only flaw in the plan was that the ship didn't make it home. Got caught in a blow and seized up on the Bermuda rocks. Nobody knew there was anything on board worth worrying about."

Sanders said, "Did the man in Havana admit this?"

"Hell, no! He makes all manner of lugubrious references to the sinking of the fleet and the loss of the King's jewels. That put me off for a while."

"I think you're reaching: he might have done this, he could have done that. It's all supposition."

Treece nodded. "I thought so, too, until about four o'clock this morning." He paused, enjoying the game. "What was the King of Spain's name?"

"Come on," Sanders said, feeling manipulated. "Philip."

"Aye. And what was his new wife's name?"

Sanders sighed. "The duchess of Parma."

"No!" Treece smiled. "Not her title, her name." He waited, but they had no answer.

"Her name was . . . Elisabetta Farnese."

It took a second for the initials to register. Gail's mouth dropped open. Sanders was stunned.

Treece grinned. "There's still one unanswered question."

Sanders thought for a few seconds, then laughed and said, "I know."

"What?" The grin lit up Treece's face.

"The question is, Did King Philip ever get laid?"

"Right! And about that, you contentious bastard," he said, slapping Sanders' shoulder, "I would not presume to make a guess."

Sanders tried to share Treece's joviality, but his mind was crowded with conflicting images: jewels and drugs and explosives, the sight of Coffin's twisted body, the tattered linen doll, the leer on Slake's face. "How much is it worth?" he said.

"No telling. Depends what's still down there, what we can get at, how much was lost, and how much the man in Havana made off with. What we have now is worth, I'd say, somewhere near a quarter of a million dollars—that is, once we can firm up the provenance. We have to find at least one jewel that's on the list I've got, for the provenance to be perfect."

"What are we going to do about the drugs?" Gail said.

"I've thought about it. There's not a chance of our getting the lot up, not before Cloche makes his move. You know the numbers. What do you figure the value of the ampules we've got now is?"

"I don't know for sure how many ampules we have, but take a round figure—say we get a hundred thousand altogether. That's over a million dollars, maybe two million."

"That leaves a bloody heap of glass out there for him. But of course, he doesn't know that, does he?" Treece was talking more to himself than to them. "He doesn't know what we've got and what's still there."

"So?"

"So we'll go for the jewels; they're much more important. Let him think we're digging for glass."

"We can't just leave the rest of the drugs for him."

"No, we won't, but you have to weigh your risks. There's one thing certain: Cloche will try to get us out of the way, more'n likely by killing us." Treece paused, letting silence give emphasis to his words. "If he kills us, you might say who gives a damn what he gets; it's not our worry. But I care. I don't want him to get those drugs, and I *really* don't want him to get any of the jewels; dizzy bastard'd melt 'em down and sell the bloody gold, destroy 'em forever. That treasure is unique. It'd be criminal to let it fall into the hands of someone who doesn't understand what it represents. If we work the glass until he tries something, we'll lose the jewels. Even if he doesn't kill us, he can keep us off the wreck—blow it up out of sheer perversity if he wanted to. But if we get the jewels, then we can take whatever time we've got left to work the glass. *We*

257

can blow 'em up if we want to; Christ, I'd relish the chance." There was no objection from David or Gail. "Let's go down cellar." He stood up and opened a drawer.

"You've got a cellar?" Sanders said.

"After a fashion." Treece took a strip of maroon velvet from the drawer and wrapped the cameo, the medallion, the crucifix, the chain, and the pine cone. "Have to have something to anchor this shack in a breeze; else, she'd tumble off the cliff."

He led them into the living room and moved a chair. Under the chair, a small brass ring was countersunk into the floor. Treece pulled on the ring, and a four-by-four-foot section of cedar boards separated from the floor. He set the trap door aside and took a flashlight from the mantelpiece, then sat on the floor and let his legs dangle into the hole. "It's about a five-foot drop, not much more than crawl space, so mind your heads." He dropped into the hole and ducked down.

The cellar was a packed-dirt square as large as the living room above, walled with heavy stones held together by mortar.

The Sanderses followed Treece's crouched figure to a far corner of the cellar.

"Count three stones up from the floor," Treece said, shining his light in the corner.

Sanders touched the third stone above the floor.

"Now move four to the right."

Sanders ran his fingers along the wall until they came to rest on a cantaloupe-size rock. "This?"

"Aye. Pull."

Sanders could barely get his hand around the stone, but once he had a good grip, the stone slid easily from the wall.

There were two pieces of paper in the hole; behind them, another stone. "My birth certificate," Treece said, reaching in and removing the papers.

Gail wondered what the other piece of paper was, and in the reflected glow of the flashlight she could make out a last name—*Stoneham*—and three letters of a first name: *lla*. Priscilla, she thought: his wife's birth certificate.

"What's that?" Sanders said, pointing to something small and shiny in the hole.

Quickly, Treece shifted the light away from the hole and put his hand inside. "Nothing." He removed the object.

Gail thought, his wedding ring.

"Now reach in and pull that other rock."

Sanders did as he was told. His arm went in the hole almost up to the elbow.

When the other stone was free, Treece placed the velvet-wrapped jewels in the back of the hole. "Okay, put it back."

Sanders replaced the rear stone, Treece returned the papers and the shiny object and set the front stone back into the wall.

Treece said, "All you have to remember is, three up, four over."

"I don't want to remember it," said Gail. "It's none of our—"

"Just a precaution. I might take a wrong turn and walk

off a cliff. Any of us might. Better we all know where things are."

They went up into the house. "Might's well have a bite to eat," Treece said as he pushed the chair over the brass ring in the floor. "This is going to be a long day."

They reached the reef at eleven o'clock in the morning. It was a clear, calm day, with an offshore breeze barely strong enough to keep the boat off the rocks. They could see twenty or thirty people, in twos and threes, on the Orange Grove beach, and a mother playing with her child in the wave wash.

While Treece set the anchor, Sanders found a pair of binoculars and focused them on the patch of sand where he had found Coffin's body. "They've raked it clean; you can see marks."

"Aye. Don't want to leave anything that might upset the tourists. Hundred a day doesn't include a corpse on the beach."

Gail grimaced at the coarse, matter-of-fact dismissal of Coffin. She started to speak, but Treece, anticipating her, cut her off.

"A man dies, girl, he isn't any more, least not down here. Respect and all that crap doesn't serve the dead; it just makes the living feel better. The dead one, maybe he *is* somewhere else—maybe all he needs to be somewhere else is to believe he will be somewhere else. I won't deny a man his belief, and I don't know any more'n you about souls and all that stuff. But I know this: Speaking good or bad about something that isn't any more is a bloody waste of time. I can't feature Saint Peter sitting up there saying; 'Hey, Adam, there's folks bad-mouthing you down there. What'd you do to merit that?'"

Gail did not respond. She waited a moment, then said, "I can dive today."

"No. Stay here. There won't be much lugging. If we get all's down there, it won't be more'n a bag or two. And I want someone on the boat, today specially."

"Why?"

"Because I think we might have a little excitement today." Treece checked the shotgun. "Just be sure you remember how to use this and how to shut off the compressor. If nothing happens, the least you'll get is a royal fine suntan." He started the compressor.

Treece and Sanders returned to the cove in the reef where they had found the pine cone. The tide carried the sand from the air lift away to the right, so they had a clear view of the bottom.

For the first few minutes, they found nothing but single ampules, ten in all. Sanders reached to take them from the hole, but Treece waved him off and let the ampules rattle up the aluminum tube. One shattered, and a small billow of pale liquid puffed from the end of the tube. Treece dug deeper, inching closer to the reef.

There was a change in the way the sand moved under the air lift's suction. Instead of coming away smoothly in an unbroken pattern, now it moved in a rough V, as if it were surrounding something. Treece cupped his left hand over the mouth of the tube, cutting off its suction, and gestured with his hand for Sanders to dig in the hole.

Sanders rubbed the center of the V with his fingers and felt something hard. He brushed sand away and saw gold. It was a rose, about three inches high and three inches wide, and each of its golden petals had been finely etched with a jeweler's tool. Sanders picked it from the sand, held it by the delicate stem for Treece to see, then put it in a canvas bag.

Treece nosed the air lift against the base of the reef. Lying on his stomach a foot from the mouth of the tube, Sanders saw more gold under a rock overhang. He tapped the air lift, and Treece backed off. Sanders reached under the rock, his fingers closed on the gold and pulled. It moved, but it felt heavy, as if it were attached to something. When his hand was clear of the reef, Sanders looked at his palm and saw a gold chameleon with emerald eyes. The chameleon's mouth was open, and there was an opening near the tail. From the chameleon's belly protruded a sharp, finlike spike of gold. Two strands of gold chain led from a ring on the animal's back down into the reef. Sanders tugged at the chain, and, slowly, it came from the reef—ten feet of it, spilling in coils beneath Sanders' face.

Treece took the chameleon from Sanders and held it to his mask. He pursed his lips and mimed blowing inside his mask at the chameleon's head, telling Sanders that the figurine served as a whistle. Then he turned the animal on its back, curled his lip, and jabbed the spike toward his teeth: the spike was a toothpick.

They had been down for nearly five hours and had collected four gold rings (one with a large emerald); two huge almond-shaped pearls joined by a gold plate etched with the letters "E.F." on one side, a Latin inscription on the other; a belt of thick gold links; and two pearl-drop earrings. Then Treece spotted the first gold rope. It was deep in the reef, almost invisible except when shafts of sunlight caught the woven strands of gold and the tiny pearls held in place by the intricate weaving. Treece directed Sanders to reach for the rope.

Sanders was bitterly cold. Despite his wet suit, the hours of immersion had sucked heat from his body, and by now he was shivering constantly. He obeyed Treece without thinking, without worrying that something alive might be in the hole. His trembling hand reached into the reef, fingers closed around the gold and pulled: the rope was stuck, wrapped around a rock, perhaps, or covered with stones. Sanders withdrew his hand and shook his head at Treece.

Treece raised his right index finger and pointed at Sanders, saying: Watch. He made punching gestures at the reef with the air lift, then cupped his hands and pointed at Sanders.

Sanders didn't understand what Treece was saying. He shook his head; a cold tremor ran up his back and made his head quiver. He could not concentrate on Treece's gestures.

Treece pointed at the surface, set the air lift in the reef between two rocks, and started up. Sanders grabbed the canvas bag and followed.

"That's the one," Treece said when they were aboard. "There's our bloody provenance."

"I know." Sanders unzipped his wet-suit jacket and rubbed the goose flesh on his chest.

"We'll have a rest and let you warm up a bit; then we'll

go get her." He looked at the sun, then at Gail. "Coming up on five o'clock. Any trouble?"

"No. I'm frying, that's all."

Sanders said, "What were you trying to tell me down there?"

"We'll have to break up the reef to get at the rope. I'll bang the gun against the coral, and as pieces break off, you take 'em and set 'em aside. Don't want 'em to fall into the hole." He walked toward the cabin. "Get you a pry bar. Gun'll break up the coral all right, but it won't move boulders."

They rested for half an hour. Sanders lay on the cabin roof, warming in the lowering sun.

Ashore, the few remaining people on the beach straggled toward the elevator, which moved up and down in the shadows of the cliffs and flashed as it rose into the sunlight.

"Let's go," Treece said. He touched Gail's shoulder with a finger, and a circle of white appeared in her pink-brown skin and faded away. "Stay out of the sun. It'll burn you, even this late in the day."

"I will."

"Go below and stretch out if you like. Charlotte'll raise a din if anyone snoops around."

The men went overboard—Treece with a canvas bag, Sanders with a crowbar. Gail watched until she could no longer see their bubbles, then went below.

The work on the reef was slow and, because of the diminishing light, difficult: every time Treece rammed the nose of the air lift into the coral, a cloud of fine coral dust would rise from the broken piece; Sanders had to grope blindly to catch the coral before it fell out of reach into the hole. The rope of gold was wrapped around the base of a large oval rock, most of it underneath the rock—as if it had fallen loosely into the reef and been forced, by centuries of wave and tide action, into every crevice and cranny around the rock. Sanders had wanted to use the crowbar to tip the rock backward, but Treece stopped him, demonstrating with his hands the possible danger: the rope might have snaked around the back of the rock, too, and tipping it backward would crush the soft, fine gold strands beneath the sand.

It took them an hour to widen the hole three feet. Now Sanders could put his head and arms and shoulders into the hole and guide the mouth of the air lift along the gold rope, gently prying it free, inch by inch, as the sand was stripped from it. The pearls were set at three-inch intervals along the rope. Sanders counted the pearls already free— seventeen. If Treece's research was correct, if there were thirty-eight pearls per rope, there were five more feet of gold rope yet to come.

The work became dreamy, unreal: encased in water, hearing nothing but the sound of one's own breathing and the distant chug of the compressor relayed through the air hose, motionless save for the rote movement of fingertips— Sanders fantasized that he was doing multiplication tables in a cocoon.

Gail was sitting on one of the bunks, trying to concentrate on an article in an old yellowed newspaper, when she heard the dog bark. Then she heard an engine noise, drawing near, stopping. Then more barks, then voices. She held her breath.

"She empty."

"Seem so, 'cept for the dog."

"Hey, dog! How your ass?"

"Hush your mouth. Sound carry."

"How carry? Down the water? Shit."

The dog barked twice, growled.

A third voice, familiar. "Cut that yammering. Rig up."

Gail put a hand on the deck and crept off the bunk. Keeping her head below the starboard porthole, she crawled to the ladder. She stopped at the bottom of the ladder, hearing the beat of her pulse, breathing as quietly as possible through her mouth, thinking: If the other boat was abeam of *Corsair*, she could crawl into the cockpit without being seen, keep her back to the bulkhead, stand up, and reach the shotgun. If the boat was astern, they'd see her the second she poked her head out of the cabin.

She listened to the sounds of equipment being readied: the clink of buckles, the hiss of valves opened and closed, the thud of tanks on the deck. The sounds seemed to be coming directly from the left, abeam, so Gail climbed the short ladder and flattened herself against the bulkhead. The shotgun lay on the shelf by the steering wheel, four or five feet away. To reach it, her hand would have to pass in front of the window.

"How many loads you got for that thing?"

"This and two more."

"You?"

"Same. Shit, man, only three down there, and one a splittail."

"Just mind you don't mess with the pink hose. We gon' need it."

266

Now, Gail thought; they won't be looking this way. She extended her arm, leaned forward, and grabbed the butt of the shotgun. She lifted it off the shelf with no trouble, but, at arm's length, it was heavier than she remembered: the barrel sank a few inches and struck the steering wheel.

"What that noise?"

"What noise?"

Gail clutched the shotgun to her middle, one hand around the trigger guard, the other on the pump slide.

"*That* noise."

"I don't hear no noise."

"Well, I do. Somethin' on that boat."

"Shit. Dog only thing on that boat."

"Somethin' in*side* that boat."

"You jumpy, man."

"You go 'head over. I gon' cuddle this boat up to that boat and have me a look."

A laugh. "You be careful. That dog bite your ass."

"I shoot that sucker with a spear gun."

A splash, another, a few incoherent words, then silence.

Gail waited. She heard the sound of a paddle sweeping through the water, looked aft, and saw the shadow of the other boat drawing near.

She stepped around the bulkhead, the shotgun at her waist. The man was in the stern of the other boat, looking down at the water and paddling. She didn't have to see his face; the angry red scar shone black against his dark chest: Slake.

"What do you want?"

Slake looked up.

In the brief glimpse Gail had of his face, she saw surprise, then glee. What followed seemed a single motion: he dropped the paddle, bent to the deck, righted himself. Something shiny in his hand. A twanging sound, tightened elastic released. A flash of metal. The thunk of a steel spear in the bulkhead six inches from her neck.

Then (she would not remember all of this) the *click-clack* of the shotgun cocking. The roaring *boom* of the twelve-gauge shell exploding. The sight of Slake, three yards away, as the nine pellets struck him in the sternum—a baseball-size hole, red ooze flecked with white—staggering backward across the cockpit, striking the windward gunwale, sagging, hands clutching at his chest. A gurgling rush of breath. Echo of the explosion across the still water. Eyes rolling up in his head. Skin color graying as the blood left the head. Slump to the deck.

The steady chug of the compressor.

Open-mouthed, she watched the twitching body. The slap of water against *Corsair*'s hull brought her out of shock. She put the shotgun on the deck, walked aft to the compressor, found the wing nut, and turned it. The motor sputtered and died.

Sanders freed the last two inches of gold rope. He tapped the aluminum tube and saw it withdraw from the hole, gathered the rope in his right hand, and backed out onto the reef. The light was fading fast, but in the blue-gray mist he could still see Treece and the reflections off the air lift and the outline of the reef. Assuming that they would keep digging for more gold, Sanders opened his wet-suit jacket and stuffed the gold rope inside.

Sanders sensed a change in the sound patterns; something was missing. He exhaled, drew another breath, and realized what was missing: the compressor. He strained to fill his lungs one last time, looked at Treece, and saw a glint and a shadow falling toward him. The glint moved—a knife. Treece's air hose stiffened, the glint slashed back and forth, and the air hose went limp. Treece turned and raised his arms over his head.

Two men struggled in a twisting ball of shadows, a flurry of arms and hoses and bubbles, the shape of the knife falling to the bottom. Thrashing and kicking, the forms rose toward the surface.

Sanders held his breath, fighting panic. He kicked off the bottom and followed the thrashing figures, rising slowly, remembering to exhale, searching for other shadows in the gloom.

The shape of the figures changed. He could see Treece clearly now, his long body extended vertically, flippers kicking steadily. His hands were clasped around the other man's head. The man's regulator and mouthpiece floated away from his tank. For a moment, Sanders thought Treece was helping the man reach the surface. Then, as he saw the man's arms—pinned to his sides—struggling to wrestle free, saw the legs kicking feebly, Sanders knew what Treece was doing: his hand was clamped over the man's mouth and nose, preventing him from exhaling. The compressed air in the man's lungs would be expanding as he was dragged to the surface. With no exit from mouth or nose, the air would be forced through the lining of the lungs.

Sanders had a split-second recollection of a diagram he had seen in a diving book: a ruptured lung, a pocket of air in the chest cavity collapsing the lung, forcing still more air into the chest cavity, that air ramming the collapsed lung and other organs across the chest cavity and collapsing the other lung. Bilateral spontaneous pneumothorax. The man might well be dead before he reached the surface. Briefly, Sanders wondered if the man would feel pain or would simply pass out and die of anoxia.

Sanders was ten feet from the surface, and now all he could think of was getting air. The tightness in his chest lessened as he rose nearer the top; he knew he could make it. But what was up there waiting for him?

Suddenly his head was snapped backward, and he was pulled toward the bottom. Something had grabbed his air hose. He reached for his mask, trying to wrench it off his head, but the pressure on the straps was too great. His flailing hands found the hose and pulled against the downward force. In the twilight blue, he could only see a few feet of the yellow hose. Then there was a flicker of steel, and he saw, rising at him—climbing his air hose—a man with a spear gun.

Sanders' head throbbed with the need for oxygen. He yanked frantically at the hose, but the man had a firm grip.

They were six feet apart when the man released the air hose, raised the spear gun, and aimed it at Sanders' chest. Sanders kicked at the gun with his flippers, hoping to deflect the aim, but the man was patient. His cold eyes watched and waited for an interval between kicks.

A fuzz of dizziness passed through Sanders' brain, and he

knew he was dead. He waited for the flash of pain that would come as the spear pierced his wet suit and stabbed between his ribs. Maybe he would pass out first. . . .

The man fired. Sanders saw the spear coming at him, felt the blow as it struck his chest, waited for the pain. But there was no pain.

A yellow blur. The spear gun jerked upward, spun out of the man's hand, and fell. The man's fingers tore at his throat; the mouthpiece flew from his mouth. Huge, gloved hands on each side of his neck knotted a length of air hose around his throat.

Then Sanders fainted. The pain in his head was gone, and he felt as if he were flying through a warm darkness.

He awoke on the surface. Gail's hands cradled his face, holding the back of his head against the diving platform. He became aware of a face against his, a wet mouth engulfing his mouth, a blast of breath rattling down his throat. His eyes fluttered open and saw Treece's face pull away.

"Welcome back," Treece said.

Sanders' mind was still foggy. "Did I drown?"

"Gave it a try. Another couple of seconds, you'd've been up there with Adam giving us the celestial eyeball. You'd better be glad the duchess was a greedy bitch."

"What do you mean?"

"That bastard hit you full in the chest with his spear. If it hadn't been for the gold, you were dead."

Sanders looked down and saw a neat hole in his wet suit. The spear had penetrated the rubber but had caromed off the gold rope he had stuffed inside his jacket.

Gail put her hands under Sanders' armpits and, with Treece pushing from below, hauled Sanders onto the platform.

"How many were there?"

"Three. One's floating out there somewhere, making terms with the devil. Your girl splashed another one all over their boat. The third one's here." Treece yanked his right hand, and a rubber-hooded head popped out of the water, a piece of yellow hose still wrapped around his neck.

Sanders looked at Gail. "You killed one?"

"I didn't mean to. I had no choice. He . . ."

Treece said, "What'd I tell you? When you're up against it, you do the damnedest things."

Sanders rolled onto his stomach and stood up.

"Here," Treece said, extending the still body to Sanders. "Take this trash and haul it aboard while I dive to fetch the gear."

Sanders took the hose. "Is he dead?"

"I imagine. But don't take it for granted. Dump him on the deck and put the shotgun on him till I get back."

"Don't you want to start the compressor?" Gail asked.

"No, just toss me a mask. If I can't make it on one good heave, it's time to find another line of work."

While Gail looked for a face mask, Sanders pulled the inert man onto the platform. He let go of the hose, bent down, and took the man's arms.

"Don't bother with that," Treece said. "Just haul him up with the hose."

"I . . ." Sanders knew that, practically, Treece was

272

right: it would be much easier to pull the man aboard by the hose around his neck. But he couldn't do it. If he knew the man was already dead, that would be one thing. If he wasn't dead . . . Sanders was not ready to be his executioner.

"Don't be so delicate," Treece said. "He's as good as dead." He took the mask from Gail, hyperventilated for a few seconds, breathed deeply one last time, and slipped below the surface.

"What did he mean by that?" Gail said.

"I don't know. Help me with this, will you?"

Each holding one arm, they pulled the man over the transom and lay him on the deck.

"He's heavier than he looks," Gail said.

"Dead people are."

"Why?"

"I don't know. I read it somewhere."

"You mean really heavier, or just heavier than they look?"

"I don't know. Where's the shotgun?"

"Over there." Gail pointed. "I don't think you'll need it." She looked at the still black form and shivered.

Sanders picked up the gun, sat on the gunwale, and rested the gun across his knees. "What was it like?" He nodded toward the other boat. Sanders found that he envied Gail for having killed Slake. The thought of killing the man who lay helpless at their feet was repulsive. Unfair. But to kill a man in pure self-defense, to take up the challenge and beat the man who was trying to kill you—a fair fight. Vengeance.

"It was horrible," Gail said. "I didn't know what I was doing, not till afterward."

It was dark now; the moon was creeping over the horizon, and the stars were pale dots against the black sky. Sitting on opposite gunwales, David and Gail saw each other as faceless silhouettes.

They did not see the first faint tremors in the black rubber body on the deck, nor the opening of the eyes, nor the slight movement of fingers toward the calf of the left leg; did not hear the soft snap of the strap on the sheath around the leg or the sliding of the blade from the sheath.

The dog was the first to hear the new sounds. It whined.

Sanders looked toward the bow, and as he turned his head, the body sprang into a crouch and screamed—a high-pitched guttural yowl that sounded like a cat fight.

Sanders whirled back and leveled the gun. "Hey . . ."

He did not finish the command. The man leaped at him. Sanders squeezed the trigger. Nothing. The gun wasn't cocked. He pulled on the pump slide, leaning backward to gain one extra tenth of a second. He saw the blade swooping down at him, raised an arm in self-defense, and fell overboard. The slide snapped forward, and as Sanders hit the water, feeling a new, unspecific pain—in his arm or his side; he couldn't tell which—his finger squeezed the trigger. The shotgun fired into the air.

The man turned to Gail—crouching, waving the knife slowly in front of him, daring her to grab for it. He murmured low, throaty sounds, yips and growls and half-words, feinted with the knife, and, little by little, moved closer. Moonlight illuminated his face, and Gail saw his eyes—wild, fevered—and saw a trickle of drool on his chin. She wanted to talk to him, plead with him, but she was not sure the man even knew where he was or what he was doing. He yowled again.

Gail backed against the gunwale, glanced down at the water, and wondered if she should dive overboard. No: he'd be on her in an instant. She hedged forward along the gunwale, hoping that, when the man lunged, she could dodge him in the darkness of the cockpit.

The man screamed and jumped, swinging the knife in a wide arc.

Gail ducked and threw herself to the left, hearing the sound of breaking glass: the momentum of his swing had carried the man's hand through the pane of glass in the bulkhead. She crouched by the steering wheel.

The man turned, whispering incomprehensible curses, searching for her in the shadows. He saw her and raised the knife.

A noise behind him stopped his move. He half-turned.

Gail decided to dash for the stern. She took a step, then saw that escape was unnecessary: there was a heavy thump, the man's eyes rolled back in his head until only two slivers of white were showing, and he fell to the deck.

Sanders stood where the man had been, a wrench in his right hand. He had hit the man with the flat side of the wrench, and it was matted with blood and hair.

Sanders said, "Are you all right?"

"Yes," Gail said. She saw that he was holding his left arm across his chest, as if in a sling. "You're hurt."

Sanders touched his arm. "I can't tell, but I don't think it's too bad."

They heard Treece come aboard.

"He try something?" Treece said, noticing how the body now lay on the deck.

"Yeah. I wasn't quick enough."

"Well, looks like you made up for it." Treece bent over and felt for a pulse on the man's neck. "Iced him clean."

"He's dead?" Sanders said.

"I'll say." Treece went below.

Sanders still held the wrench. He looked at it, then at the body on the deck. A moment before, it had been a man, alive; now it was a corpse. One swing of one arm, and life had become death. Killing should not be that easy.

Sanders heard Treece say, "Where's the shotgun?"

He looked up and saw Treece playing a flashlight over the water, searching for the other boat.

"In the water," Sanders said. "I'm sorry."

"Did you get a sudden attack of the mercies? They can be fatal."

"No. I tried to shoot him, but the gun wasn't cocked."

"You're lucky." Treece handed him the flashlight, dove overboard, swam to the other boat, boarded it, walked forward, found a length of rope, and made it fast to a cleat on the bow. Then he dove off the bow, holding the free end of the rope, and towed the boat to *Corsair*.

He lay the dead man on the gunwale and tied the rope around his neck.

"What are you doing?" Gail asked.

Treece looked at her, but said nothing. He found a

knife, slit the corpse's belly, and before any viscera could ooze onto the deck, rolled the man overboard.

"What are you *doing?*" Gail said again.

"Feedin' him to the sharks."

"But why?"

"A warning. Cloche is loading these animals with some fiery shit, to hop 'em up, turn 'em into kamikazes. It's all bush, but you feed a bird like that hallucinogenics and then talk bush to him, and he's a rightful maniac. Believes he's serving some crazy-ass god, and when he wakes up in the morning he'll be in Valhalla or some such. But they believe the only way you'll get there is whole; can't have anything missing, so being lunch is bad bush. Cloche's people find what's left of that fellow hanging off the bow rope, maybe they'll think twice before pulling a stunt like this again."

They could see the other boat, outlined against the moonlight. The corpse's head bobbed to the surface, jerked up by the rope, then sank again.

Gail turned away and said, "My God!"

"Don't waste sympathy on him," Treece said. "He can't feel a thing."

There was a thump against the leeward side of *Corsair*, followed by a grunt and another thump.

"What's that?" Sanders said, worried that, somehow, more of Cloche's divers were attacking. He looked over the side and saw white foam boiling up beside the boat.

Treece shined the light on the water, then quickly turned it off and said, "Next thing, they'll eat the boat." He went forward.

Sanders felt an acid pool rise in his throat, and he gagged

at the taste. The few seconds of light had branded a night-mare image on his brain. What had thumped against the boat was a body, not that of the man tied to the other boat, but of the man Treece had killed earlier by preventing him from exhaling. And what had slammed the body against the boat was the broad, flat head of a shark. The head was the size of a manhole cover. Two nostrils flared on the snout, and the jaws snapped as the tail thrust forward, forcing more and more rubber and flesh into the mouth. The eyes looked sleepily evil, two-thirds covered by a white shield of membrane. While Sanders had watched, the head shook fiercely from side to side, and a two-foot crescent of flesh had begun to tear away.

Now, in darkness, Sanders could still see the white foam and hear the slapping of the tail and the crunch of teeth against bone and sinew.

"What is it?" Gail asked.

Sanders shook his head, trying not to vomit.

Gail looked out over the dark water at the receding shape of the other boat. "It's so quiet," she said.

"Aye," Treece said, standing at the wheel. "Death is that." He started the engine.

The trip back to St. David's didn't take long, for the night was calm and the moonlight bright.

They were still several hundred yards at sea when the offshore breeze brought them the strident sounds of taxi horns.

XI

When he had secured the boat to the dock, Treece shut off the engine. Above the low murmur of wind they could hear the distant bleat of several taxi horns, apparently stationed at intervals around the island. The horns were blown in staccato bursts, with no rhythm or organization.

Treece frowned. "What the *hell* is he up to now?"

"He?" Sanders said. "That's Cloche? Those taxis?"

"Aye. There are no cabs on St. David's. He's making bush again."

A shiver touched Sanders' spine. "I've about had it. I hope he's not going to try anything more tonight."

"If he was, you wouldn't think he'd announce it. Besides, what's he think he'll get from another visit? He doesn't know anything about the cave, and he's not fool enough to believe he can make us tell him."

"Then why . . . ?"

"I don't know. He's saying something, that's for sure. If I had to guess, he's spooking the Islanders, telling 'em to stay indoors—all bush. But you're right: If he's doing that, it'd seem he's planning to pay us a visit."

Treece snapped his fingers at the dog and pointed to the path. "Well, whatever. I'll go get a couple of Kevin's cannons and fix him a royal welcome. Too bad we lost that shotgun. It was a fine people-eater."

There was no rebuke in Treece's voice, so all Sanders said was "Yeah."

Treece started up the path after the dog, with the Sanderses following. "Any weapon's only as good as the man using it," Treece said, "and a good man can make a good weapon out of most anything. Ever kill a man with a knife?"

"Me?" Sanders said. "No."

"There's right ways and wrong ways. Most knives have three elements to 'em: the point, the sharp side, and the dull side. Depending on what you want to do to the fellow . . ."

Bringing up the rear, Gail tried to block out the conversation ahead of her. It was all becoming unreal, inhuman . . . terrifying. It seemed that a new Treece was speaking now—not a wounded man or a compassionate man or a sensitive man: a killer. But perhaps this wasn't new, perhaps it was the boy talking, the boy who played by his own rules, and when the rules called for killing, he killed. What scared her most was that the man Treece was talking to, explaining the rules to, was her husband. She heard Sanders say, "Yeah, but he could still—"

"Not if you go deep enough," Treece said. "You snip that spinal cord just like a thread, he goes all to jelly."

"Stop!" Gail's voice was so loud that it scared her.

"Hush, girl! Christ, you'll wake the dead."

The cut on Sanders' arm had stopped bleeding; a caked crusty streak of brownish red showed through his wet suit.

Treece handed him a bottle full of a dark, viscous brown liquid. "Here. Wash your arm off and lard some of this on it. I'm going to bury the jewels in the wall."

"What is it?"

"My grandmother used to make it; bloody junk defies chemical analysis. There's some mango derivative in it, and berry juice, and something that might or might not come from spirea bark. Rest of it's a mystery. But it works."

When she heard Treece's feet hit the cellar floor, Gail said to David, "I'm frightened."

"I don't blame you."

"Not for me. For you. Treece thinks this is a war."

"That was talk."

"*Talk*. We killed three people."

"We didn't have much choice." Sanders finished swabbing the medicine on his arm. "They tried to kill us."

Gail heard the trap door close in the living room, and the sound of the chair scraping across the floor. "This has gone far enough," she whispered. "I can't take much more."

Treece came into the kitchen. From a cabinet he took what looked like a brick of modeling clay, the bottom half of a champagne bottle, some plastic-coated wire, a small rectangular magnet, an egg timer, and a little cardboard box. He set the paraphernalia on the table and made himself a drink.

"Looks like shop," Sanders said.

"What?" Treece sat down at the table.

"Shop class. In grade school. You know: modeling, carving, making things for Mom."

"Aye." Treece smiled. "But if you came home from school with this, your mom would run like a rabbit." Treece pulled chunks of the gray claylike substance off the brick and stuffed them into the bottom of the champagne bottle. "Ever use this stuff?"

"What is it?" asked Gail.

"It's called C-4. Plastic explosive. Fine stuff."

"What do you use it for?"

"Normally, salvage work. Clearing harbors, knocking down piers, getting old wrecks out of the way, banging holes in reefs so ships can get through. But this time we're gonna put what's left of the drugs away for good."

"Thank God," said Gail.

"How? With that?" Sanders said.

"Not alone, no." Treece had filled the bottle-half to the top. He opened the cardboard box, gingerly removed a blasting cap, and set it in the bed of explosive. Then he began to attach the coated wire to the cap. "But set this

C-4 up against a load of other explosives—say a cargo of live ammunition—and you've got enough to make Bermuda's own Grand Canyon. Military term for it's a shape charge. These champagne bottles are indented on the bottom; a lump goes up inside 'em. Pack the C-4 around it, and when you set it off, the lump sort of aims the force of the explosion where you want it." Treece tipped the bottle on its side. "You lay it up against an artillery shell like this." He put his hand against the blasting cap. "All the power's directed at the shell. Boom!"

"How do you get out of the way?"

Treece held up the egg timer. "That's what this is for. I'm going to dive down, wire the charge to the timer, and set it for maybe five minutes. That'll give me time to scoot to the surface and get the hell out of there. Don't want to be closer than a few hundred yards when she goes off. The ammunition would turn any ship nearby into an instant wreck."

Gail said, "When are you going to do this?"

"Tomorrow morning, after we've had a last look-around. Then we'll come back and smash the ampules we've got." Treece finished wiring the charge and stood up. "I'm going to nip down to Kevin's and borrow a gun or two. I'll leave Charlotte here. She'll let you know if there are any Peeping Toms about."

The dog barked twice and jumped onto the window sill.

Treece looked out the window. "Nothing." He patted the dog's head. "Getting goosy, just like . . ." Then he heard something, cocked his head, and listened. "Sonofa-bitch."

"What is it?" Sanders asked.

"There's a *boat* down there."

Treece opened a drawer and rummaged through a tangle of kitchen knives. He took out a long, thin-bladed filleting knife and passed it to Sanders. "Remember what I told you; this thing'll skin an alligator." He removed a cleaver from a rack on the wall and handed it to Gail.

She recoiled, refusing to take it. "What am I supposed to do with *that?*"

"Just have it." He put it in her hand. "Got no esteem for yourself. You showed what you can do."

"What do you want me to do?"

"Come along." He selected a carving knife for himself—the cutting edge of the blade worn into a crescent by countless honings—and shut the drawer. Then he closed the window. "Stay in the house, Charlotte. Don't need you raising an untimely ruckus." On his way to the kitchen door, Treece stopped at a cabinet and found a waterproof flashlight.

They went out into the empty yard. The moonlight shone on the slick leaves of the bushes at the edge of the cliff. Treece motioned for David and Gail to stay low, and they ran, crouching, to the top of the path leading to the dock.

Looking down, they could see a boat at the mouth of the cove, barely moving. They heard a few muted clanks above the far-off drum sounds.

"Is it Cloche?" Gail whispered.

"Must be, but I'm damned if I know how he found out about the cave. You stay up here; keep in the shadows. We'll go have a look. Could be they're just snooping."

Treece tucked the flashlight in the belt of his wet-suit pants and told Sanders to follow. They started down the path.

The high foliage shaded the path into complete darkness. Twice Sanders stumbled into bushes, heard Treece's warning, "Sssshhhhh!" Then he found he could follow Treece by looking at the tops of the bushes: as Treece passed below and brushed a branch, the upper leaves shimmered in the moonlight.

A few feet from the bottom of the path, Treece stopped and waited for Sanders. The movement on the boat was clearly audible, and fighting that and the sound of the horns above, Treece had to put his lips to Sanders' ear to be heard.

"Stay here. I'm going out along the dock, see what's up." He touched the knife in Sanders' hand. "Comfortable with that?"

Sanders nodded.

Treece stepped to the end of the path and, with animal stealth, crept along the narrow space between the dock and the bushes.

Sanders rested on one knee, clutching the knife. He felt all the symptoms of fear, but they were soothed by a sense of confidence in Treece. Like a young child on an expedition with his older brother, he felt excited—scared but comforted by the belief that he could take his cues from Treece.

So he was doubly surprised when he felt a thick, muscular arm slam into his throat, a hand push his head forward, cutting off his breathing, and a great weight knock him to the ground and blanket him with slippery, sweaty flesh.

He tried to scream, but the pressure against his throat reduced the scream to a gurgle. He still held the knife—blade pointing upward, as Treece had shown him—and he jabbed it at the flesh, but a knee jammed his wrist into the ground. His left arm was pinned to his side by the body on top of him. He was helpless.

He relaxed his body, hoping desperately—through a film of waning consciousness—that he could convince his attacker that he was dead. But when the man felt muscle resistance ease, he tightened his grip.

Then, as suddenly as the weight had fallen on him, it left him. He was free. He drew a painful, rattling breath.

He heard Treece's voice whisper, with bitterness and feral ferocity unlike anything he had ever heard, the single word "Kevin!"

Sanders raised himself on one elbow and looked. Kevin lay on his back, Treece kneeling on his chest and pulling his hair so his head tilted at a cockeyed angle. With his other hand, Treece held the carving knife at Kevin's throat. Kevin's legs kicked, then fell to the dirt.

"You told him!" Treece whispered. "Why?" Kevin said nothing. "*Why?* For money?" Treece's voice was no longer angry; it was choked with the sorrow of betrayal. "For *money?*" Still Kevin was silent.

In the reflections of moonlight off the water, Sanders could see their eyes: Kevin's flat and expressionless, looking through Treece with a kind of blank resignation; Treece's shiny, enraged, unbelieving.

"Oh, you sorry, sorry bugger," Treece said, and when the last whispered word had faded, he punched the point of the knife into Kevin's throat and drew the blade quickly across the neck. There was a black line of blood, a foam of bubbles, and a wet, wheezing sigh. Treece hung his head and closed his eyes.

A beam of light swept across the cove toward them, and Sanders heard Cloche's voice call, "Kevin?"

Sanders whispered, "Treece?"

Treece did not answer.

"Treece!"

The light moved closer, and Sanders knew that in a few seconds it would illuminate half of Treece's back. He rose to his knees and lunged at Treece, hitting him with his shoulder and knocking him to the ground. The light swept over them, stopped, and moved back to the water.

"Kevin?" Cloche called again. "Idiot!"

Lying on the ground, with Sanders next to him, Treece gradually shook off his stupor. "All right," he said. "All right. At least now we know." He crawled on his stomach to the end of the path, looked at Cloche's boat, and returned to Sanders. "Looks like there's two or three divers, plus a couple fellas they'll leave on the boat. We'll wait till the divers are overboard, then try to get to *Corsair* and throw on tanks and go down."

"The tanks have bad air."

"Not all. I only filled two that night. The others were already full. There should be four good ones aboard."

"Then what?"

"We'll see how many men there are and how they're working. If they're working two at a time in the cave, with hand lights, we've a chance to pick 'em off. Odds are, the divers won't be armed. They'll have their hands full with the glass."

"Pick them off?" Sanders said. "Why?"

"To stop 'em before they get the ampules. *We* can't get the glass up with those yahoos around, and I'm damned if I'm about to let Cloche have what's down there."

"What do we do? Stab them?"

"Only if you have to. Try to grab the regulator hose and cut it and get the hell out of his way. A man with a sudden-cut air hose is a bloody menace; he'll grab a baby's mouthpiece."

"But if we cut their air hoses, they'll just come up; they'll be waiting for us on the surface."

"It's my bet these chaps are still a bit wary of the water. Put 'em in a panic, they're like as not to hold their breath on the way up, or lose their way and drown in the cave. But even suppose they don't. If we cut all their air hoses, they'll be spooky as hell about going back down there. And Cloche doesn't have extra equipment."

"So they wait for us to come up and then shoot us."

"We won't come up. It's dark. They'd have a hell of a time following a bubble trail. We'll stay on the bottom, go out of the cove and around the corner. There's a place about fifty yards down where we can land."

"He won't give up—especially when he finds that guy floating off the reef."

"No, he'll be back. But all we need is the rest of tonight to get that glass out of there and destroy it."

Sanders paused briefly, then said, "Okay."

They heard splashes and fragments of conversation.

Someone said, "Where's Kevin at?" and Cloche replied, "Drunk, I suppose. He is of no consequence now; he gave us full value."

A few more splashes, then silence.

Treece waited for ten or fifteen seconds, then crept out into the open. Cloche's boat floated twenty yards out in the cove, off *Corsair*'s stern, so *Corsair* protected them from view as they moved along the dock. They slipped into the cockpit and lay on the deck.

"Fins, mask, and tank," Treece whispered. "Don't fool with weights. They'll make too much noise."

The necks of the steel air tanks gleamed in the moonlight, and Sanders saw that it would be impossible to pull the tanks out of the rack without being seen.

"Old Indian trick," Treece said, removing a two-pound lead weight from a nylon belt. He reached to the transom and uncleated the stern line, letting the stern swing a few feet away from the dock, then recleated the line. "When you hear the splash, grab a tank and go over the side between the boat and the dock. I'll be right along." He threw the weight as hard as he could—a straight-arm arc that used the muscles of the shoulder, not the arm—and the weight cleared the bridge of the other boat by several feet and splashed into the water beyond.

Sanders rose, removed a tank from the rack, held it overboard, and slid into the water after it, aware of the sounds of footsteps and voices and the cocking of a rifle. Treece joined him. They checked each other's tanks, making sure the air valves were turned on, and the air was good. "Hold my hand till we get to the bottom," Treece said. "We'll stay there for a minute and have a look-see. Their light'll tell us where they are."

Hand in hand, they sank below the surface and kicked to the bottom.

Kneeling in the bushes at the top of the hill, Gail heard the splash and the voices. She got to her feet in a stooped stance, ducked as a beam of light swept toward her, then rose again and looked down, half-expecting, dreading, to hear a gunshot. But there was nothing, only the incessant taxi horns. Holding the cleaver—scared of it but glad of it, as she had been of the shotgun—she started down the path.

Near the bottom of the path, with her hands in front of her like a blind person in a strange room, she stepped on one of Kevin's legs. Shocked, she lurched backward and fell into the bushes, cracking branches as she fell.

She heard a voice: "Kevin?"

She held her breath.

"Go over there and look around."

A splash; sounds of a man swimming.

She exhaled and inhaled, and her nostrils filled with the stench of feces. Terrified, she extricated herself from the bushes and scrambled up the hill.

On the bottom of the cove, Sanders and Treece knelt together, still holding hands. Forty or fifty feet away, the cave was as visible as a proscenium stage in a dark theater, illuminated not by hand-held lights but by huge floodlights. As they watched, a diver swam out of the cave and turned on a flashlight. He carried a mesh bag full of ampules. Two other divers passed him, heading for the cave, switching off their flashlights as they entered the pool of light.

Treece tugged at Sanders' hand, and they kicked toward the cave. When they were within ten feet of the entrance, just outside the range of the floodlights, Treece let go of Sanders' hand and gently pushed him against the face of the cliff, signaling for him to wait.

Treece dropped to his stomach and pulled himself along the sand until he could look inside the cave. Then he withdrew from the light. He flicked on his flashlight, located Sanders, and swam to him.

Treece held the flashlight in his left hand and shined it on his right, pointing to Sanders, then to the near side of the cave, then to himself, then—in an arching motion—to the far side of the cave. Then he shined the light on Sanders' face, to see if he understood. He did: he was to position himself at one side of the entrance, Treece at the other.

They flattened themselves against the cliff and waited. In the shimmering light, Sanders caught an occasional glimpse of Treece's face, of the shining knife blade in his hand.

Moving water disturbed sand at the entrance to the cave: something was coming out. Sanders saw Treece's knife rise and hold steady.

The man on Treece's side came out first, a few feet ahead of his companion. His head appeared, looking down at the sand, then his shoulders.

Treece jumped him: a flash of red-brown skin, an explosion of bubbles, a fist grabbing the man's air hose and wrenching the mouthpiece from his mouth, drawing the hose taut, the knife slicing easily through the rubber tube.

The head of the second man emerged from the cave. Sanders raised his knife.

The man looked up and saw Sanders. His eyes widened, hands flew to his head as Sanders leaped.

The man knocked Sanders' knife hand away and reached for Sanders' mask.

Sanders dodged. His shoulder hit the man's chest, and they tumbled to the bottom, clawing at each other. They rolled along the bottom, punching and kicking, each trying to keep his head away from the other's grasp. Sanders breathed in spurts, holding his breath after each inhalation, fearful of having his hose cut when his lungs were empty.

They were several yards inside the cave now, floating and bumping on the sand in a grotesque waltz: the man held Sanders' right wrist, keeping the knife away from his neck. Sanders' left arm was wrapped around the man's side, pinning his right arm. Sanders could not stab the man, could not cut his air hose; he was waiting for Treece. Frantically, he looked to the mouth of the cave, expecting to see Treece swimming toward him. Instead, Treece was poised in a fighter's crouch, facing out of the cave, awaiting the two flashlights that moved swiftly toward him.

The man's right arm wiggled free. His hand inched upward and slammed into Sanders' groin, fingers clawing at his balls. Sanders kicked upward with his left leg, deflecting the hand. Then he saw the hole in the cave wall, a dark tunnel above a pile of stones.

He touched a foot to the bottom and pushed off, dancing the man toward the wall. The man's heels hit a rock, and he tripped, but he did not release Sanders' wrist. Sanders leaned against him, forcing him onto the wall, butting him to make him jerk his head back toward the hole.

The man's head was a few inches below the hole. Sanders' foot found purchase on a rock, and he shoved again, driving the man up, exposing the black flesh and puffed arteries.

The pig eyes—beads in the slimy green head—showed in the hole, the mouth waving hungrily, half open.

The moray struck, needle teeth fastening on the man's neck, throat convulsing as it pulled back toward the hole. Blood billowed out the sides of the moray's mouth.

The man's mouth opened, releasing his mouthpiece, and roared a noisy shriek of panic.

Their arms parted. Sanders wondered if he should stab the man, to make sure, but there was no need: his mouthpiece floated behind his head. Half his throat was engulfed in the moray's mouth, and already his flails were weaker, his eyes dimmer.

Sanders turned back to the entrance of the cave. Treece was still crouched, the two flashlights closer to him but not moving. He feinted toward them, and they backed away.

Sanders knew Treece was waiting for him. If Treece had wanted to escape, he could have swum off into the darkness. The lights would soon have lost him, and even if the men could have kept track of him, they could not hope to catch him underwater.

The flashlights flicked off; the figures faded into the darkness. Treece turned on his light and swept the area in front of the cave. Sanders tapped him on the shoulder to let him know he was there. Treece pointed to the surface and turned off his light.

Rising through the glow cast by the floodlights in the cave, Sanders felt naked. He knew Cloche's men could see him. He kicked hard, reaching for darkness.

Something rammed his back. Legs wrapped around his middle; his head was pulled back. He sucked on the mouthpiece and breathed water: his regulator hose had been cut. The legs released him.

The salt water made him gag. He clamped his teeth together and forced himself to exhale, fighting the physical impulse to gasp for air.

He reached the surface, coughed, and drew a ragged breath. A light shone on his face. He threw his head to the right and dove underwater as a bullet slapped the surface, ricocheted, and struck the stone cliff. Holding his breath a few feet below the surface, he saw the beam of light playing across the water. It moved to the left, so he swam to the right. His hands touched the cliff face and, slowly, he inched upward.

They had lost him; the light was sweeping the surface several yards to his left. It started back toward him. He ducked until it had passed, then rose again to breathe. He heard Cloche's voice.

"Treece!" No answer. "We are at an impasse, Treece. You cannot stop us; we are too many. Leave while you can. We will take no more than is in the cave, you have my word. A fair compromise." No answer.

Sanders felt something touch his foot. He jerked his leg

upward and drew a breath, expecting to be dragged beneath the surface, determined to struggle, but fearfully, hopelessly convinced that he lacked the strength to survive.

Treece's head broke the surface next to his. "Chuck your tank," Treece whispered, unsnapping his own harness and letting his tank sink to the bottom.

Cloche called twice more, but Treece didn't reply. He led Sanders toward shore, swimming a silent breast stroke.

"Die, then!" Cloche said angrily.

They reached the end of the dock, crawled out of the water, and when they heard Cloche order his divers to come aboard, dashed for the path.

Gail was waiting for them at the top of the hill. "What . . ."

Treece ran past her toward the house. "Come on!"

In the kitchen, Treece examined the shape charge. He checked the wires, then taped the magnet to the side of the bottle.

"Did you hear what Cloche said?" Sanders asked. "About the compromise?"

"Aye. Lying bugger. He'll go for the lot; bet on it. But if we're lucky, we'll beat him to it. There's the tank and a regulator out by the compressor. Get 'em for me. And one of the hand lights, too, while you're there."

Sanders hurried out the kitchen door, and Gail said to Treece, "Where are we going?"

"Orange Grove. We'll take Kevin's car." Treece picked the shape charge off the table and held it in both hands.

"You're going to plant that thing tonight?"

"No choice, not if we want to get rid of the ampules before Cloche goes for them." He saw Sanders returning from the compressor shed and said, "Let's go. If we don't get there first, it's all down the drain."

As they hurried along the path, Sanders said, "What about the rest of the jewels?"

"If there's anything left down there . . . well, maybe Philip's ghost can have a romp with the good duchess. We can't take a chance on the drugs."

The dog followed them to the gate, but Treece stopped her there and ordered her to stay.

They heard the engine of Cloche's boat chug to life and turn southwest toward Orange Grove. Treece broke into a run.

He drove the Hillman as fast as it would go, leaning his body against the turns in the narrow road, cursing when the small engine faltered on steep hills. Sanders sat beside Treece, Gail in the back seat, steadying the shape charge with her hand.

On a long South Road straightaway the speedometer nudged seventy. Bracing himself against the dashboard, his feet pressed against imaginary brake pedals, Sanders said, "Suppose a cop stops you."

"Any police who values his life will not stop me tonight." Treece did not speak again until he had parked the car in the Orange Grove lot and was running toward the stairs that led to the beach. "You run an outboard?" he said then.

"Sure," Sanders said.

"Good. I need a chauffeur."

The moon was high, and as they ran down the stone stairs, they could see the white hulls of the Boston Whalers on their dollies.

Treece looked out to sea, to the left, at the white lines of reef. "Light's good. We'll see him coming." He handed Gail the shape charge, grabbed the painter of the nearest Whaler, spun the dolly around, and, alone, dragged the boat into the water. Then he took the charge from Gail and said, "Stay here."

"No."

"Aye, you'll stay here."

"I will not!"

Her defiance surprised him. "It'll be hairy out there, and I don't want you around."

"It's my decision. It's my life, and I'm going." She knew she was being unreasonable, but she didn't care. She could not stay on the beach, a helpless observer.

Treece took her by the arm and looked into her eyes. "I have killed one woman," he said flatly. "I'll not be responsible for killing another."

Gail glared back at him and, in anger, without thinking, said, "I am not your wife!"

Treece relaxed his grip. "No, but . . ." He seemed embarrassed.

Gail touched his hand. "You said it yourself. I'm here. I'm me. Protecting me won't do a thing for her."

Treece said to Sanders, "Get in the boat." He helped Gail into the boat after Sanders, walked the boat into water deep enough for the propeller shaft, and climbed aboard.

They went over the reefs, to a spot above the remains of *Goliath*. There they let the boat wallow.

Treece rigged the scuba tank, put it on his back, and sat on the starboard gunwale, resting the shape charge against his thighs. The hand light hung from a thong on his wrist. "I'll go rig the charge," he said. "Be right back. Then, soon's we see him coming, I'll nip over again and set the timer."

"Okay," said Sanders.

"Now . . . an order. If anything happens, get the hell out of here in a hurry. Don't play Boy Scout."

Sanders had no intention of leaving Treece, but he did not reply.

Treece rolled off the gunwale, turned on the light, and swam for the bottom.

Moments later, Sanders saw the first splash—sparkling white eruptions of water over the bow of a boat that was moving full-speed along the outer reef. "Look!" he said, pointing.

Gail saw the boat, then looked overboard. Treece's light was steady on the bottom. "How long will it take him to rig that thing?"

"I don't know. Too long."

Sanders heard the high whine of a bullet passing overhead, followed a second later by the crack of a rifle shot. He ducked, and another bullet whirred by.

As Cloche's boat drew nearer, there were more shots, but the Whaler, riding low in the water, was a bad target. All the shots were high.

Crouching in the bottom of the Whaler, Gail said, "He said to go."

"The hell with him."

Treece's head popped up beside the Whaler. He started to say something, but stopped when he heard a shot.

"Go!" he said.

Sanders said, "No! You . . ."

"Go, goddammit! I'll set the timer and follow you in. Get into the shallowest water you can find." Treece disappeared below the surface.

For a few seconds, Sanders didn't move.

"We've got to go!" Gail said.

"But he'll—"

"Do you *want* to die?"

Sanders looked at her. He started the engine and spun the boat toward shore.

Two more bullets chased the Whaler inshore. When he felt that they were out of practical range, Sanders slowed the boat and turned the bow seaward.

"He said to find shallow water," Gail said.

"This is shallow enough."

Cloche's boat was stopped over *Goliath*. A light flickered on, then another, and, one by one, figures dropped into the water.

"Divers," Gail said.

"Don't pay attention to them!" Sanders snapped. "Look for Treece. If we don't get him out of the water before that thing goes off, he's dead. He *must* have finished by now."

But Treece had not finished. A wire had come loose from the timer, and he was resetting it, using his thumbnail as a screw driver. He tightened the screw and turned the timer dial to five minutes. Then the first light found him.

Sanders could not wait any longer. "Screw this!" he said, and he pushed the gear lever forward, heading for the reef.

"What are you *doing?*" Gail screamed.

"I don't know! We've got to get him out!" Sanders guessed they were five hundred yards from Cloche's boat.

There were two lights around Treece now. He was holding his breath, for his air hose had been cut. He turned in slow circles, trying to keep both divers in sight.

They were quick. One man circled with Treece, keeping always behind him, and when he saw a chance for a move, he darted forward and plunged his knife into Treece's back.

Treece felt a deep, fiery ache. He held the timer to his chest and turned the dial to zero.

The Whaler was three hundred yards from the reef when the sea exploded.

David and Gail saw the bow of the Whaler rise toward them, and then they were flying away from it. They spun through the air, aware of fragmented images that flashed by their eyes: the sudden mountain of water rising, then rupturing; bits of Cloche's boat flying in every direction, pieces cast impossibly high; a body, spread-eagle, cartwheeling across the sky.

Sanders hit the water on his back. His eyes were open, but he was not truly conscious. He heard bits of debris falling around him, felt stinging sensations as pieces of rock and coral hit his face. His legs dangled below him, and as he exhaled, he sank a few inches, then rose again as he inhaled. He saw the stars and the shimmering shafts of moonlight, and he thought vaguely: This isn't what they say death is like.

The gentle swells carried him slowly toward shore.

A voice that sounded faint and far away was calling, "David?"

He rolled onto his stomach and, testing his limbs with the first tentative strokes, swam stiffly toward the voice.

Gail was treading water twenty yards away. She saw him coming and said, "You okay?"

"Yeah. You?"

"I don't know. I can't move one of my arms."

He helped her to shore, and they staggered out of the water. The beach looked like an endless field, the elevator a mile away.

They turned and looked back at the water. There was a new gap in the reef line, and pieces of flotsam were washing up in the waves. Otherwise, the sea was unchanged.

Leaning against each other, they walked toward the base of the cliff, where a crowd was already beginning to gather.

AUTHOR'S NOTE

This is a work of fiction. But while it is true that none of the characters bears any intentional resemblance to anyone living or dead, many of the facts about Bermuda, about shipwrecks, and about the Spanish trade with the New World were gleaned from historical sources.

It would be impractical to list all the reference works consulted, but a few were of particular help: *Pieces of Eight*, by Kip Wagner, as told to L. B. Taylor, Jr.; *The Treasure Diver's Guide*, by John S. Potter, Jr.; *Marine Salvage*, by Joseph N. Gores; *Diving for Sunken Treasure*, by Jacques-Yves Cousteau and Philippe Diolé; *Treasures of the Armada*, by Robert Sténuit; *Port Royal Rediscovered*, by Robert F. Marx; and *Diving to a Flash of Gold*, by Martin Meylach, in collaboration with Charles Whited.

Finally, I am deeply indebted to a friend, mentor, and walking encyclopedia—Teddy Tucker.

P.B.